The Duke's
by Mic

"About last night," Charles said. "I've had a change of heart."

Uh oh.

"Now that I know what I'll be missing," he added, "maybe I won't be co-operating with the royal family after all."

Oh yes, kissing him had been a really bad idea.

He was coming closer with that look in his eyes, like any second he planned to ravish her. And she wanted him to. Desperately.

He'd managed to turn the tables on her.

"I mean, what's the worst that can happen?" he said.

Hopefully something really bad. "Renouncement? Hanging?" she offered.

He only smiled. He was standing so close now that he could reach out and touch her.

**Convenient Marriage,
Inconvenient Husband
by Yvonne Lindsay**

**If she was to have any man's child,
by choice, it would be Brent's.
Which left only one option.**

One man.

Could she carry it off? Could she withhold the truth from him long enough to get him to father a child with her?

Amira's stomach churned at the thought of using him. But they'd had a passionate relationship before. Could she hope to stoke that fire of attraction between them again to trick him into impregnating her?

Available in February 2010 from Mills & Boon® Desire™

The Executive's Valentine Seduction
by Merline Lovelace

&

Valente Must Marry
by Maxine Sullivan

Blackmailed Into a Fake Engagement
by Leanne Banks

&

Tempted Into the Tycoon's Trap
by Emily McKay

Featuring a bonus story by Maureen Child

The Duke's Boardroom Affair
by Michelle Celmer

&

Convenient Marriage, Inconvenient Husband
by Yvonne Lindsay

THE DUKE'S
BOARDROOM
AFFAIR

BY
MICHELLE CELMER

CONVENIENT
MARRIAGE,
INCONVENIENT
HUSBAND

BY
YVONNE LINDSAY

⊙™ MILLS & BOON®

All the characters in this book have no existence outside the imagination of the author, and have no relation whatsoever to anyone bearing the same name or names. They are not even distantly inspired by any individual known or unknown to the author, and all the incidents are pure invention.

All Rights Reserved including the right of reproduction in whole or in part in any form. This edition is published by arrangement with Harlequin Enterprises II B.V./S.à.r.l. The text of this publication or any part thereof may not be reproduced or transmitted in any form or by any means, electronic or mechanical, including photocopying, recording, storage in an information retrieval system, or otherwise, without the written permission of the publisher.

This book is sold subject to the condition that it shall not, by way of trade or otherwise, be lent, resold, hired out or otherwise circulated without the prior consent of the publisher in any form of binding or cover other than that in which it is published and without a similar condition including this condition being imposed on the subsequent purchaser.

® and ™ are trademarks owned and used by the trademark owner and/or its licensee. Trademarks marked with ® are registered with the United Kingdom Patent Office and/or the Office for Harmonisation in the Internal Market and in other countries.

First published in Great Britain 2010
Harlequin Mills & Boon Limited,
Eton House, 18-24 Paradise Road, Richmond, Surrey TW9 1SR

The publisher acknowledges the copyright holders of the
individual works as follows:

The Duke's Boardroom Affair © Michelle Celmer 2009
Convenient Marriage, Inconvenient Husband © Dolce Vita Trust 2009

ISBN: 978 0 263 88159 2

51-0210

Harlequin Mills & Boon policy is to use papers that are natural, renewable and recyclable products and made from wood grown in sustainable forests. The logging and manufacturing processes conform to the legal environmental regulations of the country of origin.

Printed and bound in Spain
by Litografia Rosés S.A., Barcelona

THE DUKE'S
BOARDROOM AFFAIR

BY
MICHELLE CELMER

Bestselling author **Michelle Celmer** lives in southeastern Michigan with her husband, their three children, two dogs and two cats. When she's not writing or busy being a mum, you can find her in the garden or curled up with a romance novel. And if you twist her arm really hard you can usually persuade her into a day of power shopping.

Michelle loves to hear from readers. Visit her website at www.michellecelmer.com or write to her at PO Box 300, Clawson, MI 48017, USA.

Dear Reader,

Welcome to book four of my ROYAL SEDUCTIONS series! The story of Charles Mead, Duke of Morgan Isle, and his personal assistant, Victoria Houghton.

I've never been the corporate type – most days I don't change out of my pyjamas until it's time to make dinner – so Victoria intrigued me from the start. She's so confident and determined. And tough. At least, that was what I saw, until I scratched the surface and realised that she has just as many insecurities as the rest of us. And Charles, a shameless and hopeless flirt, uses every single one to his advantage.

Their interactions are intense, their dialogue witty and sharp and their physical attraction off the charts. It was fun to sit back and see who would tackle whom first. It might surprise you.

You'll even meet a new family member…but I don't want to give too much away. I hope you enjoy it!

I'll see you again soon for the next book in the ROYAL SEDUCTIONS series, when you'll meet the royal family of Thomas Isle and their crown prince, the *Royal Seducer*.

Best,

Michelle

To my Aunt Janet, who,
besides being totally cool and tons of fun,
told me my first dirty joke when I was a kid.
Why does a honeymoon only last six days?
I think you remember the rest…

One

Victoria Houghton had never been so humiliated.

Watching her father lose in a hostile takeover the hotel that had been in their family for generations had been almost more than she could bear—and now she was expected to be a personal assistant to the man who was instrumental in sealing the deal?

The Duke of Morgan Isle, Charles Frederick Mead, lounged casually behind his desk, smug and arrogant beneath the facade of a charming smile, the crisp blue of the Irish Sea a backdrop through a wall of floor-to-ceiling office windows behind him. Dressed in a suit that was no doubt custom-made, his casual stance was at odds with the undeniable air of authority he oozed from every pore.

"I was told I would be taking on a managerial

position," she told him. And along with it a generous salary and profit sharing. Or had they changed their minds about that part, too?

He leaned back and folded one leg casually atop the other. "Until the second phase of the hotel opens, there's nothing for you to manage. And since my personal assistant recently left, you will temporarily replace her."

He must have thought her daft if he believed she would buy that flimsy excuse. She would work in housekeeping, changing linens and scrubbing commodes, if it meant not seeing this man every day. He may have looked pleasant and easygoing, but underneath he was cold and heartless.

"So put me in the part of the hotel that's already completed," she said. "I'll do anything."

"There aren't any openings."

"None?"

He shook his head.

Of course there weren't. Or so he said. To men like him, lying was as natural as breathing. And what of their financial agreement? Surely he didn't expect to pay an assistant the exorbitant salary they had quoted in her contract? "What about my salary and profit sharing?"

He shrugged. "Nothing in the terms of your contract will change."

Her brow perked up in surprise. What was he trying to pull?

"If you consult your attorney, he'll confirm that we're honoring our end of the deal," he assured her.

According to her father, their own attorney had sold them out to get in good with the royal family, so unfortunately he wouldn't be much help. She doubted there was a single attorney on the island who would take on the monarchy, so basically, she was screwed.

"And if I refuse?" she asked, though she already knew the answer.

"You violate the terms of your contract."

He had no idea how tempted she was to do just that. She'd never wanted this job. But refusing it would devastate her father. The sale of his hotel—her legacy—to the royal family for their expansion project had been contingent on her being hired as a permanent manager, and at nearly twice the salary she had been making before. Not to mention incredible benefits. He wanted assurances that she would be well taken care of. And she was helpless to object.

Losing the hotel had put unneeded strain on his already weakening heart. Despite sitting on the prime resort land of the island, since the opening of the newly renovated Royal Inn hotel, occupancy in their much smaller facility had begun to drop. The way the lawyers for the royal family had begun buying up ocean-side property, both she and her father feared it would only be a matter of time before their number was up.

And they had been right.

In his fragile state, more bad news might be all it took to do him in. Since the day her mother and older brother were killed in an automobile accident, when Victoria was only five, he had been her entire life. He had sacrificed so much for her. She couldn't let him down.

With renewed resolve, she squared her shoulders and asked, "When do you expect the second phase of the hotel to open?"

"The additions and renovations are scheduled for completion by the beginning of the next tourist season."

The next tourist season? But that was nearly six months away! Six *days* would be too long to work for this man, as far as she was concerned. But what choice did she have?

Something that looked like amusement sparked in his deep, chocolate-brown eyes. Did he think this was funny?

"Is that a problem?" he asked.

She realized the duke was baiting her. He *wanted* her to violate the terms of her contract so he could get rid of her. He didn't want her services any more than she wanted his charity.

Well, she wouldn't give him the satisfaction of seeing her buckle. He may have broken her father, but there was no way he was going to break her.

She raised her chin a notch and looked him directly in the eye, so he would see that she wasn't intimidated. "No problem."

"Excellent." A satisfied and, though she hated to admit it, *sexy* grin curled the corners of his mouth. Which she didn't doubt was exactly what he wanted her to think.

He opened the top drawer of his desk, extracted a form of some sort, and slid it toward her. "You'll need to sign this."

She narrowed her eyes at him. "What is it?"

"Our standard nondisclosure agreement. Every employee of the royal family is obligated to sign one."

Another trick? But after a quick scan of the document, she realized it was a very simple, basic agreement. And though she wouldn't be working directly for the royal family but instead for the hotel chain they now owned, she didn't feel it was worth arguing. Their secrets would be safe with her.

Yet, as she took the gold-plated pen he offered and signed her name, she couldn't escape the feeling that she had just sold her soul to the devil.

She handed it back to him and he tucked it inside his desk, then he rose from his chair. Short as she was, she was used to looking up to meet people in the eye, but he towered over her. At least a foot and a half taller than her measly five foot one. And he looked so…perfect. His suit an exact fit, his nails neatly trimmed and buffed, not a strand of his closely cropped, jet-black hair out of place.

But men like him were never as perfect as they appeared. God knows she'd met her share of imperfect men. Despite his looks and money and power, he was just as flawed as the next guy. Probably more so. And being that he was an attorney, she wouldn't trust him as far as she could throw him—which, considering their size difference, wouldn't be very far.

"Welcome to the company, Victoria." He extended a hand for her to shake and, determined to be professional, she accepted it.

His hand enfolded her own, gobbling it up, big and warm and firm. And she felt a strange stirring in the pit of her belly. A kind of fluttering tickle.

His hand still gripping hers, he said, "Why don't we discuss your duties over lunch?" But his eyes said he had more than just lunch in mind. Was he *hitting* on her?

You have got to be kidding me.

She came this close to rolling her eyes. The tabloids

were forever painting him as a shameless, ruthless womanizer, but she had always assumed that was just gossip. No man could possibly be that shallow. Perhaps, though, they weren't so far off the mark.

If he believed for an instant that he would be adding her to his list of female conquests, he was delusional.

As graciously as possible she pried her hand loose. "No. Thank you."

He regarded her curiously. Maybe he wasn't used to women telling him no. "My treat," he said, dangling the word in front of her like bait.

Did he really think she was that hard up?

"We're going to be working somewhat closely," he added, and she could swear she heard a hint of emphasis on *closely*. "We should take the time to get to know one another."

They wouldn't be working *that* closely. "I prefer not to mix business with pleasure."

She wondered if he would insist, citing it as part of their contract, but he only shrugged and stepped around his desk. "Well, then, I'll show you to your office."

Instead of taking her back through the outer office, past the grim-faced, aged secretary she'd met on the way in, he led her through a different door to a smaller, sparsely decorated, windowless office with little more than an empty bookcase, a comfortable-looking leather office chair, and an adequately sized desk. On it's surface sat a phone, a laptop computer and a large manila envelope.

"Everything you need is on your computer," he explained. "You'll find a list of all your duties, along with any phone numbers you may need as well as a copy of my personal schedule. If you're unsure of how to use the program you can ask Penelope, my secretary, for help."

"I'm sure I can figure it out."

He picked up the envelope and handed it to her. "Inside is a badge for this building, and another that will give you access to the business offices at the palace—"

"The *palace?*" She never imagined that going to the palace would be a part of the job description.

"I keep an office there and often attend meetings with King Phillip. Have you ever been there?"

She shook her head. She'd only seen photographs. Not that she hadn't imagined what it would be like.

"Well, then, I'll have to give you a tour."

Okay, maybe there would be *some* perks to this job. The idea of being in the palace, and possibly meeting members of the royal family, filled her with nervous excitement. Then she reined in her wayward emotions by reminding herself that this was not going to be a fun job. And given the choice, she would rather be anywhere but here.

"You'll also find a set of card keys," he continued, "for both your office and mine. They're marked accordingly. And in a separate envelope is your personal security code for my house."

Why on earth would he give her access to his house?

"My driver will be at your disposal twenty-four hours a day. Unless, of course, I'm using him, in which case you will be reimbursed for your petrol use."

A driver? She couldn't imagine what she would need that for. This job just kept getting stranger and stranger.

He gestured to a second door, adjacent to the one connecting their offices.

"That door leads to Penelope's office and will be the entrance that you use. She'll take you on a tour of the building, show you the break room and facilities. If you need to speak to me specifically, call first. The line to my office is marked on the phone. If I don't answer that means I'm busy and not to be disturbed."

"All right."

"My business calls go through Penelope, but any personal calls will be routed through your office or to the cell phone I'll supply you."

Answering phones and taking messages? Not the most challenging job in the world. But the duke was obviously a man who liked things done a certain way, and if nothing else she respected that. More than once her employees at the Houghton had suggested she was a little too rigid when it came to her business practices, but she had never felt an ounce of regret for running a tight ship.

She had been working since the age of twelve, when her father let her help out in the Houghton Hotel office after school. But only after earning her master's degree in business at university was she promoted to manager. Her father had insisted she earn her education, should she ever need something to fall back on.

And, boy, had she fallen back.

"Take some time to look over your duties, then we can discuss any questions you have," he said.

"Fine."

"I have to warn you, I've been without an assistant for a week now, and I'm afraid things are in a bit of a mess."

Honestly, how hard could it be, being a glorified secretary? "I'm sure I can manage."

"Well," the Duke said, with one of those dazzling smiles, "I'll leave you to it, then."

He turned and was halfway through the door before she realized she had no idea how she was supposed to address him. Did she call him Sir, or Sire? Did she have to bow or curtsy?

"Excuse me," she said.

He turned back to her. "Yes?"

"What should I call you?" He looked puzzled, so she added, "Mr. or Sir? Your Highness?"

That grin was back, and, like his handshake, she felt it all the way to the pit of her belly.

Stop that, she warned herself. He only smiled that way because he *wanted* her to feel it in her belly.

"Let's go with Charles," he said.

She wasn't sure if that was proper. Calling him by his first name just felt too…casual. But he was calling the shots, and she wasn't going to give him any reason to accuse her of violating the contract. "All right."

He flashed her one last smile before he closed the door behind him, and she had the distinct feeling he knew something she didn't. Or maybe that was just part of the game. Either way, she refused to let him intimidate her. If they thought they were going to force her out, they had no idea who they were dealing with. She hadn't earned her reputation as a savvy businesswoman by letting people walk all over her.

She took a seat at her new desk, finding the chair to be as comfortable as it looked. But the office itself was cold and impersonal. Since she would be spending at least six months here, it wouldn't hurt to bring a few photos and personal items into work.

She opened the laptop and booted it up. On the desktop were the documents he had mentioned. Convinced this job couldn't get any worse, she opened the one titled *Duties*. Starting at the top, she read her job description, working her way down the two-page, single-spaced list, her stomach sinking lower with each line, until she could swear it slipped all the way down near the balls of her feet. *Personal assistant, my foot*.

She had just agreed to be Charles Frederick Mead's indentured slave.

Two

Charles sat at his desk, watching the time tick by on his Rolex. He gave Victoria five minutes before she stormed into his office in a snit about her employment duties. And he'd bet his ample net worth that she'd forget to call first.

For a woman with her education and experience, the backward step from managing a five-hundred-room hotel to the duties of a personal assistant would be tough to navigate. If it were up to him, he'd have found her a position in the hotel. But it wasn't his call. His cousins, King Phillip and Prince Ethan, were calling the shots.

The Houghton Hotel hadn't been acquired under the best of circumstances—at least, not for the Houghton family—and the royal family needed to know if Victoria was trustworthy before they allowed her into the fold. The logical way to do that was to keep her close.

He could see that she was still distraught over the loss of their hotel and property, but, sadly, the buyout had been inevitable. If not the Royal Inn, some other establishment would have swooped in for the kill. At least with the royal family they were given a fair deal. Other prospective buyers, with less interest in the country's economy, might have been far less accommodating. But it was possible that Victoria and her father, Reginald Houghton, didn't see it that way. But at the very least, she could show a little bit of gratitude. The royal family had saved them the embarrassment of both professional and personal financial devastation.

He'd barely completed the thought when his phone rang. Three short chirps, indicating the call originated from Victoria's office. She remembered.

He glanced at his watch. She was early. Only three and a half minutes.

He answered with a patient, "Yes, Victoria."

"I'm ready to discuss my duties," she said, and there was a distinct undertone of tension in her voice that made him grin.

"That was quick," he said. "Come on in."

The door opened a second later, and she emerged, a look on her face that could only be described as *determined*. For a woman her size, barely more than a nymph, she had a presence that overwhelmed a room. A firestorm of attitude and spunk packed neatly into a petite and, dare he say, *sexy* package. He usually preferred women with long, silky hair—and typically blond—but her shorter, warm brown, sassy style seemed to fit her just right.

He wasn't typically drawn to strong-willed women, but Victoria fascinated him. And he wouldn't mind at all getting to know her better. Which he would, despite what she seemed to believe. It was a simple fact: women found him irresistible. It was exhausting at times, really, the way women threw themselves at him. He didn't help matters by encouraging them. But he just couldn't help himself. He loved everything about women: Their soft curves and the silky warmth of their skin. The way they smelled and tasted. In fact, when it came to the female form, there wasn't a single thing he didn't adore.

This time, he had his sights set on Victoria. And he had yet to meet a woman he couldn't seduce.

"You have questions?" he asked her.

"A few."

He leaned back in his chair and folded his arms. "Let's hear it."

She seemed to choose her words very carefully. "I assumed my duties would be limited to more of a…secretarial nature."

"I have a secretary. What you'll be doing is handling every aspect of my private affairs. From fetching my dry cleaning to screening my e-mail and calls. Making dinner reservations and booking events. If I need a gift for a friend or flowers for a date, it will be your responsibility to make it happen. You'll also accompany me to any business meetings where I might require you to take notes."

She nodded slowly, and he could see that she was struggling to keep her cool. "I understand that you need to fill the position, but don't you think I'm a little *over*-qualified?"

He flashed her a patient and sympathetic smile. "I realize this is quite a step down from what you're used to. But as I said before, until the second phase opens…" He shrugged, lifting his hands in a gesture of helplessness. "If it's any consolation, since my last assistant left, my life has been in shambles. There will be plenty to keep you busy."

For a second she looked as though she might press the issue, then thought better of it. It wasn't often anyone outside of the family contradicted him. It was just a part of the title.

She spared him a stiff, strained smile. "Well, then, I guess I should get started."

He was sure that once she got going, she would find managing his life something of a challenge. He wished he could say the same for seducing her, but he had the sneaking suspicion it would be all too easy.

Charles hadn't been kidding when he said his life was in shambles.

After a quick tour of the building with Penelope, who had the personality and warmth of an iceberg, Victoria started at the top of his to do list. Sorting his e-mail. She had to go through his personal account and first weed out the spam that had slipped through the filter, then compare the sender addresses on legitimate mail to a list of people whose e-mails were to be sorted into several separate categories. Which didn't sound like much of an undertaking, until she opened the account and discovered over *four hundred* e-mails awaiting her attention.

There were dozens from charities requesting his donation or endorsement, and notes from family and friends, including at least three or four a day from his mother. A lot of e-mails from women. And others from random people who admired him or in some cases didn't speak too fondly of him. Cross-referencing them all with the list of addresses he'd supplied her would be a tedious, time-consuming task. And it seemed as though for every e-mail she erased or filed, a new one would appear in his inbox.

When eyestrain and fatigue had her vision blurring, she took a break and moved down to number two on the list. His voice mail. Following his instructions, she dialed the number and punched in the PIN, and was nearly knocked out of her chair when the voice announced that he had two hundred and twenty-six new messages! She didn't get that many personal calls in a month, much less a week. And she couldn't help wondering how many of those calls were from women.

It didn't take long to find out.

There was Amber from the hotel bar, Jennifer from the club, Alexis from the ski lodge, and half a dozen more. Most rang more than once, sounding a bit more desperate and needy with each message. The lead offender for repeated calls, however, was Charles's mother. She seemed to follow up every e-mail she sent with a phone call, or maybe it was the other way around. No less than *three* times a day. Sometimes more. And she began every call the exact same way. *It's your mum. I know you're busy, but I wanted to tell you...*

Nothing pressing as far as Victoria could tell. Just

random tidbits about family or friends, or reminders of events he had promised to attend. A very attractive woman from a good family she would like him to meet. And she seemed to have an endless variety of pet names for him. Pumpkin and Sweetie. Love and Precious. Although Victoria's favorite by far was Lamb Chop.

His mother never requested, or seemed to expect, a return call, and her messages dripped with a syrupy sweetness that made Victoria's skin crawl. How could Charles stand it?

Easily. By having someone else check his messages.

She spent the next couple of hours listening to the first hundred or so calls, transcribing the messages for Charles, including a return phone number should he need to answer the call. Any incoming calls she let go directly to voice until she had time to catch up. Between the e-mail and voice mail, it could take days.

"Working late?"

Startled by the unexpected intrusion, she nearly dropped the phone. She looked up to find Charles standing in the doorway between their two offices. She couldn't help but wonder how long he'd been standing there watching her.

"I'm sorry, what?" she said, setting the phone back in the cradle.

Her reaction seemed to amuse him. "I asked if you're working late."

She looked at her watch and realized that it was nearly eight p.m. She'd worked clear through lunch and dinner. "I guess I lost track of the hour."

"You're not required to work overtime."

"I have a lot of work to catch up on." Besides, she would much rather have been busy working than sitting home alone in the flat she had been forced to rent when her father could no longer afford to keep the family estate. Since she was born, that house had been the only place she had ever called home. But there was a new family living there now. Strangers occupying the rooms that were meant to belong to her own children some day.

Every time she set foot in her new residence, it was a grim, stark reminder of everything they had lost. And Charles, she reminded herself, was the catalyst.

He held up what she assumed was to be her new phone. The most expensive, state-of-the-art gadget on the market. "Before Penelope left she brought this in."

She felt a sudden wave of alarm. His secretary was gone? Meaning they were alone?

She wondered who else was in the building, and if working alone with him was wise. She barely knew him.

"Is everyone gone?" she asked in a voice that she hoped sounded nonchalant.

"This is a law firm. There's always someone working late on a case or an intern pulling an overnighter. If it's safety you're concerned about, the parking structure is monitored by cameras around the clock, and we employ a security detail in the lobby twenty-four seven."

"Oh, that's good to know." Still, as he walked toward her desk to hand her the mobile phone, she tensed the tiniest bit. He was just so tall and assuming. So…*there*.

"It's a PDA as well as a phone. And you can check e-mail and browse the Internet. If you take it to Nigel in tech support on the fourth floor tomorrow morning, he'll set everything up for you."

"Okay." As she took it from him their fingers touched and she had to force herself not to jerk away. It was barely a brush; still, she felt warmth and electricity shoot across the surface of her skin. Which made no sense considering how much she disliked him.

"I've been going through your phone messages," she told him. "Your mother called. Many times."

"Well, there's a surprise," he said, a definite note of exasperation in his voice. "I should probably warn you that when it comes to dealing with my mother, you have to be firm or she'll walk all over you."

"I can do that." Being *firm* had never been a problem for her. In fact, there had been instances when she'd been accused of being *too* firm. A necessity for any woman in a position of power. She had learned very early in her career how not to let people walk all over her.

"Good." He glanced at his watch. "I'm on my way out, and since it would seem that neither of us has eaten yet, why don't you let me take you out to dinner?"

First a lunch invitation, now dinner? Couldn't he take no for an answer? "No, thank you."

Her rejection seemed to amuse him. He shrugged and said, "Have it your way."

What was that supposed to mean? Whose *way* did he expect her to have it? His?

"I'm going to the dry cleaners tomorrow to pick up your laundry," she said. "Do you have anything dirty at home that I should take with me?"

"I do, actually. My housekeeper is off tomorrow

morning but I'll try to remember to set it by the door before I leave for work. Would you like my car to pick you up?"

"I can drive myself." Her father had always had a driver—until recently, anyway—but she never had felt comfortable having someone chauffer her around. She was too independent. She liked to be in control of her environment and her destiny. Which had been much easier when her father owned the company. When she was in charge. Answering to the whims of someone else was going to be…a *challenge*.

He shrugged again. "If that's what you prefer. I guess I'll see you in the morning."

Unfortunately, yes, he would. And nearly every morning for the following six months. "Good night."

For several very long seconds he just looked at her, then he flashed her one of those devastating, sexy smiles before he walked out of her office, shutting the door behind him.

And despite her less-than-sparkling opinion of him, she couldn't help feeling just a tiny bit breathless.

Victoria checked her caller ID when she got home and saw that her father had called several times. No doubt wondering how her first day had gone. All she wanted to do was fall into bed and sleep, but if she didn't call him back he would worry. She dialed his number, knowing she would have to tread lightly, choose her words carefully, so as not to upset him.

He answered sounding wounded and upset. "I thought you wouldn't call."

It struck her how old he sounded. Too frail for a man of sixty-five. He used to be so strong and gregarious. Lately he seemed to be fading away. "Why wouldn't I call?"

"I thought you might be cross with me for making you take that job. I know it couldn't have been easy, working for those people."

That was the way he'd referred to the royal family lately. *Those people.* "I've told you a million times, Daddy, that I am not upset. It's a good job. Where else would I make such a generous salary? If it does well, the profit sharing will make me a very wealthy woman." She found it only slightly ironic that she was regurgitating the same words he had used to convince her to take the position in the first place.

"I know," he conceded. "But no salary, no matter how great, could make up for what was stolen from us."

And she knew that he would live with that regret for the rest of his life. All she could do was continually assure him that it wasn't his fault. Yet, regardless of whose mistake it was, she couldn't help feeling that she would spend the rest of her life paying for it.

"Is it a nice hotel?" he asked grudgingly.

"Well, I didn't actually see the hotel yet."

"Why not?"

Oh, boy, this was going to be tough to explain. "There isn't a manager's position open in the hotel right now," she said, and told him about the job with the duke, stressing that her contract wouldn't change.

"That is completely unacceptable," he said, and she could practically feel his blood pressure rising, could just imagine the veins at his temples pulsing. He'd already had two heart attacks. One more could be fatal.

"It's fine, Daddy. Honestly."

"Would you like me to contact my attorney?"

For all the good that would do her. "No."

"Are you sure? There must be something he can do."

Was he forgetting that it was his attorney who was partially to blame for getting them into this mess?

"There's no need, Daddy. It's not so bad, really. In fact, I think it might be something of a challenge. A nice change of pace."

He accepted her lie, and some of the tension seemed to slip from his voice. He changed the subject and they went on to talk about an upcoming party for a family friend, and she tried to remain upbeat and cheerful. By the time she hung up she felt exhausted from the effort.

Performing her duties would be taxing enough, but she could see that creating a ruse to keep her father placated would be a long and arduous task. But what choice did she have? She was all her father had left in the world. He had sacrificed so much for her. Made her the center of his universe.

No matter what, she *couldn't* let him down.

Three

Charles lived in an exclusive, heavily gated and guarded community fifteen miles up the coast in the city of Pine Bluff. His house, a towering structure of glass and stone, sat in the arc of a cul-de-sac on the bluff overlooking the ocean. It was a lot of house for a single man, but that hardly surprised her. She was sure he had money to burn.

Victoria pulled her car up the circular drive and parked by the front door. She climbed out and took in the picturesque scenery, filled her lungs with clean, salty autumn air. If nothing else, the duke had impeccable taste in real estate. As well as interior design, she admitted to herself, after she used her code to open the door and stepped inside the foyer. Warm beiges and deep hues of green and blue welcomed her inside. The foyer opened up into a spacious living room with a rustic stone fireplace that climbed to the peak of a steep cathedral ceiling. It should have looked out of place with the modern design, but instead it gave the room warmth and character.

She had planned to grab the laundry and be on her way, but the bag he had said he would leave by the door was conspicuously not there. Either he hadn't left yet or he'd forgotten. She was guessing the latter.

"Hello!" she called, straining to hear for any signs of life, but the house was silent. She would have to find the clothes herself, and the logical place to look would be his bedroom.

She followed the plushly carpeted staircase up to the second floor and down an open hallway that overlooked the family room below. The home she had grown up in was more traditional in design, but she liked the open floor plan of Charles's house.

"Hello!" she called again, and got no answer. With the option of going either left or right, she chose right and peered into each of the half-dozen open doors. Spare rooms, mostly. But at the end of the hall she hit the jackpot. The master suite.

It was decorated just as warmly as the living room, but definitely more masculine. An enormous sleigh bed—unmade, she noted—carved from deep, rich cherry dominated the center of the room. And the air teemed with the undeniable scent of the woodsy cologne he had been wearing the day before.

She tried one more firm "Hello! Anyone here?" and was met with silence.

Looked like the coast was clear.

Feeling like an interloper, she stepped inside, wondering where the closet might be hiding. She found it off the bathroom, an enormous space in which row upon row of suits in the finest and most beautiful fabrics she had ever seen hung neatly in order by color. Beside them hung his work shirts, and beside them stood a rack that must have had three hundred different ties hanging from its bars. She wondered if he had worn them all. The opposite side of the closet seemed casual in nature, and in the back she discovered a mountain of dirty clothes overflowing from a hamper conveniently marked Dry Cleaning.

It was shirts mostly. White, beige, and a few pale blue. She also noted that his scent was much stronger here. And strangely familiar. Not the scent of a man she had known only a day. Perhaps she knew someone who wore the same brand.

Purely out of curiosity she picked up one of the shirts and held it to her face, inhaling deeply.

"I see you found my laundry."

She was so startled by the unexpected voice that she squealed with surprise and spun around, but the heel of her pump caught in the carpet and she toppled over into a row of neatly hung trousers, taking several pairs with her as she landed with a thump on the floor.

Cheeks flaming with embarrassment, she looked up to find Charles standing over her, wearing nothing but a damp towel around his slim hips and an amused smile.

She quickly averted her gaze, but not before she registered a set of ridiculously defined abs, perfectly formed pecs, wide, sturdy shoulders, and biceps to die for. Damn her pesky photographic memory.

"I didn't mean to startle you," he said. He reached out a hand to help her up and she was so tangled she had no choice but to accept it.

"What are you doing here?" she snapped when she was back on her feet.

He shrugged. "I live here."

She averted her eyes, pretending to smooth the creases from her skirt, so she wouldn't have to look at all that sculpted perfection. "I'd assumed you'd left for work."

"It's only seven-forty-five."

"I called out but no one answered."

"The granite in the master bath was sealed yesterday, so I was using the spare room down the hall."

"Sorry," she mumbled, running out of places to look, without him realizing she was deliberately not looking at him.

"Something wrong with that shirt?" he asked.

She was still clutching the shirt she had picked up from the hamper, and she realized he must have seen her sniffing it. What could possibly be more embarrassing?

"I was checking to see if it was dirty," she said, cringing inwardly at that ridiculously flimsy excuse.

Charles grinned. "Well then, for future reference, I don't make a habit of keeping clean clothes in the hamper."

"I'll remember that." And she would make a mental note to never come into his house until she was entirely sure he wasn't there, or at the very least fully clothed. "Well, I'll get out of your way."

She turned and grabbed the rest of the clothes from the hamper, stacking them in her arms. He stepped out of her way and she rushed past him and through the doorway.

"Might as well stick around," he said.

She stopped and turned to him, saw that he was leaning casually in the closet doorway. She struggled to keep her eyes from wandering below his neck. "Why?"

"I was going to call my driver, but since you're here, I'll just catch a ride into work with you."

He wanted to ride with *her?* "I would, but, um, I have to stop at the dry cleaners first. I don't want to get you to work late."

"I don't mind." He ran his fingers through the damp, shiny waves of his hair, his biceps flexing under sun-bronzed skin. She stood there transfixed by the fluidity of his movements. His pecs looked hard and defined, and were sprinkled with fine, dark hair.

He may have been an arrogant ass, but God, he was a beautiful one.

"Give me five minutes," he said, and she nodded numbly, hoping her mouth wasn't hanging open, drool dripping from the corner.

"There's coffee in the kitchen," he added, then he turned back into the closet, already loosening the knot at his waist.

The last thing she saw, as he disappeared inside, was the towel drop to the floor, and the tantalizing curve of one perfectly formed butt cheek.

Charles sat in the passenger side of Victoria's con-vertible two-seater, watching her through the window of the dry cleaner's. He would have expected her to drive a more practical car. A sedan, or even a mini SUV. Not a sporty, candy-apple-red little number that she zipped around in at speeds matched only on the autobahn. And it had a manual transmission, which he found to be a rarity among females. Sizewise, however, it was a perfect fit. Petite and compact, just like her. So petite that his head might brush the top had he not bent down.

She was full of surprises today—the least of which was her reaction when he greeted her wearing nothing but a towel. To put it mildly, she'd been flustered. After her chilly reception last night in the office, he was beginning to wonder if she might be a bit tougher to seduce than he had first anticipated. Now he was sure that she was as good as his. Even if that meant playing dirty. Like deliberately dropping his towel before he cleared the closet door.

Victoria emerged from the building with an armload of clean clothes, wrapped in plastic and folded over one arm. She tucked them into the trunk, then slipped into the driver's seat. Her skirt rode several inches up her thighs, giving him a delicious view of her stocking-clad legs.

If she noticed him looking, she didn't let on.

"They got the stain out of your jacket sleeve," she told him, as she turned the key and the engine roared to life. She checked the rearview mirror for oncoming traffic, then jammed her foot down on the accelerator and whipped out onto the road, shifting so smoothly he barely felt the switch of the gears.

She swung around a corner and he gripped the armrest to keep from falling over. "You in a hurry?"

She shot him a bland look. "No."

She downshifted and whipped around another corner so fast he could swear the tires on one side actually lifted off the pavement.

"You know, the building isn't going anywhere," he said.

"This is the way I drive. If you don't like it, don't ask to ride with me." She took another corner at high speed, and he was pretty sure she was doing it just to annoy him.

If she drove this way all the time, it was a wonder she was still alive. "Out of curiosity, how many accidents have you been in?"

"I've never been in an accident." She whipped into the next lane, cutting off the car directly behind them, whose driver blared its horn in retaliation.

"Have you caused many?"

She shot him another one of those looks. "No."

"Next you'll try to tell me you haven't gotten a speeding ticket."

This time she stayed silent. That's what he figured.

She took a sharp left into the underground parking at his building, used her card key to open the gate, zipped into her assigned spot, and cut the engine.

"Well, that was an adventure," he said, unbuckling his seat belt.

She dropped her keys in her purse and opened her door. "I got you here alive, didn't I?"

Only by the grace of God, he was sure.

They got out and walked to the elevator, taking it up to the tenth floor. She stood silently beside him the entire time. She could never be accused of being too chatty. Since they left his house she hadn't said a word that wasn't initiated by a question. Maybe she was in a snit about the towel. She had enjoyed the free show, but didn't want to admit it.

The elevator doors opened at their floor, and as they stepped off he rested a hand on the small of her back. A natural reaction, but she didn't seem to appreciate his attempt to be a gentleman.

She jerked away and shot lasers at him with her eyes. "What are you doing?"

He held his hands up in a defensive gesture. "Sorry. Just being polite."

"Do you touch all of your female employees inappropriately?"

What was her problem? Here he thought she'd begun to warm to him, but he couldn't seem to get an accurate read on her.

"I didn't mean to offend you."

"Well, you did."

A pair standing in the hallway outside his office cut their conversation short to look at him and Victoria.

"Why don't we step into my office and talk about this," he said quietly. She nodded, then he almost made the monumental error of touching her again, drawing his hand away a second before it grazed her shoulder.

He couldn't help it; he was a physical person. And until today, no one had ever seemed to have a problem with that.

Penelope was already sitting at her desk, tapping away at her keyboard. The only hint of a reaction as he ushered Victoria to his office door was a slight lift of her left brow. He liked that about his secretary. She was always discreet. He also knew exactly what she was thinking. He'd lost another assistant already. Not all that unusual, until he factored in that he hadn't even slept with this one yet.

"Penelope, hold my calls, please." He opened the door and gestured Victoria inside, then closed it behind them. "Have a seat."

Her chin jutted out stubbornly. "I'd rather stand, thank you."

"Fine." He could see that she wasn't going to make this easy. He rounded his desk and sat down. "Now, would you like to tell me what the problem is?"

"The *problem* is that your behavior today has been completely inappropriate."

"All I did was touch your back."

"Employers are not supposed to walk around naked in front of their employees."

He leaned forward and propped his elbows on the desk. "I wasn't naked."

"Not the entire time."

So, she had been looking. "Need I point out that you were in *my* house? When I walked into *my* closet I had no reason to expect you would be there. Sniffing my shirts."

Her cheeks blushed pink, but she didn't back down. "And I suppose the towel accidentally fell off."

"Again, if you hadn't been ogling me, you wouldn't have seen anything."

Her eyes went wide with indignation. "I was not ogling you!"

"Face it, sweetheart, you couldn't keep your eyes off me." He leaned back in his chair. "In fact, I felt a little violated."

"*You* felt violated?" She clamped her jaw so tight he

worried she might crack her teeth. She wasn't easy to rile, but once he got her going…damn.

"But I'm willing to forgive and forget," he said.

"I've read your e-mails and listened to your phone messages. I know the kind of man that you are, and I'm telling you to back off. I don't want to be here any more than you want me to, but you have done such a thorough job of ruining my family that I need this position. The way I see it, we're stuck with each other. If you're trying to get me to quit, it isn't going to work. And if you continue to prance around naked in front of me and touch me inappropriately I'll slap a sexual harassment suit on you so fast you won't know what hit you."

He couldn't repress the smile that was itching to curl the corner of his mouth. "I was *prancing?*"

Her mouth fell open, as though she couldn't believe he was making a joke out of this. "You really are a piece of work."

"Thank you."

"That wasn't a compliment! You have got to be the most arrogant, self-centered—" she struggled for the right word, but all she could come up with was "—*jerk* I have ever met!"

He shrugged. "Arrogant, yes. Self-centered, occasionally. But anyone will tell you I'm a nice guy."

"Nice?"

"And fair."

"Fair? You orchestrated the deal that ruined my father. That stole from us the land that has been in our family for five generations, and you call that fair? We

lost our business and our home. We lost *everything* because of you."

He wasn't sure where she was getting her information, but she was way off. "We didn't *steal* anything. The deal we offered your father was a gift."

Her face twisted with outrage. "A *gift?*"

"He wouldn't have gotten a better deal from anyone else."

"Ruining good men in the name of the royal family doesn't make it any less sleazy or wrong."

This was all beginning to make sense now. Her lack of gratitude toward the royal family and her very generous employment contract. And there was only one explanation. "You have no idea the financial shape that the Houghton was in, do you?"

She instantly went on the defensive. "What is that supposed to mean? Yes, my father handled the financial end of the business, but he kept me informed. Business was slow, no thanks to the Royal Inn, but we were by no means sinking."

Suddenly he felt very sorry for her. And he didn't like what he was going to have to do next, but it was necessary. She deserved to know the truth, before she did something ill-advised and made a fool of both herself and her father.

He pressed the intercom on his desk. "Penelope, would you please bring in the file for the buyout on the Houghton Hotel."

"What are you doing?" Victoria demanded.

Probably making a huge mistake. "Something against my better judgment."

Victoria stood there, stiff and tight-lipped until Penelope appeared a moment later with a brown accordion file stuffed to capacity. She handed it to Charles, but not before she flashed him a swift, stern glance. Penelope knew what he was doing and the risk he was taking. And it was clear that she didn't approve. But she didn't say a word. She just walked out and shut the door behind her.

"The contents in this file are confidential," he told Victoria. "I could be putting my career in jeopardy by showing it to you. But I think it's something you need to see. In fact, I know it is."

At first he thought she might refuse to read it. For several long moments she just stared at him. But curiosity must have gotten the best of her, because finally she reached out and took the file.

"Take that into your office and look it over," he said.

Without a word she turned and walked through the door separating their offices.

"Come see me if you have questions," he called after her, just before she shut the door firmly behind her. And he was sure she would have questions. Because as far as he could tell, everything her father had told her was a lie.

Four

Victoria felt sick.

Sick in her mind and in her heart. Sick all the way down to the center of her soul. And the more she read, the worse she felt.

She was barely a quarter of the way through the file and it was already undeniably clear that not only had the royal family not stolen anything from her and her father, they had rescued them from inevitable and total ruin.

Had they not stepped in, the bank would have foreclosed on mortgages she hadn't even been aware that her father had levied against the hotel. And he was so far behind in their property taxes, the property had been just days from being seized.

The worst part was that the trouble began when Victoria was a baby, after her grandfather passed away and her father inherited control of the hotel. All that time he'd been riding a precarious, financial roller coaster, living far above their means. Until it had finally caught up to him. And he had managed to keep it a secret by blatantly lying to her.

She had trusted him. Sacrificed so much because she thought she owed him.

Because of the royal family's generous offer, she and her father had a roof over their heads. And she had the opportunity for a career that would launch her further than she might have ever dreamed possible. Yet she still felt as though the rug had been yanked violently from under her. Everything she knew about her father and their business, *about her life,* was a lie.

And she had seen enough.

She gathered the papers and tucked them neatly back into the file. Though she dreaded facing Charles, admitting her father's deception, what choice did she have? Besides, he probably had a pretty good idea already that something in her family dynamic was amiss. If nothing else, she owed him an apology for her unfounded accusations. And a heartfelt thank-you for… well…*everything*. His family's generosity and especially their discretion.

And there was only one thing left to do. Only one thing she *could* do.

She picked up the phone and dialed Charles's extension. He answered on the first ring. "Is now a good time to speak with you?"

"Of course," he said. "Come right in."

She hung up the phone, but for several long seconds

just sat there, working up the courage to face him. And she thought yesterday had been humiliating. Getting her butt out of the chair and walking to his office, tail between her legs, was one of the hardest things she'd ever done.

Charles sat at his desk. He had every right to look smug, but he wore a sympathetic smile instead. And honestly she couldn't decide which was worse. She didn't deserve his sympathy.

She handed him the file. "Thank you for showing me this. For being honest with me."

"I thought you deserved the truth."

She took a deep breath. "First, I want to thank you and the royal family for your generosity. Please let them know how much we appreciate their intervention."

"'We'?" he asked, knowing full well that her father didn't appreciate anything the royal family had done for them.

Although for the life of her, she couldn't imagine why. Pride, she supposed. Or stubbornness. Whatever the reason, she was in no position to make excuses for him. Nor would she want to. He had gotten them into this mess, and any consequences he suffered were his own doing.

"And while I appreciate the opportunity to work for the Royal Inn," she said, removing her ID badge and setting it on his desk, "I'm afraid I won't be accepting the position."

His brow furrowed. "I don't understand."

She had taken this job only to appease her father, and now everything was different. She didn't owe him anything. For the first tine in her life she was going to make a decision based entirely on what *she* wanted.

"I'm not a charity case," she told Charles. "I owe you too much already. And unlike my father, I don't care to be indebted to anyone."

"You've seen the file, Victoria. We were under no obligation to your father. Do you honestly believe we would have hired you if we didn't feel you were qualified for the position?"

She didn't know what to believe anymore. "I'm sorry, but I just can't."

"What will you do?"

She shrugged. She was in hotel management, and the Royal Inn was the biggest game on the island. She would never find a position with comparable pay anywhere else. Not on Morgan Isle, anyway. That could mean a move off the island. Maybe it was time for a change, time to stop leaning on her father and be truly independent for the first time in her life. Or maybe it was he who had been leaning on her.

"I'll find another job," she said.

"What will you do until then?"

She honestly didn't know. Since the buyout, what savings she'd had were quickly vanishing. If she went much longer without a paycheck, she would be living on the streets.

"I have an idea," Charles said. "A mutually beneficial arrangement."

She wasn't sure she liked the sound of that, but the least she could do was hear him out. She folded her arms and said, "I'm listening."

"You've seen the shambles my life is in. Stay, just long enough to get things back in order and to hire and train a new assistant, and when you go, you'll leave with a letter of recommendation so impressive that anyone would be a fool not to hire you."

It was tempting, but she already owed him too much. This was something she needed to do on her own.

She shook her head. "You've done too much already."

He leaned forward in his seat. "*You* would be the one doing *me* the favor. I honestly don't have the time to train someone else."

"I've been here *two* days. Technically someone should be training me."

"You're a fast learner." When she didn't answer he leaned forward and said, "Victoria, I'm desperate."

He did look a little desperate, but she couldn't escape the feeling that he was doing it just to be nice. Which shouldn't have been a bad thing. And she should have been jumping at his offer, but she couldn't escape the feeling that she didn't deserve his sympathy.

"Do this one thing for me," he coaxed, "and we'll call it even. You won't owe me and I won't owe you."

She would have loved nothing more than to put this entire awful experience behind her and start fresh.

"I would have to insist you pay me only an assistant's wage," she said.

He looked surprised. "That's not much."

"Maybe, but it's fair."

"Fine," he agreed. "If that's what you want."

"How long would I have to stay?" she asked.

"How about two months."

Yeah, right. "How about one *week?*"

He narrowed his eyes at her. "Six weeks."

"Two weeks," she countered.

"Four."

"Three."

"Deal," he said with a grin.

She took a deep breath and blew it out. Three weeks working with the duke. It was longer than she was comfortable with, but at the very least it would give her time to look for another job. She had interviewed hundreds of people in her years at the Houghton, yet she had never so much as put together a résumé for herself. Much less had to look for employment. She barely knew where to begin.

"I'll have Penelope post an ad for the assistant's position. I'll leave it to you to interview the applicants. Then, of course, they'll have to meet my approval."

"Of course."

"Why don't we catch an early lunch today and discuss exactly what it is I'm looking for?" His smile said business was the last thing on his mind.

Were they back to that again?

If she was going to survive the next three weeks working for him, she was going to have to set some boundaries. Establish parameters.

"I'm not going to sleep with you," she said.

If her direct approach surprised him, he didn't let it show. He just raised one brow slightly higher than the other. "I don't know how you did things at the Houghton, but here, *lunch* isn't code for sex."

On the contrary, that's exactly what it was. Practically everything he said was a double entendre. "I'm not a member of your harem."

One corner of his mouth tipped up. "I have a harem?"

Was he forgetting that she'd listened to his phone messages? "I just thought I should make it clear up front. Because you seem to believe you're God's gift to the female race."

He shot her a very contrived stunned look. "You mean I'm *not?*"

"I'm sorry to say, I don't find you the least bit attractive." It was kind of a lie. Physically she found him incredibly attractive. His personality, on the other hand, needed serious work.

He shrugged. "If you say so."

He was baiting her, but she wouldn't give him the satisfaction of a response. "Have a list of employment requirements to me by end of day and I'll see that the ad is placed." She already had a pretty good idea of the sort of employee he was looking for. More emphasis on looks than intelligence or capability. But she was going to find him an assistant who could actually do the job. And she would hopefully be doing it sooner than three weeks. The faster she got out of here, the better.

"You'll have it by five," he said.

"Thank you. I should get back to work." She still had a backload of e-mail and phone messages to sort through.

She was almost to her office when he called her name, and something in his voice said he was up to no good. She sighed quietly to herself, and with her hand on the doorknob, turned back to him. Ready for a fight. "Yes?"

"Thank you."

"For what?" she asked, expecting some sort of snappy, sarcastic comeback or a sexually charged innuendo.

Instead, he just said, "For sticking around."

She was so surprised, all she could do was nod as she opened the door and slipped into her office. The really weird thing was, she was pretty sure he genuinely meant it. And it touched her somewhere deep down.

If she wasn't careful, she just might forget how much she didn't like him.

It was almost four-thirty when Charles popped his head into her office and handed Victoria the list of employment requirements. And early, no less.

"Are you busy?" he asked.

What now? Wasn't it a bit early for a dinner invitation? "Why?"

"You up for a field trip?"

She set the list in her urgent to-do pile. "I guess that all depends on where you want to go." If it was a field trip to his bedroom, then no, she would pass.

"I have a meeting at the palace in half an hour. I thought you might want to tag along. It would be a chance for you to learn the ropes."

A tickle of excitement worked its way up from her belly. Anyone who lived on Morgan Isle dreamed of going to the palace and meeting the royal family.

But honestly, what was the point? "Why bother? I'll only be working for you for three weeks."

"Yes, but how will you train your replacement if you don't learn the job first?"

He had a point. Although his logic was a little

backward. But the truth was, she really *wanted* to go. After all, when would she ever get an opportunity like this one again?

"When you put it that way," she said, pushing away from her desk, "I suppose I should."

"A car is waiting for us downstairs."

She grabbed her purse from the bottom desk drawer and her sweater from the hook on the back of the door, then followed him through the outer office past Penelope—who didn't even raise her head to acknowledge them—to the elevator. He was uncharacteristically quiet as they rode down and he led her through the lobby to the shiny, black, official-looking Bentley parked out front. Not that she knew him all that well, but he always seemed to have something to say. Too much, usually.

They settled in the leather-clad backseat, and the driver pulled out into traffic. She wasn't typically the chatty type, but she felt this irrational, uncontrollable urge to fill the silence. Maybe because as long as they were talking, she didn't have to think about the overpowering sense of his presence beside her. He was so large, filled his side of the seat so thoroughly, she felt almost crowded against the door. It would take only the slightest movement to cause their knees to bump. And the idea of any sort of contact in the privacy of the car, even accidental, made her pulse jump.

When she couldn't stand the silence another second, she heard herself ask, "Not looking forward to this meeting?"

The sound of her voice startled him, as though he'd forgotten he wasn't alone. "Why do you ask?"

"You seem…preoccupied."

"Do I?"

"You haven't made a single suggestive or inappropriate comment since we left your office."

He laughed and said, "No, I'm not looking forward to it. Delivering bad news is never pleasant."

He didn't elaborate, and though she was dying of curiosity, she didn't ask. It was none of her business. And honestly, the less she knew about the royal family's business, the better.

The drive to the palace was a short one. As the gates came into view, Victoria's heart did a quick shimmy in her chest. She was really going to visit the royal palace. Where kings and queens had lived for generations, and heads of state regularly visited. Though she had lived on Morgan Isle her entire life, not ten miles from the palace, she never imagined she would ever step foot within its walls. Or come face-to-face with the royal family.

Charles leaned forward and told the driver. "Take us to the front doors." He turned to Victoria. "Normally you would use the business entrance in the back, but I thought for your first visit you should get the royal treatment."

The car rolled to a stop, and royally clothed footmen posted on either side of the enormous double doors descended the stairs. One opened the car door and offered a hand encased in pristine white cotton to help her out. It was oddly surreal. She'd never put much stock in fairy tales, but standing at the foot of the palace steps, she felt a little like Cinderella. Only she wasn't there for a ball. And even if she were, there were no single princes in residence to fall in love with her. Just an arrogant, womanizing duke.

Which sounded more like a nightmare than any fairy tale she'd ever read.

She and Charles climbed the stairs, and as they approached the top the gilded doors swung open, welcoming them inside.

Walking into the palace, through the cavernous foyer, was like stepping into a different world. An alternate reality where everything was rich and elegant and larger than life. She had never seen so much marble, gold, and velvet, yet it was tastefully proportioned so as not to appear gaudy. She turned in a circle, her heels clicking against marble buffed to a gleaming shine, taking in the antique furnishings, the vaulted and ornately painted ceilings.

Though she had seen it many times in photos and on television documentaries, and on television documentaries, those were substitute for the real thing.

"What do you think?" Charles asked.

"It's amazing," she breathed. "Does everyone who visits get this kind of welcome?"

"Not exactly. But I feel as though everyone should experience the entire royal treatment at least one time. Don't you think?"

She nodded, although she couldn't help wondering if he had done this out of the kindness of his heart or if instead he had ulterior motives. She knew from experience that men like him often did. How many other women had he brought here, hoping to impress them with his royalty? Not that she considered herself one of his *women*. But he very well might. In fact, she was pretty sure he did. Men like him objectified women, saw them as nothing more than playthings.

And she was buying into it. Playing right into his hand. Shame on her for letting down her guard.

She put a chokehold on her excitement and flashed him a passive smile. "Well, thank you. It was a nice surprise."

"Would you like to meet the family?" he asked.

Her heart leapt up into her throat. "The f-family?"

"We have a meeting scheduled, so they should all be together in the king's suite."

The *entire* family? All at once? And he said it so casually, as if meeting royalty was a daily occurrence for her.

But what was she going to tell him? *No?*

"If it's not a problem," she said, although she didn't have the first clue what she would say to them.

"They're expecting us."

Expecting them?

She went from being marginally nervous to shaking in her pumps.

He stepped forward, toward the stairs, but she didn't budge. She couldn't. She felt frozen in place, as though her shoes had melted into the marble.

He stopped and looked back at her. "You coming?"

She nodded, but she couldn't seem to get her feet to move. She just stood there like an idiot.

Charles brow furrowed a little. "You okay?"

"Of course." If she ignored the fact that her legs wouldn't work and that a nest of nerves the size of a boulder weighed heavy in her gut.

A grin curled one corner of his mouth. "A little nervous, maybe?"

"Maybe," she conceded. "A little."

"You have nothing to worry about. They don't bite." He paused then added, "Much."

She shot him a look.

He grinned and said, "I'm kidding. They're looking forward to meeting you." He jerked his head in the direction of the stairs. "Come on."

She didn't pitch a fit this time when Charles touched a hand to the small of her back to give her a gentle shove in the right direction. But he kept his hands to himself as he led her up the marble staircase to the second floor, gesturing to points of interest along the way. Family portraits dating back centuries, priceless heirlooms and gifts from foreign visitors and dignitaries.

It all sounded a bit rehearsed to her, but the truth was, as the family lawyer, he'd probably taken lots of people on a similar tour. Not just women he was hoping to impress. And it did take her mind off of her nerves.

"The family residence is this way," he said, leading her toward a set of doors guarded by two very large, frightening-looking security officers. He gestured to the wing across the hall. "The guest suites are down that way."

Feeling like an interloper, she followed him toward the residence. The guards stepped forward as they approached, and Victoria half-expected them to tackle her before she could make it through the doors. But instead they opened the doors and stepped aside so she and Charles could pass. Inside was a long, wide, quiet hallway and at least a dozen sets of double doors.

Behind one of those doors, she thought, waited the entire royal family. And what she hadn't even considered until just now was that each and every one of them knew the dire financial situation she and her father had been in. For all she knew, they might believe she was responsible. She could only hope that Charles had told them the truth.

"Ready?" he asked.

Ready? How did one prepare herself for a moment like this? But she took a deep breath and blew it out, then looked up at Charles and said, "Let's do it."

Five

Victoria was tough, Charles would give her that.

Typically when people were introduced to members of the royal family, it was one or two at a time. Victoria was meeting King Phillip and Queen Hannah; Prince Ethan and his wife, Lizzy; and Princess Sophie and her fiancé, Alex, all at the same time.

Everyone was gathered in the sitting room of Hannah and Phillip's suite, and they all rose from their seats when he and Victoria entered.

If she was nervous, it didn't show. Her curtsy was flawless, and when she spoke her voice was clear and steady. It never failed to intrigue him how a woman so seemingly small and unassuming could dominate a room with sheer confidence. He could see that everyone was impressed. And though it was totally irrational, he felt proud of her. Hiring her had in no way been his idea. He had merely been following orders.

After the introductions and several minutes of polite small talk, an aide was called in to give Victoria a tour of the business offices and familiarize her with palace procedure.

"I like her," Sophie said, the instant they were gone. It had been at her insistence that they had hired Victoria in the first place.

Charles nodded. "She's very capable."

"And attractive," Ethan noted, which got him a playful elbow jab in the side from his very pregnant wife, Lizzy.

"Stunning," Hannah added.

"Quite," Charles agreed. "And she would have been an asset to the Royal Inn."

"Would have been?" Phillip asked.

Sophie narrowed her eyes at Charles. "What did you do?"

"Nothing!" He held both hands up defensively. "I swear."

He explained Victoria's outburst and admitted to showing her the file on the Houghton sale. "She seems to think we see her as some sort of charity case. She has no idea her expertise. Nor does she have the slightest clue how valuable she is. Had it not been for her, I think the Houghton would have collapsed years ago."

"Then it will be up to you to see that she learns her value," Phillip said.

Easier said than done when she was suspicious of his every move. "She's stubborn as hell. But I'm sure I can convince her."

"Stubborn as hell," Alex said, glancing over at Princess Sophie. "She'll fit right in, won't she?"

Now she narrowed her eyes at him. "Is it so wrong that I don't want my wedding to be a spectacle? That I prefer small and intimate?"

"You have other news for us?" Phillip asked Charles, forestalling another potential wedding argument.

Yes, it was time they got to it. Charles took a seat on the couch beside Sophie, rubbing his palms together.

"I gather the news isn't good," Ethan said.

"The DNA test confirmed it. She's the real deal," Charles told them. "Melissa Thornsby is your illegitimate sister and heir to the throne."

"We have a sister," Sophie said, as though trying out the sound of it. Phillip and Hannah remained quietly concerned.

"And here I believed I had the distinction of being the only illegitimate heir to the throne," Ethan quipped, even though he was the one who had taken the time to investigate their father's notorious reputation with women, and the possibility of more illegitimate children. But who could have imagined that King Frederick would have been so bold as to not only have an affair with the former prime minister's wife but to father a child with her? And he never told a soul. Had Ethan not stumbled across a file of newspaper clippings King Frederick had left hidden after his death, they might never have learned the truth.

"She's older than Phillip?" Lizzy asked.

"Twenty-three days," Charles said.

Everyone exchanged worried glances, but Hannah

broached the subject no one else seemed willing to speak aloud. "Could she take the crown?"

This was the part Charles hadn't been looking forward to. "Technically? Yes, she could. Half Royal or not, she's the oldest."

Hannah frowned. "But she wasn't even raised here."

"She was born here, though. She's still considered a citizen."

In an uncustomary show of emotion, Phillip cursed under his breath. Losing the crown for him wouldn't be an issue of status or power. Phillip truly loved his country and had devoted his entire life in the preparation to become its leader. To lose that would devastate him. "We'll fight it," he said.

"I don't think it will come to that," Charles said. "She doesn't seem the type to take on the role as the leader of a country. Despite a first-rate education, other than heading up a host of charities, she's never had a career."

"As a proper princess wouldn't," Phillip said, sounding cautiously optimistic. "Meaning she could very well fit right in."

"Would she be the type to go after our money?" Sophie asked.

Charles shook his head. "I seriously doubt it."

"Why?"

"Because she has almost as much money as you do. She inherited a considerable trust from her parents on her twenty-first birthday, and her aunt and uncle left her a fortune. She's at the top of the food chain in New Orleans high society."

"How did she take the news?" Hannah asked.

"According to the attorney, it was definitely a shock, but she's eager to meet everyone. So much so that she's dropping everything so that she can move here. Temporarily at first. Then she'll decide if she wants to stay."

"Her place is here with her family," Sophie said.

"We can't force her to stay," Lizzy pointed out.

"True," Hannah said, looking pointedly at Phillip. "But if we make her feel welcome she'll be more inclined to."

It was no secret that when Ethan joined the family, Phillip had been less than welcoming to his half brother. But in Phillip's defense, Ethan had gone out of his way to be difficult. Since then, they had put their differences aside and now behaved like brothers. Not that they didn't occasionally butt heads.

"When will she come?" Phillip asked.

"Saturday."

"We'll need to see that a suite is prepared," Sophie said. "I suggest housing her in the guest suite at first, with restricted privileges to the residence."

"I agree," Phillip said. "Lizzy, can you please handle the details?"

Lizzy nodded eagerly. Going from full-time employment to royal status had been rough for her. And despite a somewhat trying pregnancy, she was always looking for tasks to keep her busy until the baby arrived. "I'll take care of it immediately."

Phillip turned to Sophie, who handled media relations. "We'll have to issue a press release immediately. I don't want to see a story in the tabloids before we make a formal announcement."

Sophie nodded. "I'll see that it's done today."

"Speaking of the tabloids," Alex said, "you know they're going to be all over this. And all over her." Having recently been a target of the media himself when his ex-wife fed them false information about his relationship with the princess, he knew how vicious they could be.

"She'll be instructed on exactly what she should and shouldn't say," Charles assured him. "Although given her position in society, I don't think handling the press will be an issue."

"I'd like to keep this low-key," Phillip said, then he rose from his seat, signaling the end of the meeting. "Keep us posted."

Hannah tugged on his sleeve. "Are you forgetting something, Your Highness?"

He looked down at his wife and smiled. "You're sure you want to do this now?"

She nodded.

He touched her cheek affectionately, then announced, with distinct happiness and pride, "Hannah is pregnant."

Everyone seemed as stunned as they were excited.

Sophie laughed and said, "My gosh! You two certainly didn't waste any time. Frederick is barely three months old!"

Hannah blushed. "It wasn't planned, and I only just found out this morning. We'd like to keep it quiet until closer to the end of my first trimester. But I was too excited not to tell the family."

"I think it's wonderful," Lizzy said, a hand on her

own rounded belly. She shot Sophie a meaningful glance. "At this rate we'll have the palace filled with children in no time."

Sophie emphatically shook her head. "Not from me you won't. Alex and I have already discussed it and decided to wait until he's not traveling back and forth to the States so much."

"You say that now," Lizzy teased. "Things have a way of not working out as you plan."

She would know. Her pregnancy had been an unplanned surprise. She'd gone from palace employee to royal family member with one hasty but genuinely happy *I do*.

"What about Charles?" Sophie said, flashing him a wry grin. "He's not even married yet. Why not pick on him?"

"When it comes to marriage," Phillip said, sounding only slightly exasperated, "*yet* is not a word in Charles's vocabulary."

Phillip was absolutely right. And this was not a conversation Charles cared to have any part of. The last thing he needed was the entire family meddling in his love life.

"Wow," he said, glancing down at his watch. "Would you look at the time. I should be going."

"What's the matter, Charles?" Sophie asked. "Have you got a hot date?"

In fact he did. Even though the "date" in question didn't know it yet.

Phillip just grinned. "If you hear anything else from Melissa or her attorney, you'll let us know?"

"Of course." He said the obligatory goodbyes, then

made a hasty retreat out into the hall. Before he could escape the residence, Ethan called after him.

"Charles, hold up a minute." He wore a concerned expression, which was enough to cause Charles concern himself. Ethan was one of the most easygoing people he knew.

"Is there a problem?" he asked.

Ethan paused for a moment, then sighed and shook his head. "I guess there's really no tactful way to say this, so I'm just going to say it. The family is asking, as a personal favor, that you not have an affair with Victoria."

For an instant, Charles was too stunned to speak. Then all he could manage was "I beg your pardon?"

"You heard me."

Yes, he had. But he must have been mistaken. He'd devoted his life to his family, true, but that didn't give them the right to dictate who he could or couldn't sleep with. "What are you suggesting, Ethan?"

Ethan lowered his voice. "I don't have to *suggest* anything. It's common knowledge that the employees you sleep with don't last. Normally that isn't a problem because they're *your* personal employees, and how you run your firm is your own business. But Victoria is an employee of the royal family, as are you, and as such, policy states there can be no personal relationship. If we can convince her to stay, her expertise will be a great asset to the Royal Inn. That isn't likely to happen if you and she become…*intimately* involved."

"That's a little hypocritical coming from you," Charles said. "Seeing as how you knocked up a palace employee."

It was a cheap shot, but the arrow hit its mark.

Ethan's expression darkened. "Make no mistake Charles, this is something the *entire* family is asking. Not just me."

And what if Charles said no? What if he slept with her and she refused to stay? Would he be ousted as the family attorney? "This sounds a bit like a threat to me."

"It's nothing more than a request."

Though only a cousin, Charles had always been an integral part of the royal family. For the first time in his life he felt like an outsider.

And he didn't like it.

"Do whatever it takes to make her stay," Ethan said, and there was a finality to his words that set Charles even deeper on edge.

"I need to go fetch my assistant," Charles told him, then he turned and left before he said something he might later regret.

He found Victoria in the main business office with one of the secretaries. For the life of him he couldn't remember her name. She was explaining the phone and security system to Victoria. As he approached they both looked up at him.

"Finished already?" Victoria asked.

Charles nodded. "Ready to go?"

"Sure." She thanked the secretary, whose name still escaped him, grabbed her purse, and followed Charles out. She practically had to jog to keep up with his brisk, longer stride. He led her out the back way this time, where she would come and go should the position ever call for her coming back to the palace.

"Meeting not go well?" she asked from behind him, as they passed the kitchen.

"What makes you think that?"

"You're awfully quiet. And you seem to be in a terrible rush to leave," she said, sounding a touch winded.

He made an effort to slow his pace. It wasn't the meeting itself that was troubling him. That had gone rather well, all things considered. "It was fine," he said.

The car was waiting for them when they stepped out of the back entrance. They got in, and he almost directed the driver to take them back to the office, but then he remembered that he was treating Victoria to dinner.

Instead he told him, "The Royal Inn."

"Why are we going to the Royal Inn?" she asked.

"I'm taking you to Les Régal De Rois for dinner," he said. He expected an argument or an immediate refusal. Instead she just looked amused, which rubbed his already frayed nerves.

"Is that an invitation?" she asked.

"No. Just a fact."

"Really?"

He nodded. "Yep."

"What about my car?"

"It'll be fine in the parking garage overnight. I'll arrange for my car to pick you up in the morning."

She mulled that over, looking skeptical. He steeled himself for the inevitable argument. In fact, he was looking forward to it. He needed a target to vent a little steam. Even though he was supposed to be convincing her to stay, not using her for target practice.

Instead she said, "Okay."

"Okay?"

"I'll go to dinner with you, but only if I get to choose the restaurant."

He shrugged. "All right."

"And you have to let me pay."

Absolutely not. He never let women pay. It had been hammered into him from birth that it was a man's duty—his *responsibility*—to pick up the check. As far as his mother was concerned, chivalry was alive and kicking.

"Considering your current employment status, it might be wise to let me cover it," he said.

She folded her arms across her chest. "Let me worry about that."

Would it hurt to let her *think* she was paying? But when it came time to get the bill, he would take it. It's not as if she would wrestle it out of his hand. At least, he didn't think she would. She may have been independent, but he knew from experience that deep down, all women loved to be pampered. They liked when men held doors and paid the check. Expected it, even.

"Fine," he agreed.

She leaned forward and instructed the driver to take them to an unfamiliar address in the bay area. For all he knew she could be taking him to a fast-food establishment.

The driver looked to Charles for confirmation, and he nodded.

What the heck. He was always up for an adventure.

Six

It wasn't a fast food restaurant.

It was a cozy, moderately priced bistro tucked between two upscale women's clothing stores in the shopping district. The maître d' greeted Victoria warmly and Charles with the proper fuss afforded royalty, then seated them at a table in a secluded corner. It was quiet and intimate and soaked in the flickering glow of warm candlelight. Their waiter appeared instantly to take their drink orders—a white wine for Victoria and a double scotch for him—then he listed the specials for the evening.

"I recommend the prime rib," Victoria said, once he was gone.

Charles drew the line at letting his date order for him, and he used the term *date* very loosely. Besides, his encounter with Ethan had pretty much killed his appetite.

"I take it you come here often," he said.

"I love this place," Victoria said with a smile. An honest to goodness, genuine smile. And the force of it was so devastating it nearly knocked him backward out of his chair. She might not have smiled often, but it was certainly worth the wait.

The waiter reappeared only seconds later with their drinks. Charles took a deep slug of scotch, relishing the smooth burn as it slid down his throat and spread heat through his stomach. Three or four more of these and he would be right as rain, but he'd never been one to find solace in a bottle.

Victoria took a sip of her wine, watching him curiously. "Would you like to talk about it?"

"Talk about what?"

"Whatever it is that's bothering you." She propped her elbow on the table, dropped her chin in her hand, and gazed across the candlelight at him, her eyes warm, her features soft in the low light.

She really was stunning. And not at all the sort of woman he was typically attracted to. But maybe that was the appeal. Maybe he was tired of the same old thing. Maybe he needed to spice things up a bit.

The family had put the kibosh on that, though, hadn't they? And since when did he ever let anyone tell him whom he could or couldn't pursue?

"What makes you think something is bothering me?"

"That's why I agreed to dinner," she said. "You looked as though you needed a sympathetic ear."

She certainly looked sympathetic, which for some reason surprised him. He never imagined her having a soft side. But he wasn't one to air his troubles. Although, would it hurt to play the pity card this one time? And maybe, in the process, do his job and convince Victoria to stay with the hotel?

He pulled in a deep, contemplative breath, then blew it out. "Family issues," he said, keeping it cryptic. Baiting her. But if he expected her to try to drag it out of him, boy, had he been wrong.

She just sat there sipping her wine, waiting for him to continue.

He dropped another crumb. "Suffice it to say that the family wasn't happy to hear that you're not staying with the Royal Inn."

"I'm sorry to hear that."

"I've been instructed to do whatever it takes to convince you to stay."

If she was flattered, it didn't show on her face. "But that isn't what's bothering you," she said.

Who was baiting whom here?

Though he'd had no intention of telling her what was really said, he supposed that if anyone could understand a backstabbing, meddling family, it was her.

"I've been asked by the family not to pursue you socially."

A grin tipped up the corners of her mouth. "In other words, don't sleep with me."

Her candor surprised him a little, but then, what did she have to lose? This was only a temporary position for her. "That was the gist of it, yes."

"And that upsets you?"

"Wouldn't it upset you?"

"I suppose. But then, I don't have a notorious reputation for sleeping with my employees."

He couldn't help but wonder where she'd heard that. "According to whom?"

"The girls in the palace office talk."

He couldn't exactly deny it, but still he felt... offended. Whom he dated was no one's concern. Especially the girls in the office. "What else did the *girls* have to say about me?"

"Are you sure you want to know?"

Did he? Did it even matter? When had he ever cared what people thought of him?

But curiosity got the best of him. "I'm a big boy. I think I can handle it."

"They told me that your assistants never last more than a few weeks."

Again, he couldn't deny it. But that was just the nature of business. Assistants' positions notoriously had a high turnover rate. Most were overworked and underpaid.

Were the girls in the office taking that into account?

Not to say that he was an unfair employer. But he didn't owe anyone an explanation.

"And I'm not your usual type."

"I have a type?"

"Tall, leggy, impressed by your power and position."

Could he help that people were impressed by his title?

"Oh, and they told me that you objectify women," she added. "But I already knew that."

Wait, what? He *objectified* women? "No, I don't."

She looked a little surprised by his denial. "Yes, you do."

"I have nothing but respect for women. I *love* women."

"Maybe that's part of the problem."

"What the hell is that supposed to mean?" And why did he even care what she thought of him?

"This is upsetting you," she said. "Maybe we should just drop it."

"No. I want to know how it is that I objectify women."

She studied him for a minute, then asked, "How many different women have you dated in the last month?"

"What does that have to do with anything?"

"Humor me."

"Eight or ten, maybe." Maybe more. In fact, if he counted the casual encounters in bars or clubs that led back to his bedroom, that number was probably closer to fifteen. But that didn't mean anything. Wanting to play the field, not wanting to settle down yet, did not equate into disrespect for the opposite sex.

"What were their names?" she asked.

That one stopped him. "What do you mean?"

"Their names. The women you dated. They had names, right?"

"Of course."

"So, what were they?"

He frowned. That was a lot of names. Faces he could remember, or body types. Hair color, even eye color. Names he wasn't so good with.

"I'll make it easy for you. Of the last twenty girls you dated, give me *three* names," she said.

Three names? What about the blonde from the bar last week. The bank teller with the large and plunging… portfolio. It was something simple. A *J* name. Jenny, Julie, Jeri. Or maybe it was Sara.

He was usually pretty good under pressure, but now he was drawing a blank.

"You can't do it, can you?" Victoria said, looking pleased with herself. "Here's an easy one. How about your last assistant? What was her name?"

Now this one he knew. Tall, brunette. Low, sultry voice…

It was right there, on the tip of his tongue.

"Oh, come on," she said. "Even I know this."

He took a guess, which he knew was probably a bad idea. "Diane."

"Her name was Rebecca."

"Well, she looked like a Diane to me." Mostly he'd just called her honey, or sweetheart, so he wouldn't *have* to remember her name. Because after a while they all just sort of bled together. But that didn't mean anything.

She shook her head. "That's really sad."

"So I'm not great with names. So what?"

"Name the last five male clients you met with."

They popped into his head in quick succession. One after the other, clear as if he'd read them on a list. And though he said nothing, she could read it in his expression.

The smile that followed was a smug one. "Easier, isn't it?"

He folded his arms across his chest, not liking the direction this was taking. "What's your point?"

"You remember the men because you respect them. You see them as equals. Women on the other hand exist only for your own personal amusement. They're playthings."

Though his first reaction was to deny the accusation, it *was* an interesting…hypothesis. And one he had no desire to contemplate at that particular moment, or with her.

He downed the last of his drink and signaled the waiter for the check. "We should go."

"We haven't eaten yet."

"I have to get an early start in the morning."

Her smug smile grew, as though she was feeding off his discomfort. To make matters worse, before he could take the bill from the waiter, she snatched it up. "My treat, remember?"

There didn't seem much point in arguing. And since it was only drinks, he would let her have her way this once.

She paid in cash, leaving a generous tip considering they hadn't even eaten, then they rose from their chairs and walked in silence to the door. The car was already waiting for them out front.

"I'll see you tomorrow," she said.

"You don't want a ride?"

She shook her head. "No, thanks."

"It's quite chilly."

"I'm just a few blocks from here. I could use the fresh air."

"I'll walk you," he said, because God forbid she would also accuse him of not being a gentleman.

"No, I'm fine," she said, with a smile. "But I appreciate the offer."

There was something very different about her tonight. He'd never seen her so relaxed. So pleasant and…happy.

At his expense, no doubt.

"See you tomorrow at the office." She turned to

walk away, but made it only a step or two before she stopped and turned back. "By the way, have you decided what to do?"

"What do you mean?"

"Your family? Not pursuing me. Will you listen to them?"

Good question. And despite all the hemming and hawing and claims that no one could tell him who he could or couldn't see, he had an obligation to the family. Ultimately, there was really only one clear-cut answer.

He shrugged. "I don't really have much choice."

"Well, in that case…"

Another one of those grins curled her mouth. Playful, bordering on devious, and he had the distinct impression that she was up to no good.

She stepped closer, closing the gap between them, then reached up with one hand and gripped his tie. She gave it a firm tug, and he had no choice but to lean over—it was that or asphyxiation. And when he did, she rose up on her toes and kissed him. A tender, teasing brush of her lips against his own.

Before he could react, before he could cup the back of her head and draw her in for more, it was over. She had already let go of his tie and backed away. His lips burned with the need to kiss her again. His hands ached to touch her.

He wanted her.

"What was that for?" he asked.

She shrugged, as though she accosted men on the street on a regular basis. "Just thought you should know what you're missing."

* * *

Victoria knew that kissing Charles was a really bad idea, but he had looked so adorably bewildered by their conversation in the restaurant, so hopelessly confused, she hadn't been able to resist. She thought it would be fun to mess with his head, knock him a little further off base. But what she hadn't counted on, what she hadn't anticipated, was the way it would make *her* feel.

She'd kissed her share of men before, but she felt as though, for the first time in her life, she had *really* kissed a man. It was as if a switch in her brain had been flipped and everything in her being was saying, *He's the one.*

Which was as ridiculous as it was disturbing.

Yet her legs were so wobbly and her head so dizzy that once she'd rounded the corner and was out of sight, she collapsed on a bench to collect herself.

What was wrong with her? It was just a kiss. And barely even that. So why the weak knees? The frantically beating heart and breathless feeling? Why the tingling burn in her breasts and between her thighs?

Maybe that was just the effect he had on females, something chemical, or physiological. Maybe that was why he dated so many women. They genuinely couldn't resist him.

That was probably it, she assured herself. Pheromones or hormones or something. And the effect was bound to wear off. Eventually she would even grow immune to it altogether.

She just hoped to God that he hadn't noticed. That before she let go he hadn't felt her hands shaking, that he hadn't seen her pulse throbbing at the base of her throat or the heat burning her cheeks. That he hadn't heard the waver in her voice before she turned and walked away. If he knew what he did to her, he could potentially make her life—the next few weeks, anyway—a living hell.

When she felt steady enough, she walked the two blocks to her flat. She unlocked the outer door and headed up the stairs to the third floor. The building was clean and well tended, but the flat itself was only a fraction the size of her suite at the family estate.

She stepped inside and tossed her keys and purse on the table by the door. It would be roomier once she emptied all of the boxes still sitting packed in every room. But her heart just wasn't in it. It didn't feel like home.

The light on her answering machine was flashing furiously. She checked the caller ID and saw that every one that day was from her father. He was probably eager to talk to her about the royal family, tell her more lies to cover his own mistakes.

Well, she wasn't ready to talk to him. The sting of his betrayal was too fresh. She would end up saying something she would later regret.

She erased the messages without listening to them and turned off the ringer on her phone. At times like this she wished she had a best girlfriend to confide in. Even a casual friend. Only now, with her career in the toilet, was she beginning to realize what she'd missed out on when she made the decision to devote herself entirely to her career. For the first time in her life she truly felt alone. And when she thought of her father's betrayal, the feeling intensified, sitting like a stone in her belly.

All those years of dedication and hard work, and what had it gotten her? Thanks to her father, she had lost nearly everything.

But was it fair to blame it all on him? Didn't she shoulder at least a little bit of the blame? Had she allowed it to happen by not questioning his handling of the finances? By not checking the books for herself?

By trusting him?

But what reason had he given her not to?

She shook her head and rubbed at the ache starting in her temples. Self-pity would get her nowhere. She needed to get over it, pick up the pieces, and get on with her life. And the first thing on her agenda: finding Charles a new assistant and finding herself a new job. Despite their desire to keep her in their employment, she would never feel comfortable working for the royal family. She couldn't shake the idea that their job offer had nothing to do with skill, that they had hired her out of pity.

She would never feel as though she truly fit in.

First thing in the morning she would place an ad for the assistant's position and phone her contacts at the various employment agencies in the bay area. In no time she would have Phillip a new assistant. A *capable* assistant.

And until then, she would stay as far from Charles as humanly possible.

Seven

So much for keeping her distance from Charles.

As promised, he sent his car to fetch Victoria before work the next morning. When she heard the knock at her flat door, she just assumed it was the driver coming up to get her. But when she opened the door, Charles stood there.

He leaned casually against the doorjamb, looking attractive and fit in a charcoal pinstripe suit, a grin on his face. And not a trace of the ill ease he'd worn like a shroud the night before.

"Good morning," he said, then added, "*Victoria.*"

Okay. "Good morning…Charles."

"I thought you would be impressed. I remembered your name."

He'd apparently taken what she said to heart. She

was genuinely and pleasantly surprised. It didn't last long, though.

"I'd say that I deserve a reward," he said, with an exaggerated wiggle of his brows.

The man was a shameless flirt, and though she hated to admit it, his teasing and innuendo wasn't nearly as offensive as it used to be.

And to be fair, he had remembered her name right from the start. Which meant nothing when she considered that she and her father were the topic of many a conversation prior to her employment with him. Of course he would remember her.

You're rationalizing, Vic.

The best response was no response at all.

"I just need to grab my jacket," she said. "Wait right here."

She dashed off to her bedroom, grabbed her suit jacket, and slipped it on. She was gone less than a minute, but when she returned to the door, it was closed and he wasn't there.

Had he gone back to the car?

"Nice view," she heard him say, and turned to find him standing in her cluttered living room gazing out the window.

He was *in* her flat.

The fact that it was in total disarray notwithstanding, he was just so *there*. Such a distinct and overpowering presence in a room that until that very moment had always felt open and spacious. Now they might as well have been locked in a closet together for the lack of breathing room.

Just relax. This is not as bad as it seems. You're completely overreacting.

She folded her arms across her chest, doing her best to sound more annoyed than nervous. "You don't take direction well, do you?"

He turned to her and smiled, and she felt it like a sucker punch to her belly. The worst part was that she was pretty sure he knew exactly what that smile was doing to her. And he had intended exactly that.

You just had to kiss him, didn't you?

He gestured out the window. "You have an ocean view."

Barely. Only a few snippets of blue through the buildings across the road. Nothing like the view from his home. Although it was looking decidedly more pleasing with him standing there.

Ugh. She really had to stop these random, destructive thoughts.

"I don't recall inviting you inside," she said.

"Yeah, you might want to work on those manners."

She shook her head. "God, you're arrogant."

He just grinned and gestured to the city street below. "How do you like living in the heart of the city?"

It was different. Her father's estate, *their* estate, had been in a rural setting, but she'd spent the majority of her time working in the city. A home in the bay area seemed the logical choice. "It's…convenient. Besides, I needed a change of pace. A place that didn't remind me of everything I've lost."

She cringed inwardly. Why had she told him that? It was too personal. Too private. She didn't want him getting the idea that she liked him. She didn't want to *like* him.

He nodded thoughtfully. "And how is that working out for you?"

Lousy, but he probably already figured that out.

"I'm ready to go." She walked to the door, grabbing her keys and purse from the table.

He didn't follow her. He just stood there, grinning, as though he knew something she didn't. "What's the rush?" he asked.

She looked at her watch. "It's eight-twenty."

He shrugged. "So?"

"Isn't the car waiting?"

"It's not going anywhere without us."

She didn't like the way he was looking at her. Or maybe the real problem was she liked it too much. Yesterday she would have considered his probing gaze and bone-melting grin offensive, but this morning it made her feel all warm and mushy inside.

Kissing him had definitely been bad idea.

"I've been doing some thinking," he said, taking a few casual steps toward her.

Her heart climbed up in her throat, but she refused to let him see how nervous he was making her. "About?"

"Last night."

She was tempted to ask, *Which part?* but she had the sinking feeling she already knew. So instead she asked, in what she hoped was a bored and disinterested tone, "And?"

He continued in her direction, drawing closer with every step. "I think I've had a change of heart."

Uh-oh.

She hoped he meant that he'd had a change of heart

about the way he objectified the opposite sex, but somehow she didn't think so.

"Now that I know what I'll be *missing,* maybe I won't be cooperating with the family after all."

Oh, yeah, kissing him had been a *really* bad idea.

He was coming closer, that look in his eyes, like any second he planned to ravish her. And the part that really stunk was that she wanted him to. Desperately. She had assumed that playing the role of the aggressor last night, socking it to him when he was all confused and vulnerable—and a little bit adorable—would somehow put her in a position of control.

Boy, had she been wrong.

He'd managed to turn the tables on her. At that moment, she'd never felt more *out* of control in her life. And the really frightening thing was, she kind of liked it.

"I mean, what's the worst that will happen?" he said.

Hopefully something really bad. "Hanging?"

He was standing so close now that he could reach out and touch her. And though every instinct she possessed was screaming for her to back away, she wouldn't give him the satisfaction of so much as a flinch.

"And then I got to thinking." He leaned in, his face so close to hers she could smell the toothpaste on his breath. "Who says they even have to know?"

Bloody hell, was *she* in trouble. If he decided to kiss her right now, she would have no choice but to kiss him back. And then he would know the truth. That she wasn't nearly as rigid as she'd led him to believe.

His eyes locked on hers. Deep brown irises with flecks of black that seemed to bleed out from his pupils.

Full of something wicked and dangerous. And exciting. And God knew she could have used a little excitement in her life.

No, no, no! Excitement was bad. She liked things even-paced and predictable. This was just chemical.

It took everything in her, but she managed to say, with a tone as bland as her expression, "Are you finished?"

"Finished?"

"Can we go to work now?"

The grin not slipping, he finally backed away and said, "You're tough, Victoria Houghton."

Didn't she wish that were true. Didn't she wish that her heart wasn't pounding so hard it felt as though it might beat right through her rib cage. That her limbs didn't feel heavy with arousal. That her skin would stop burning to feel his touch.

Don't let him know.

"Yes, I am," she lied.

A playful, taunting grin lifted the corners of his lips, and he reached past her to open the door. "But I'm tougher."

By three o'clock that afternoon Victoria managed to catch up on the backlog of calls and e-mails. No thanks to Charles, who, in a fraction of that time, proved himself to be a complete pain in the neck.

He popped into her office a minute after three, for what must have been the fifth time that day. "I heard the phone ring. Any answer to the employment ad?"

He knew damned well that she had just placed the ad with the employment agency that morning and they weren't likely to hear anything until at least tomorrow.

He parked himself behind her chair, hands propped on the back, his fingers brushing the shoulders of her jacket. The hair on her arms shivered to attention and she got that tingly feeling in the pit of her belly. But telling him to back off would only give him the satisfaction of knowing that he was getting to her.

"It was your mother," she told him, leaving off the *again* that could have followed. The woman was ruthless. The kind of mother who drove her children away with affection. It probably didn't help matters that Charles was an only child and the sole focus of her adoration.

No wonder he didn't want to settle down. He was already smothered with all the female attention he could handle.

"What are you working on?" he asked, leaning casually down to peer at her computer monitor, his face so close she could feel his breath shift the hair by her ear.

"A template for an updated, more efficient call and e-mail log."

He leaned in closer to see, his cheek nearly touching hers, and, did he smell delicious. She wanted to bury her face in the crook of his neck and take a long, deep breath. Nuzzle his skin. Maybe take a nibble.

"How does it work?" he asked.

"Work?"

"The spreadsheet."

Oh, right. "When I input the number or e-mail address, it automatically lists all the other pertinent information, so you don't have to waste any time looking it up yourself. It's color-coded by urgency."

"That's brilliant," he said.

She couldn't tell if he meant it or was just being sarcastic. "Oh, yes, I'm sure they'll award me the Pulitzer. Or maybe even the Nobel Peace Prize."

The rumble of his laugh vibrated all the way through her. "You said my mother called again. What did she want this time?"

She swiveled in her chair and stuck a pile of phone messages in his face, so he had no choice but to back off or get a mouthful of fuchsia paper. "To remind you about your father's birthday party. She wanted to confirm that you're spending the *entire* weekend with them."

He took the messages and sat on the edge of her desk instead, riffling through them. "What did you tell her?"

"That you would be there. *All* weekend. And you're really looking forward to it."

He shot her a curious look. "Seriously?"

She flashed him a bright and, yes, slightly wicked smile. "Seriously."

He narrowed his eyes at her. "You didn't really."

"Oh, I did."

She could have sworn that some of the color drained from his face. "That's odd, because I seem to recall telling you to tell her that I wouldn't be able to stay the whole weekend."

"Did you?" she asked innocently. "I guess I forgot."

He knew damned well that she hadn't forgotten anything.

"That's evil," he said.

She just smiled. That was what he got for messing with her—although, in all fairness, she had been the one to kiss him. But she had the feeling that there would be nothing fair about this unspoken competition they had gotten themselves into.

"Just for that, I should drag you along with me," he told her.

A duke bringing his personal assistant home for a weekend visit with the folks. Like that would ever happen. She had the sneaking suspicion that being royals, they clung to slightly higher standards. Or maybe they would make her stay in the staff quarters and take her meals in the kitchen.

Was that what she had been reduced to? Servant's status?

She and her father may not have been megarich, but they had lived a very comfortable lifestyle. The outer edges of upper crust. And to what end? Had he only been honest, lived within their means, she wouldn't be in this mess.

But now was not the time or the place to rehash her father's betrayal.

"I could ring her and tell her you don't want to stay," she told Charles. "That you have better things to do than spend time with your parents. Although, you know, they're not getting any younger."

"Wow," he said, shaking his head. "You and my mother would get along great."

She doubted that. His mother didn't strike her as the type to socialize with the hired help.

"Was there anything else you needed?" she asked, wanting him off her desk. He was too close, smelled too good. "I'd like to get back to work."

"Pressing business?" he asked.

"Keeping up on all the calls and e-mails from your female admirers is a full-time job."

"Maybe, but right now," he said, locking his chocolate eyes on hers and leaning closer, so she was crowded against the back of her chair. "I only have one special woman in my life."

Uh-oh.

Please, please, Victoria silently pleaded, *let it be anyone but me.*

He held up the message slips. "And I'd better go call her and tell her just how much I'm looking forward to the party."

She let out a quiet, relieved breath.

He rose from the corner of her desk, but his scent lingered as he walked to the door. "Buzz me if you hear about the ad."

"The second I hear anything," she promised. Hoping this would be the last time she saw him until it was time to leave for the evening.

Even that would be too soon. Maybe she could just sneak out unnoticed.

It was a dangerous game they had begun playing, but she wasn't about to surrender. She wouldn't let him win. He needed to be knocked down a peg or two. Put in his place. And she was just the woman to do it.

Eight

Charles's mother rang back not fifteen minutes later. The woman was ruthless.

Victoria struggled to sound anything but exasperated by her repeated calls. "I'm afraid he's in a meeting," she said, just as he had instructed her. In a meeting, on another line. He never took personal calls at work. "But I would be happy to take a message."

"I don't mean to bother," she said, which is how she began all of her phone conversations, whether it was the first or tenth call of the day. "I'm just calling about the party, to extend a formal invitation."

Again? Hadn't Victoria already sent an RSVP for him? How many times did she have to invite her own son? "I'll let Charles know," she said automatically.

"Oh, no, not for Charles," she said. "For *you*."

For *her?* But…

Oh, no, he didn't. He *wouldn't.* "For *me,* ma'am?"

"He told us you'll be joining him for the weekend," she gushed excitedly. And the weird thing was, she actually sounded *happy.* "I just wanted you to know how eager we are to meet you. Charles rarely brings his lady friends home."

Lady friends? Did she think…? "Ma'am, I *work* for Charles."

"Oh, I know. But he values your friendship. And any friend of Charles is a friend of ours. His father and I just wanted you to know that you're welcome."

Friendship? Since when were she and Charles friends?

"So, we'll see you then?" his mother asked.

Did Victoria really have the heart to tell her the truth? She sounded so genuinely eager to meet her. How could she tell her it was nothing more than a cruel trick?

So she said the only thing she could. "Yes, of course. I'll see you then."

Victoria was out of her chair before she hung up the phone. Not bothering to knock, she barged into Charles's office. And got the distinct feeling he'd been waiting for her to do just that. He was sitting back in his chair, elbows on the armrests, hands folded across his chest. But it was too late to turn around now.

"You call *me* evil?" she said.

He smiled. "I take it my mother phoned you."

"That was low, even for you."

He looked pleased with himself. "An eye for an eye. Isn't that what they say?"

"I do not what to spend a weekend at your parents's estate."

"Neither do I. But I guess neither of us has a choice now."

"They're not *my* parents. I have no obligation to be there."

He shrugged. "So, ring her back and tell her you don't want to come. I'm sure they won't be too offended."

She glared at him.

"Or, you could come with me and you might actually have fun."

"I seriously doubt that."

"Why?"

"Why? *You* don't even want to go!"

"My parents are good people. They mean well. But when it's just the three of us it can get…stifling. I get there Friday night, and by Saturday afternoon we've run out of things to talk about. With you there it might take a little bit of the pressure off."

"I wouldn't have a clue what to say to your parents. They're completely out of my league."

His brow edged into a frown. "How do you figure?"

"I'm an *employee* of the royal family."

"So what? You're still a person. We're all just people."

Was he really so naive? Did he truly not understand the way the world worked? They were royalty, and she was, and always would be, a nobody in their eyes. Or was this just part of the game he was playing? Lure her to his parent's estate so he could humiliate her in front of his entire family?

His intentions weren't even the issue. The real problem was that she simply didn't trust him.

"You know, you don't give yourself nearly enough credit." He rose from his chair and she tensed, thinking he might come toward her, but he walked around to sit on the edge of his desk instead. Since he'd last been in her office he'd taken off his jacket, loosened his tie, and rolled the sleeves of his dress shirt to his elbows. He seemed to do that every day, after his last meeting.

Casual as he looked, though, he still radiated an air of authority. He was always in control.

Well, almost always.

"Tell me," he said. "How could a woman so accomplished have such a low self-esteem?"

"It has nothing to do with self-esteem. Which I have my fair share of, thank you very much. It's just the way the world works."

"When you met my cousins, did they look down their noses at you?"

"Of course not."

"I think my parents might surprise you. It can't hurt to come with me and find out. Besides, the party should be a blast. Good food and company. And if at any time you feel uncomfortable, I'll take you home."

If she went at all, she would be driving herself. *If* she went?

She couldn't believe she was actually contemplating this. If nothing else, out of curiosity. At least, that's what she preferred to tell herself. There were other possible motivations that were far too disturbing to consider. Like wanting to see the kind of man Charles was around his family. What he was *really* like.

"Fine. I'll go." she said. Then added, "It's not as though I have much choice."

"Smashing," he said, looking truly pleased, which had her seriously doubting her decision.

What was he up to?

"We leave in the afternoon, two weeks from this Friday and return Sunday afternoon."

"I'll meet you there," she said. She wanted her car, in case she needed a quick getaway. And surprisingly, he didn't argue.

"Pack casual," he said. "But the party Saturday night is formal."

Formal? She was expecting an intimate family gathering. Not a social event. "How many people will be there?"

He shrugged. "No more than a hundred or so."

One *hundred?* Her heart seized in her chest. All more wealthy and influential than her.

Smashing.

"You have a dress?" he asked.

From a charity event four years ago. It would be completely out of fashion by now. She didn't exactly have the money to spend on expensive gowns. And for a party like this, nothing less than the best would do.

"I'm sure I can scrounge something up," she said, hoping she sounded more confident than she was feeling.

"You're sure?" he asked. "If it's a strain on the budget right now—"

"It's fine," she snapped. That was the second time

he'd made a reference to her diminishing funds. "It isn't as though I'm destitute."

He held his hands up defensively. "Relax. I wasn't suggesting that."

My God, listen to yourself. Maybe Charles was right. Maybe her self-esteem had taken a hit lately. Maybe her confidence was shot. Why else would she be so touchy?

Maybe she needed to get out with people. Reestablish her sense of self. Or something like that.

She softened her tone. "I'm sorry. I didn't mean to snap."

"If you really don't want to go to the party—"

"I'll go," she said firmly. "For the whole weekend."

Who knows, maybe a short vacation would be good for her. A chance to forget about the shambles her life was currently in and just relax.

And who knew? She might even have fun.

Victoria unlocked her flat door at exactly seven-thirty the following evening. Early by her standards, yet it had felt like the longest day of her life.

Since she'd kissed Charles the other night, then accepted his offer to join him at his parents, the teasing and sexual innuendo hadn't ceased. When they were alone, anyway. When anyone else was around he was nothing but professional. He treated her more like a peer than a subordinate. It was his way of showing that he did indeed respect her.

And maybe the teasing wasn't as bad as it had been at first. Not so immoral. Not that she would allow it to progress to anything more than that.

She dropped her purse and keys on the hall table and headed straight for the wine rack, draping her suit jacket on the back of the couch along the way. She opened a bottle of cabernet, her favorite wine, poured herself a generous glass, kicked off her pumps, and collapsed on the couch.

Charles left work at the same time, making sure to let her know, in the elevator on the way down to the parking structure, that he had a dinner date. As if she cared one way or the other how or with whom he chose to spend his free time. Although she couldn't help wondering who the unlucky girl could be. Amber from the club, perhaps? Or maybe Zoey from the fund-raiser last Friday? Or a dozen others who had called him in the past few days. Or maybe someone new.

Whoever she was, Victoria was just glad it wasn't her.

Are you really? an impish little voice in her head asked. *Aren't you even a little curious to know what the big deal is? Why so many women fall at his feet? They can't all be after his money and title.*

It had to be the wine. It was going straight to her head. Probably because she'd skipped lunch. Again.

You'll waste away to nothing, her father used to warn her, in regard to her spotty eating habits. And it would certainly explain her peculiar lack of energy. Not to mention the noisy rumble in her stomach. She sipped her wine and made a mental list of what was in her refrigerator.

Leftover Thai from three days ago that was probably spoiled by now. A few cups of fat-free yogurt, sour skim milk and a slightly shriveled, partial head of romaine lettuce. The contents of the freezer weren't much more promising. A few frozen dinners long past their expiration date and a bag of desiccated, ice-encrusted peas.

She was weeks past due for a trip to the market, but lately there never seemed to be time. Besides, she'd never been much of a cook. There had never been time to learn. On late nights at the Houghton she ate dinner in her office, or their housekeeper doubled as a cook when the need arose. In fact, in her entire life Victoria had never cooked an entire meal by herself. She wasn't even sure if she knew how.

Nor did she have the inclination to learn.

She sat up and grabbed the pile of carryout menus on the coffee table. The sushi place around the corner was right on top.

That would work.

She grabbed the cordless phone and was preparing to dial when the bell chimed for the door. Who could that be? She hoped it wasn't her father. She hadn't returned any of his calls, and he was probably getting impatient.

Maybe if she didn't answer, whoever it was would go away.

She waited a moment, holding her breath, then the bell chimed again.

With a groan she set the phone and her nearly empty glass on the coffee table and dragged herself up from the couch, a touch dizzy from the wine, and picked her way to the door. She peered through the peephole, surprised to find not her father but Charles standing there.

What in heaven's name did *he* want?

She considered not opening the door, but he'd probably

seen her car parked out front and knew she was home. She just couldn't force herself to be rude.

She unlatched the chain, pulled the door open and asked, "What do you want?"

Despite her sharp tone, he smiled. He was still wearing his work clothes. Well put together, but with just a hint of the end-of-the-day rumples. And he looked absolutely delicious.

Bite your tongue, Vic.

"I realized I still owe you dinner," he said. In his hand he held a carryout bag from the very restaurant she had just been about to phone. As though he had somehow read her mind.

That was just too weird.

"I hope you like sushi," he said, shouldering his way past her into her flat. Uninvited yet again.

So why wasn't she doing anything to stop him?

"And if I don't like sushi?" she asked, following him to the kitchen.

"Then you wouldn't have a menu for a sushi restaurant conveniently by the phone." He set the bag on the counter. "Would you?"

How did he…?

He must have seen it there that morning. The first time he barged in uninvited. "I thought you had a date."

The idea that someone stood him up was satisfying somehow, although, what it really meant was she was his second choice. The veritable booby prize.

"I do." He set the bag on the countertop and grinned. "With you."

What was it she just felt? Relieved? Flattered?

Highly doubtful.

She folded her arms across her chest. "I don't think it can be considered a date when the other party knows nothing about it."

He pasted an innocent look on his face. "Did I forget to tell you?"

He took off his jacket and handed it to her. Like an idiot, she took it. And came this close to lifting it to her nose to breathe in his scent, rubbing her cheek against the fabric. She caught herself at the last second and folded it over her arm instead.

Stop it, Vic.

He wasn't paying attention, anyway. He was busy emptying the bag, opening the carryout containers.

The aroma of the sushi wafted her way, making her mouth water. And if she didn't eat something soon, the wine was going to give her a doozy of a headache.

"I'll have dinner with you," she said, then added, "just this once."

He shrugged, as though her refusing his company had never even crossed his mind. Could he be more arrogant? Or more cute?

No, no, no! He is not cute.

It took only a few disastrous office romances to make her vow never to get involved with a coworker again. Not to mention the other laundry list of reasons she would never get involved with a man like him.

This was just dinner.

"I wasn't sure what you liked, so I got a variety," he said.

"I guess." There was enough there to feed half a dozen people. She would have some left over for lunch and dinner tomorrow. And since he went through all this trouble, the least she could do is offer him a drink. "I just opened a bottle of cabernet."

"I thought you would never ask," he said with a grin, then gestured to the cupboards. "You have plates?"

"To the left of the sink." She draped his jacket neatly over the back of the couch over her own and poured him a glass of wine, then refilled her own glass. She really should slow down, wait to drink until she'd eaten something, but the warm glow of inebriation felt good just then. And it wasn't as if she was completely sloshed or anything. Just pleasantly buzzed.

The dining table was topped with half-unpacked boxes, so she carried their glasses to the coffee table instead. It was that or eat standing up in the kitchen, and she honestly didn't think her legs would hold her up for long. She considered going back into the kitchen to help him, but the couch looked so inviting, she flopped down and made herself comfortable. Some hostess she was, making him serve her dinner. But he didn't seem to mind.

Besides, that's what he got for showing up out of the blue.

"Do you have a serving platter?" Charles called from the kitchen.

"Somewhere in this mess," she said. The truth was she usually just ate straight from the carryout containers. "I haven't gotten that far in my unpacking." She paused, guilt getting the best of her, and called, "Do you want help?"

"No, I've got it."

Good. She rested her head back on the cushions, sipped her wine, and closed her eyes. When she opened them again, he was setting everything down on the coffee table.

"Wake up. Time to eat."

"Just resting my eyes," she said. She sat up and he sat down beside her, so close their thighs were touching. His was solid and warm. She didn't normally let her size bother her, but he just seemed so large in comparison. Intimidating, although not in a threatening way, if that made any sense at all. And, God help her, he was sexy as hell with his collar open and his sleeves rolled up.

She took a tuna roll, dipped it in soy sauce, and popped it into her mouth. He did the same. The delicious flavors were completely lost on her as she watched him eat. He even managed to chew sexy, if that was possible.

She peeled her eyes away, before he noticed her staring, just as the doorbell chimed again.

"Expecting someone?" he asked, like maybe she had a date with some other man that had slipped her mind.

"Not that I recall." She sighed irritably and dragged herself up and walked to the door.

If she weren't so relaxed from the wine, she would have remembered to check the peephole. And if she had, she would have seen it was her father standing there.

Nine

Victoria stepped into the hall and edged the door shut behind her so her father wouldn't see who was sitting on her couch. "Daddy, what are you doing here?"

"You haven't returned my calls. I was concerned."

I'll bet you were, she thought. *Concerned that all of those lies have started catching up to you.* The idea made her heart hurt, but she was too angry to cut him any slack right now.

Besides, now was not the time for that unpleasant discussion. "I'm a little busy right now."

"Too busy for your own father?" He looked old and tired, but she couldn't feel sympathy for him.

She needed another day to think about exactly what she wanted to say to him. Not that she'd thought of much else lately. Maybe she just needed time to be less angry. "I'll call you tomorrow."

His mouth fell open and he stared at her, aghast, as though he couldn't believe she would deny him entrance into her home. "Victoria, I demand to know what's going on."

The door pulled open and Charles appeared behind her wearing a concerned expression. "Everything okay, Victoria?"

She knew he meant well, he was being protective, and in many instances she might have appreciated his intervention.

Now was not one of them.

He'd just done more harm than good.

"What is he doing here?" her father said, spitting out the question.

As if she owed him any explanation at all. Or cared that he was displeased. "Having dinner."

"Dinner?" he said, not bothering to hide his disdain. "You're having dinner with *him?*"

"Yes, I am."

He looked from her to Charles, and she knew exactly what he was thinking. "Are you—?"

"It's just dinner," she said, not that it was any of his business. "And right now you should leave. We'll talk about this another time."

But her father wasn't listening. He was too angry. He knew better than to let himself get upset. It wasn't good for his heart. Or maybe his heart was just fine now, and that was a lie, too.

"How could you do this to me?" he asked. "How could you betray me this way?"

How could *she* do this? Who was he to accuse her of deception? "There's been some betrayal going on, but it certainly isn't coming from my end."

"What do you mean?" He shot Charles a venomous glare. "What has he been telling you?"

"What you should have told me a long time ago."

The angry facade slipped a fraction. "I don't know what you're talking about."

"I saw the files from the sale of the hotel, Daddy. I know about all your debt. All the lies you told me."

"He's trying to turn you against me."

He was still going to deny it? Lie to her face? At the very least she had expected a humbled apology, maybe a plea for forgiveness. Instead he continued to try to deceive her?

She wanted to grab him and shake some sense into him.

She was stunned and angry and hurt. And even worse, she was disappointed. All of her life she had looked up to him. Idolized him even. But he had changed that forever.

"The only one doing that is you, Daddy," she said sadly, knowing that she would never look at her father the same way again.

"I should go," Charles said, taking a step backward from the door. This was a little too intense for his taste. Had he known it was her father at the door, he never would have interfered. He had enough of his own family issues to deal with without taking on someone else's.

Victoria held up a hand to stop him. "No. You stay. *You* were invited. My father is the one who needs to go."

Technically, Charles had shown up unannounced and muscled his way inside. But he didn't think now was the time to argue with her.

"I can't believe you're choosing him over me," her father said.

"And I can't believe you're still lying to me," she shot back, although she sounded more resigned than angry. "Until you can be honest with me, we have nothing left to say to each other."

Before her father could utter another word, she shut the door and flipped the deadbolt, and for several seconds she just stood there. Maybe waiting for him to have a change of heart.

After a moment of silence, she rose up on her toes and peered out the peephole. She sighed quietly, then turned to face Charles and leaned against the door. "He's gone."

"Victoria, I'm really sorry. I didn't mean to—"

"It's not your fault. He's the one who lied to me. He's *still* lying to me."

"I'm sure he'll come around."

She shook her head. "I'm not so sure. You have no idea how stubborn he can be."

If he was anything like Victoria, Charles had a pretty good idea. "What are you going to do?"

"I'm not sure. But I do know what I'm not going to do."

"What's that?"

"All my life I've been doing what my father asked of me. What was *expected* of me. Not anymore."

She surprised him by taking his hand, lacing her fingers through his. She gave it a tug. "Come on."

"Where?"

"Where do you think, genius? To my bedroom."

Wait…what? How had they jumped from dinner to her bedroom? "I beg your pardon?"

He'd been out to get in her knickers since the day he met her. And it certainly wouldn't be the first time he'd taken advantage of a situation to seduce a woman—although she seemed to be doing most of the seducing now. Not to mention that he had a strong suspicion she was slightly intoxicated. Again, that had never stopped him before. Yet, something about this just didn't feel right.

He actually felt…guilty.

She tugged again and he felt his feet moving.

"Hey, don't get me wrong," he said, as he let her lead him down the hall. "I'm not one to pass up revenge sex, but are you sure this is a good idea?"

"I think it's an excellent idea." She dragged him into the bedroom and switched on the lamp beside her bed. Only then did she let go of his hand.

Like the rest of the flat, there were boxes everywhere, but in the dim light the bed looked especially inviting. And oh, so tempting.

But he knew he really shouldn't.

She turned to him and started unbuttoning her blouse.

Christ, she was making it really hard to do the right thing. "Maybe we should step back a second, so you can think about what you're doing."

She gazed up at him though thick, dark lashes. "I

know exactly what I'm doing." The blouse slipped from her shoulders and fluttered silently to the carpet.

Ah, hell.

Underneath she wore a lacy black bra. Sexier than he would have imagined for her. But he'd always suspected, or maybe fantasized, there was more to Victoria. That deep down there was a temptress just waiting to break free.

It looked like he was right.

She reached behind her to unzip her skirt, and desire curled low and deep in his gut. "Are you just going to stand there?" she asked.

"I just don't want you to do something you'll regret." Where was he getting this crap? When did he ever care if a woman had regrets? Was he, God forbid, growing a conscience?

"I'm a big girl. I can handle it." She eased the skirt down her legs, hips swaying seductively, and let it fall in a puddle at her feet. She wore a matching black lace thong and thigh-high stockings. And her body? It was damn near perfect. In fact, he was pretty sure it *was* perfect. And he was so mesmerized that for a minute, he forgot to breathe.

"You've been after me for days," she said. "Don't chicken out now."

Calling him a chicken was a little harsh, considering two days ago she'd accused him of disrespect toward the opposite sex. The woman was a walking contradiction. But an extremely sexy and desirable one.

His favorite kind.

She walked toward him—stalked him was more like

it—and reached up to unfasten the buttons of his shirt. She did look as though she knew what she was doing.

One button, two buttons. He really should stop her. It wouldn't take much. Although he suspected that if he turned her down now, he wouldn't get another chance.

Damn it. It shouldn't be this complicated. Maybe that was what was really bothering him. This had complex and messy written all over it.

One more button, then another. Then she pushed his shirt off his shoulders and down his arms. She gazed up at him, sighing with satisfaction, her eyes sleepy and soft. She flattened her hands on his chest, dragging her nails lightly across his skin all the way to his waistband. She toyed with the clasp on his slacks…

Oh, what the hell.

He circled an arm around her waist and dragged her against him. Her surprised gasp was the last thing he heard before he crushed his mouth down on hers. Hard.

She groaned and looped her arms around his neck, fingers sinking through his hair. Feeding off his mouth.

He scooped her up off her feet and they tumbled onto the mattress together. She was so small he worried he might crush her, but she managed to wriggle out from under him, push him onto his back so she could get at the zipper of his slacks. Then she shoved them, along with his boxers, down his hips, and he kicked them away.

"My goodness," she said, gazing down at him with a marginally stunned expression. "We've certainly been blessed, haven't we?"

Though he hadn't considered it until just then, she was awfully petite. What if she was that small everywhere?

"Too much for you?" he asked.

"Let's hope not." She took a deep breath and blew it out. "Condom?"

"In my wallet, in my jacket." Which was in the other room.

"Right back," she said, hopping up from the bed and darting from the room. A bundle of sexual energy. She was back in seconds, long before he had time to talk any sense into himself.

Who was he kidding? They were already well past the point of no return. Besides, she didn't appear to be having any second thoughts.

He sat up and she tossed him his wallet. He fished a condom out, then, realizing one probably wasn't going to cut it—he hoped—he grabbed one more.

"You're sure those will fit?" she asked, but he could see that she was teasing.

"They're extra large," he assured her, setting his wallet and both condoms on the bedside table.

Victoria stood beside the bed, gazing at him with hungry eyes. She unhooked the front clasp on her bra and peeled it off, revealing breasts that couldn't have been more amazing. Not very big, but in perfect proportion to the rest of her. High and firm. The perfect mouthful. And he couldn't wait to get a taste.

She walked to the bed, easing her thong down and kicking it into the pile with the rest of her clothes. He decided, now that he'd seen the whole package, she really was perfect.

And just for tonight, she was all his.

Though he usually liked to be the one in charge, he

didn't protest when she pushed him down onto his back and climbed on him, straddling his thighs, her stockings soft and slippery against his skin. What he really wanted was to feel them wrapped around his shoulders, but she had something entirely different in mind. She grabbed one of the condoms and had it out of the package and rolled into place in the span of one raspy breath.

It was a surreal feeling, lying there beneath her, and the fact that *she* had seduced him and not the other way around. She was unlike any woman he had been with before. Most tried too hard to impress him, to be what they thought he wanted. For Victoria, it just seemed to come naturally. She leaned down and kissed him, teasing at first. Just a brush of her lips, and a brief sweep of her tongue. She tasted like wine and desire. And when she touched him, raked her nails lightly down his chest, he shivered. She seemed to know instinctively what to do to drive him nuts.

They kissed and touched, teased each other until he did not think he could take much more. Victoria must have been thinking the same thing.

She locked her eyes on his, lowered herself over him and took him inside her. Tentatively at first. She was so slick and hot, so small and tight, he almost lost it on that first slow, downward slide. Then she stopped, and for an instant he was afraid he really might be too much for her, too big. But her expression said he was anything but. It said that she could handle anything he could dish out, and then some. It said that she wanted this just as much as he did.

She rose up, slowly, until only the very tip remained

inside of her. She hovered there for several seconds, torturing him, then, with her eyes still trained on his, sank back down, her body closing like a fist around him. He groaned, teetering on the edge of an explosion. In his life he'd never seen or felt anything more erotic. And if she did that one more time, he *was* going to lose it.

He rolled her over onto her back and plunged into her. She arched up against him, gasping, her eyes widening with shock because he was so deep.

He nearly stopped, to ask her if she was okay, but she was clawing at his back, hooking her legs around his hips, urging him closer, and that said everything he needed to know. He may have been bigger than her, but they fit together just fine. He stopped worrying about hurting her. All he could think about was the way it felt. The way *she* felt. And every thrust brought him that much closer to the edge.

The last coherent thought he had was that this was too good, too perfect, then Victoria shuddered and cried out, her body tensing around him, and he couldn't think at all as she coaxed him into oblivion with her.

Ten

Victoria lay in bed beside Charles, watching him sleep. Typical man. Have sex three or four times then go out like a light.

He looked so peaceful. So…satisfied. A feeling she definitely shared.

In her experience, first times always tended to be a little awkward or uncomfortable. But there was nothing awkward about the way Charles had touched her. She'd once believed that just because a man looked like he would be good in the sack didn't necessarily mean he would be, but Charles had completely blown that theory to smithereens as well.

In fact, he was so ridiculously wonderful, so skilled with his hands and his mouth and every other part of his body, it should have given her pause. He'd obviously had a lot of practice. Yet when he looked at her and touched her, it was as though there had never been anyone else.

It was almost enough to make her go mushy-brained. And she probably would have if she weren't so firmly rooted in reality.

At least now she knew what all the fuss was about.

For a minute there, when he'd first taken off his pants, she honestly thought the size difference might be an issue, but in the end the tight fit and the wonderful friction it created had been the best part. Remarkable size wasn't worth much if a man didn't know how to use it.

And, oh, he did.

The second best part was the knowledge that she was doing something totally wrong for her. Wrong on so many levels. She'd always been the obedient daughter, doing as she was told. She never imagined that a simple thing like being bad could feel *so* good.

But it's just sex, she reminded herself, lest she get carried away and start having actual feelings for him.

She was sure that things would be clearer in the morning, at which point she would realize what she'd really done and feel overwhelming regret. Especially when she got to the office. Wouldn't *that* be awkward? But until then she was going to enjoy it.

She curled up against him under the covers, soaking up his warmth. He sighed in his sleep and wrapped an arm around her.

Nice. Very nice.

She closed her eyes, felt herself drifting off. When she

opened her eyes again, the morning sunlight was peeking through the blinds, and Charles was already gone.

Sleeping with Charles had been a *really* bad idea.

Victoria stood in the elevator at work as it climbed, dreading the moment it reached her floor. The hollow *ting* as the doors slid open plucked every one of her frayed nerves.

He hadn't even had the decency to wake her before he left. He'd just skulked away in the middle of the night. Probably the way he did with all the women he slept with.

Did you really think you were any different?

She had gone from feeling sexy and desirable, feeling *bad,* to feeling…cheap.

He could have at least said goodbye before he left. Maybe given her one last kiss.

You are not going to let this bother you, she told herself as she exited the elevator and walked to her office. Penelope, who typically ignored her, lifted her head as she passed and actually looked at her. Not a nasty look. Just sort of…blank.

She knows. She knows what Charles and I did.

That was ridiculous. It was just a coincidence that she chose today to acknowledge Victoria. After all, she doubted Charles confided in his secretary about his sex life. And how else would she possibly know?

So this was what it felt like to be the office slut.

Fantastic.

Victoria nodded at the old prune, then opened her office door. Feeling edgy and unsettled, she hung her jacket, sat in her chair, and stowed her purse in the bottom desk drawer. Work as usual. This day was no different than any other. Not to mention, this situation was temporary. With any luck, she would hear from the employment agency about a suitable replacement.

She was just about boot to up her computer when the intercom buzzed, startling her half to death, and Charles's voice, in a very professional tone, said, "Would you please come in here, Victoria?"

Her heart jumped up into her throat.

Here we go, the part where he tells you it was fun but it isn't going to happen again. He certainly wasn't wasting any time. Not that she hadn't expected that.

She pressed the call button. "One minute."

The sooner it's over the better. And only once, for a millisecond, would she allow herself to admit that she was the tiniest bit disappointed it had to end. It may have only been sex, but it was damned good sex.

She remembered the invitation to spend the weekend with his family and cringed. That would just be too awkward. She would have to come up with some reason to decline. She doubted he would be anything but relieved.

What had she been thinking? One night of fantastic sex was not worth all of this complication.

She took a deep breath. No point in putting this off any longer. She rose from her chair, walked to the door and pulled it open, stepping inside his office. But he wasn't sitting at his desk.

The door closed behind her, and the next thing she knew, she was in Charles's arms.

"Morning," he said, a wicked grin on his face, and

before she could utter a sound, he was kissing her. Deep and sweet and wonderful. And though everything in her was screaming that this was wrong, she wrapped her arms around his neck and kissed him back.

She didn't care that he was kissing away her lipstick, or rumpling her hair. She just wanted to feel him. To be close to him.

Oh, this was bad.

When he broke the kiss she felt dizzy and breathless. He grinned down at her and said, "Good morning."

She couldn't resist returning the smile. Despite feeling as though her entire world had been flopped upside down, she actually felt…happy.

"If it weren't for the conference call I had this morning," he said, caressing her cheek with the tips of his fingers, "we might still be in bed."

"Conference call?" He left because he had to be at work?

"At six-thirty. You didn't get my note?"

"Note?" He left a note?

"On the pillow."

The rush of pure relief made her weak in the knees. And she didn't even care how wrong it was. "I guess I didn't see it."

A grin curled his mouth. "You didn't think I'd just up and leave without a word, did you?"

She shrugged, feeling ashamed of herself for thinking that. For judging him that way. And automatically assuming the worst. "It doesn't matter."

"Have time to take a break?" he asked with a devilish smile.

"I just got here."

He dipped his head to nibble on her neck. "I don't think your boss will mind."

Office romance. Very bad idea. But neither the affair nor the job were going to last long, so, honestly, why the hell not? Besides, it was really tough to think logically when his hands were sneaking under her clothing, searching for bare skin.

"What about Penelope?" she asked.

He shuddered and shook his head. "Definitely not my type."

She laughed. "That's not what I meant."

"I already told her that I'm not to be disturbed." He kissed her throat, her chin, nibbled the corner of her lips. "It's just you and me."

The old woman would have to be a fool not to realize what was going on, but she already disliked Victoria, so what difference did it make? Besides, Victoria had never been one to care what other people thought of her.

"I'm sure I can spare a minute or two," she said.

He smiled. "It's going to be a lot longer than a minute or two."

He lifted her up in his arms and carried her to the couch. He seemed to like doing that. Taking over, seizing control. And for some reason she didn't mind. Probably because he made her feel so damned good. He was one of those rare lovers who took pleasure for himself only after she had been satisfied first. She had always heard that men like that existed, but she'd never actually met one.

He sat on the couch and set her in his lap. But before he could kiss her, she asked, "Have you done this before?"

"What do you mean?"

"In here, with another assistant." She didn't know where the question came from, or if she even wanted to know the answer. And he looked surprised that she'd asked.

"You know what, never mind. Forget I asked."

She tried to kiss him, before she completely killed the mood, but he caught her face in his hands.

"Hold on, I want to answer that." His eyes locked on hers and he said, "No, Victoria, I haven't."

The way he said it, the way he looked her in the eye, made her believe it was the truth. She had no reason, no *right* to be relieved, but she was. And the tiny part of her that was still doubtful melted into a puddle at their feet.

She wanted this, right here, right now, and she wasn't going to be afraid to take it.

It was almost noon when Victoria finally made it back to her office. And she'd barely been there fifteen minutes, checking phone messages—there were already three from his mother—when Charles quietly opened the door and slipped inside.

She pretended not to hear him skulking around behind her, but when she felt his hands on her shoulders, his lips teasing the back of her neck, he became really hard to ignore.

"Neither of us is going to get anything done if you keep this up," she scolded, but she wasn't doing any-thing to stop him. Although, she thought, maybe she should. Unlike his office, hers didn't have a sturdy lock. In fact, she wasn't sure if it locked at all.

"Just thought I would pop in and say hello," he said, his breath warm on her skin. She couldn't deny that another hour or so in his office was tempting.

No, you have work to do.

"Your smother called," she said. "Several times."

He stopped kissing her. "My what?"

She turned to look at him. He had a quirky grin on his face. "Your mother," she repeated.

"That's not what you said."

What was he talking about? "Yes I did."

He shook his head. "No. You said *smother*. 'My smother called.'"

She slapped a hand over her mouth. Oh my gosh, had she? Had she really said it out loud? "I'm so sorry. That was completely inappropriate."

Rather than look offended, he laughed. "No. That's perfect. 'My smother.' I'll have to tell my father that one."

"No!" What would his father think of Victoria? Insulting his wife like that.

Charles just shrugged. "He knows what she's like. She drives everyone crazy. He'll think it's hilarious."

She swiveled in her chair to face him. "Please don't, Charles. It's going to be awkward enough. I would be mortified."

He didn't look like he got it, but he nodded. "All right. I won't say anything."

"Thank you."

He backed away from her. She couldn't help wondering if she'd offended him somehow, and she realized the idea truly disturbed her. How quickly she'd gone from disliking him to valuing his friendship.

Too fast.

And when he smiled at her, she realized he wasn't the least bit offended. "Can I take you out to dinner tonight?" he asked.

Two nights in a row? Then again, sitting in bed naked feeding each other sushi couldn't really be counted as having dinner out. And her first impulse was to say yes, she would love to. But did she want to make a habit of being seen with him in public? To be crowned his latest conquest? Just another fling? Even though that was exactly what she was.

"I don't think that would be a good idea," she said.

"Why?"

"We're sleeping together, not dating."

He shrugged. "What's the difference?"

"There's a *huge* difference. Sex is temporary. Superficial."

"And dating isn't? According to whom?"

He had a point. "I suppose it can be, but…it's just *different.*"

"I don't date women with the intention of a lasting relationship. So by definition, dating for me is very temporary." He paused, then his brow tucked with concern. "You're not looking for a relationship, are you?"

"With *you?* Of course not!"

He looked relieved, and she knew enough not to take it personally. He was just establishing parameters. It was what men like him did. And it was the truth. He was the last man on earth that she would ever consider for a serious relationship.

"Well, then, what's the problem?" he asked.

"Maybe another time."

He folded his arms over his chest. "You're going to make me chase you, is that it?"

"Chase me? Are you forgetting that I was the one who had to drag you to my bedroom last night?"

"Oh yeah." That devilish, sexy grin was back, and it warmed her from the inside out. He leaned in closer, resting his hands on the arms of her chair. She couldn't help but think, *Oh, boy, here we go again.* "Did I forget to tell you how much I enjoyed it?"

He'd told her several times, but what she'd found even more endearing, most appealing, was that he had been worried about her state of mind, that she might have been acting rashly and making a mistake. She hadn't expected that from a man like him.

Every time she thought she had him pegged, he surprised her.

"Don't you have work to do?" she asked.

He dipped in close and kissed her neck, just below her ear. He'd discovered last night that it was the second most sensitive spot on her body. And he used it to his advantage. "Have dinner with me, Victoria."

She closed her eyes and her head just sort of fell back on its own. "I can't."

"It doesn't have to be a restaurant." He nibbled her earlobe and she shivered. "I'll make us dinner at my place."

Dinner at his house wouldn't be so bad. *But two nights in a row? Won't that be pushing it a little?* Although what he was doing felt awfully good. Could she honestly work up the will to deny herself another night of unconditional pleasure? "I shouldn't," she said, but not with much conviction.

"I'm an excellent cook," he coaxed, pulling her blouse aside to nibble on her shoulder. "My specialty is dessert."

He kissed his way down to her cleavage and a whimper of pleasure purled in her throat. "Well, I do have dry cleaning to drop off. I suppose I could hang around for a little while. And if you happen to have dinner ready…"

He eased himself down on the floor in front of her chair, then pulled her blouse aside, exposing one lace cup of her bra. He took her in his mouth, lace and all, and bit down lightly. Though she tried to hold it in, a moan slipped from her lips.

God, he was good.

He looked up at her with that devilish gleam. "So you'll be stopping by when? Around seven?"

"Seven sounds about right," she said, aware that her door wasn't locked and anyone could walk in. Not that anyone but him ever did. But it was the sense of danger, the possibility that someone *could,* that made her so bloody hot for him. "We really shouldn't do this in here."

"Do what?" He switched to the opposite side and took that one into his mouth.

She grabbed his head, sinking her nails though his hair. "Have sex."

"Who says we're going to have sex?"

"I guess I just assumed."

"Nah." He eased her skirt up around her hips, hooked

his fingers on her thong and dragged it down her legs. He nipped at the flesh on the inside of her upper thigh, the number-one most sensitive area on her body, and she melted into a puddle in her chair.

"Well, then, what would you call it?" she asked, her voice thick with arousal.

He grinned up at her. "Afternoon snack?"

Well, whatever he called it, as he kissed his way upward, she had the sneaking suspicion that neither of them was going to get much work done today.

Eleven

Victoria woke slowly the next morning aware, even before she opened her eyes, something was different. Then it dawned on her.

She wasn't at home.

She was curled up in Charles's bed, warm and cozy between his soft silk sheets.

Too warm and cozy.

She hadn't meant to fall asleep here and risk having someone see her car parked out front. Not to mention that spending the night was just a bad idea. She had planned to go back to her own place, sleep in her own bed. Charles hadn't made it easy, though.

Last night, every time she'd made noises like she was going to leave, he would start kissing her and touching her, and she would forget what she'd been saying. And *thinking*. And when they weren't devouring each other, they lay side by side and talked. About her childhood and his. Which couldn't have been more different.

After a while it got so late, and she'd felt so sleepy. She remembered thinking that she would close her eyes for just five or ten minutes, then she would crawl back into her clothes and drive home.

So much for that plan.

He knew it, too. Charles knew she wanted to leave, and he let her sleep anyway. She wasn't sure how to take that. Most men considered letting a woman spend the night in their house too personal. Did he genuinely want her there, or was it some sort of power play? To see if he could bend her to his will. Did he do that with all of the women he *dated?*

Speaking of Charles…

She reached over and patted the mattress beside her, but encountered only cool, slippery silk.

He had one of those enormous king-size deals that a person could lie spread-eagled in and still not encounter the person lying beside them.

She reached even farther, with the very tips of her fingers, till she hit the opposite edge of the bed.

No one there.

She rose up on her elbow, pried one eye open and peered around. The curtains were drawn and Charles was nowhere to be seen.

Here we go again, she thought. Waking up alone. But how far could he have run this time, seeing as how they were in his house?

Not that he had *run* yesterday morning. He'd gone to work. And he'd left a note.

She sat up and rubbed her eyes. A robe hung over the side of the bed that she was guessing he'd put there for her to use. Thoughtful, yet she couldn't help wondering if all of the women who slept over wore it. Would it smell of someone else's perfume? Would she find strands of another woman's hair caught in the collar? Or did he have the decency to wash it between uses?

His shirt from the night before was draped over the chair across the room, so she padded across the cold wood floor and slipped that on instead. It hung to her knees, and she had to roll the sleeves about ten times, but it was soft and it smelled like him. And she could say with certainty that no other woman had worn it recently.

She stopped in the bathroom and saw that she had a serious case of bed head. An inconvenience of short hair. She rubbed it briskly and picked it into shape as best she could. Next to the sink was a toothbrush still in the package. For her, she assumed.

The man thought of everything. Convenient, if not a little disturbing. He probably had a whole closet full of them. For every woman he brought home.

She brushed her teeth and considered showering, but the stall was dry, and she recalled him saying something about the granite just being sealed the other day. She ventured out into the hallway instead, wondering where he could be.

She poked her head in a few of the rooms, called, "Hello!" But he didn't seem to be anywhere upstairs. Then she caught the scent of freshly brewed coffee wafting up from the lower level, and let her nose lead her to the source.

She found Charles in the kitchen, standing by the sink, the financial section of the newspaper in one hand, a cup of coffee in the other. He was dressed in a pair of threadbare jeans and nothing else, and his hair was even a little rumpled. Very *normal* looking. He looked up and smiled when she stepped in the room. "Good morning."

"Morning."

He eyed her up and down appreciatively. "I left a robe out for you, but honestly, I think I prefer the shirt." He put down the paper and cup, and walked toward her, a hungry, devilish look in his eye, and her stomach did a backflip with a triple twist.

They'd slept together on two separate occasions, so shouldn't that intense little thrill have disappeared by now? Before she could form another thought he wrapped her up in his arms and kissed her senseless, which made her thankful she'd taken the time to brush her teeth.

It should have been awkward or uncomfortable, but it wasn't. It was as though she had spent the night dozens of times before. Maybe he'd had so many women sleep over that it had become second nature waking with a virtual stranger in his house.

Okay, she wasn't a stranger, but still…

She sighed and rested her head on his chest. This was nice. It was…comfortable. Still, she couldn't shake the feeling she was just one insignificant piece to a much larger puzzle that was Charles's romantic life.

"You do this often?" she asked.

"Do what?"

"Sleepovers."

"I'm assuming you mean with women." He eased back to look at her. "Why do you ask?"

She shrugged. "You just seem to have a routine."

His brow perked with curiosity. "I do?"

"The robe, the toothbrush. It was just very…convenient."

"And here I thought I was being polite." He didn't look offended exactly. Maybe a little hurt.

She realized she was being ridiculous. Besides, she didn't want him to get the wrong idea, to think she was being possessive. Because she wasn't.

"I'm sorry," she said. "Forget I said anything. I'm obviously not very good at this."

He grinned down at her. "Oh, no, you were very good. And to answer your question about sleepovers— If I like a woman, and want to spend time with her, I invite her to stay over. Simple as that."

And why shouldn't he? Who was she to judge him? Who he did or didn't spend the night with was none of her business, anyway. She did appreciate his honesty, though.

"Now that we have that out of the way," he said. "Can I interest you in a nonroutine cup of coffee?"

She smiled up at him. "I'd love one."

"Cream or sugar?"

"A little of both."

He grabbed the cup that was already sitting beside his state-of-the-art coffeemaker.

"What will you be up to today?" he asked, as he poured her a cup.

"I should probably work on unpacking. Although, considering my current employment situation, I might have to look into renting a cheaper place. Just until things are settled."

He handed her a steaming cup and she took a sip. The coffee was rich and full-bodied and tasted expensive.

He leaned back against the edge of the counter. "The offer for the job at the Royal Inn is still good. I can even work on getting you out of my office and into a management position sooner if that would sweeten the deal."

She wished she could, but that was no longer an option. The only reason she had even considered it in the first place was for her father's sake.

"You know I can't do that. But thank you. I do appreciate the offer." She leaned against the opposite counter. "What are you doing today?"

"Most likely damage control."

Well, that was awfully direct. Although she wasn't sure how she felt about him referring to their night together as *damage*.

Then he held up the front section of the newspaper and she realized he wasn't talking about them. The headline read in bold type:

Royal Family Reveals Illegitimate Heir

Beside the article was a photo of an attractive woman in her early to mid-thirties who bore a striking resemblance to the king. "Another illegitimate heir?"

"She's their half sister," Charles said. "The result of King Frederick's affair with the wife of the former prime minister."

As if his family hadn't had enough scandal the past couple of years. "Oh, boy."

"Yeah. It's not going to be pretty."

She took the page from him and skimmed the article. Not only was this princess illegitimate, but she was the oldest living heir. Which, the article stated, could mean that she was the rightful heir to the crown itself.

Did this mean King Phillip would lose the crown? A move like that could potentially turn the country upside down.

She was dying of curiosity. But as the family attorney, Charles probably wouldn't be able to tell her more than was divulged in the press release.

"This is what that meeting was about the other day, wasn't it?" she asked.

He nodded. "We wanted to get the press release out as soon as possible, before the tabloids caught wind of it."

From the other room she heard her cell phone ring. It was still in her purse on the couch. "I should get that," she said.

By the time she reached the living room, opened her purse, and wrestled her cell phone out, she'd missed the call. There was no name listed and the number was unfamiliar. Then the phone chirped to indicate that a message had been left. She would listen to it later.

There were also two calls from her father from the night before. Had he called to argue, or was he ready to apologize? She didn't even want to think about that right now.

She needed to get dressed and get back to her own place, before this got too cozy. Besides, she didn't want to wear out her welcome. It would be awkward if he had to ask her to leave.

"Everything okay?"

She turned to find Charles standing in the arch between the living room and the foyer, watching her. She snapped her phone shut and stuffed it back in her purse. "Probably just a wrong number."

"I was about to jump into the shower," he said, walking toward her. "I thought you might like to join me."

Oh, that was so tempting. He was obviously in no hurry to get rid of her. Would it hurt to stay just a little bit longer…?

"I really need to go," she told him.

He didn't push the issue, although if he had, she just might have caved.

"I have family obligations this evening," he said, "but I'm free Sunday night. How about dinner?"

She wondered if he really had family obligations or just some other woman he'd already made plans to see. Although, as far as she could tell, he'd never been anything but honest with her.

She just wasn't ready to trust him yet. "Call me."

He folded his arms across his chest. "Why do I get the feeling that means no?"

She shrugged. "It means call me."

But, in all honesty, it probably did mean no. Even so, she couldn't help wondering, as she headed upstairs to get dressed, if she didn't say yes, would it just be someone else?

The possibility that it might be disturbed her far more than it should have.

* * *

It was amazing that despite being only half Mead, Melissa Thornsby looked so much like her siblings. She had the same dark hair and eyes, and the same olive complexion. She was tall and slim, and she carried herself with that undeniable royal confidence. She even shared similar expressions and gestures. Charles couldn't help wondering: if she had stayed on Morgan Isle after her parents' death, would someone have made the connection years ago?

He stood off to the side of the palace library, where this first meeting was taking place, as introductions were being made. At times like this he couldn't help feeling like an outsider. And, yes, maybe a little envious. But he had his mother, who drowned him in so much attention he couldn't imagine when he would find time for anyone else. And people wondered why he insisted on staying single. He didn't think he could handle his mother *and* a wife demanding his time.

The only catch, he thought, as he watched Phillip cradle his son, was that someday he would like to have children of his own. Not that he needed to be married for that. But he'd seen firsthand what a mess an illegitimate child could cause in a royal family.

Melissa spotted him and walked over.

"You must be Charles." She spoke with an accent mottled with varying intonation. A touch of the New Orleans South combined with a twinge of East Coast dialect, and something else he couldn't quite put his finger on. Very unusual. Especially for a princess.

He nodded. "Welcome home, Your Highness."

She took his hand and clasped it warmly. She carried herself with a style and grace that reeked of old money and privilege. "I wanted to thank you for all you've done. For making all the arrangements."

He was just doing his job. But he smiled and said, "You're welcome."

"It's not every day one is informed they may have an entire family they know nothing about. It could have been messy. I was impressed by how diplomatically the situation was handled, and I'm told that was in most part due to you."

"I really can't take the credit."

"Modest," she said, with a smile. "A good quality." She glanced around the room, as though searching for something. "Is your spouse not here with you?"

"I'm not married."

"Significant other?"

Oddly enough, the first person who came to mind was Victoria. Odd because she was no more significant than any other woman he had dated. "No one special."

"A handsome thing like you," she teased in a deep Southern drawl. "Why, in New Orleans you'd have been snapped up by some lovely young debutante ages ago."

"I could say the same for you," he said. "How could a woman so lovely still be single?"

"Oh," she said, with a spark of humor lighting her eyes, "we won't even go there."

Despite the trepidation of the rest of the family, Charles knew without a doubt that he was going to like his cousin. She had spunk and a pretty damned good sense of humor. He appreciated a woman, especially one in her social position, who didn't take herself too seriously.

Sophie stepped up beside them. "Sorry to interrupt, but I thought I might show Melissa to her suite and get her settled in."

"I certainly could use a breather," Melissa said. "It's been something of a crazy week, to say the least." She turned to Charles. "It was a pleasure meeting you. I hope we see quite a bit more of each other."

"As do I," he said, and honestly meant it. He suspected that Melissa would make a very interesting, and entertaining, addition to their family.

When they were gone, he heard Ethan ask from behind him, "So, what do you think of her?"

Charles turned to him. "I like her."

"She's quite outspoken."

"I think that's the thing about her that I like. Maybe she'll stir things up a bit."

Ethan nodded thoughtfully, and Charles had the distinct impression he felt wary of his new sibling. Which surprised him, since Ethan himself was illegitimate. If anyone were to welcome her with open arms, he would expect Ethan to. Knowing of Melissa's vast wealth, surely they didn't suspect she might be after their fortune. She had also made assurances to her attorney that she had no interest whatsoever in taking her rightful place as ruler of the country. But before Charles could question his wariness, Ethan changed the subject.

"Have you made any progress convincing Victoria to stay?"

He shook his head. "I'm working on her, though. I

think I'll have her mind changed by my father's birthday party."

Ethan's brow perked with curiosity. "She'll be there?"

Charles knew exactly what Ethan was thinking. He would never come right out and ask if Charles had slept with her, but he obviously had his suspicions.

"My mother has taken a liking to her," Charles said. "When she suggested inviting her, I figured it would be the perfect opportunity for her to get to know the family. Maybe then she would be more willing to accept our offer."

It wasn't a complete lie, more a vast stretching of the truth, but Ethan seemed to buy it.

"Good thinking. I'll make sure the others know to expect her there."

So, in other words, they would tag-team her. Try to wear her down. It couldn't hurt.

"We should see that Melissa knows she's welcome, too," Ethan said.

"I'll have my mother ring her," Charles said. Or as Victoria said, his "smother." The endearment brought a smile to his face.

He'd dated a lot of women in his life, but Victoria was different. Maybe part of the fascination was that women usually chased him, and for the first time he found himself the pursuer. And the truth was he sort of liked it. He was enjoying the challenge for a change.

All his life, things had come very easily to him. He would be the first to admit that he'd been spoiled as a child. There had never been a single thing he'd asked for that he hadn't gotten. Even if his father had said no, his mother would go behind his back.

Being told no was a refreshing change. He saw Victoria as more of an equal than just another temporary distraction. Not that he expected it to last. But why not enjoy it while he could?

Twelve

It was almost three in the afternoon when Victoria remembered the message on her cell phone and finally dialed her voice mail. As she listened to the somber voice on the other end, her heart plummeted and a cold chill sank deep into her skin, all the way through to her bones.

Her father had been admitted to the hospital with chest pains and was undergoing tests. The fact that the doctor had called, and not her father himself, filled her with dread. She called the hospital back but they refused to give her any information over the phone, other than to say that he was stable.

Was he unconscious? Dying? His cardiologist had warned that another attack, even a minor one, could do irreparable damage.

Hands trembling, heart thudding almost painfully hard in her chest, she threw on her jacket, grabbed her purse, and raced to Bay View Memorial Hospital as fast as the congested city streets would allow—damned tourists. She swore to herself that if he would just come out of this okay, she would never raise her voice to him, never be angry with him for as long as she lived.

And what if he wasn't okay? What if she got there and he was already gone? How would she ever forgive herself for those terrible things she'd said to him?

She'd lost her mum and her brother. She wasn't ready to lose him too. She couldn't bear it.

At the hospital information desk she was given a pass and directed to the cardiology wing on the fourth floor. When she reached the room, she was afraid to step inside, terrified of what she might see. Would it be like the last time? Her father hooked to tubes and machines?

With a trembling hand she rapped lightly on the door and heard her father's voice, strong and clear, call, "Come in."

She stepped inside, saw him sitting up in bed, his eyes bright and his color good, and went weak with relief. The machines and monitors she'd expected were nowhere to be seen. He didn't even have an IV line.

He was okay.

For now, at least, a little voice in her head said.

"Sweetheart," he said, looking relieved to see her. "I thought you were so angry with me you wouldn't come."

She thought she would be mad at him forever, but her anger just seemed to melt away. He held his arms out and she threw herself into them. She buried her face in the crook of his neck, squeezed him like she never wanted to let go, and he squeezed her right back.

"I'm sorry," they said at the exact same time.

"No," he said. "You had every right to be angry with me. I shouldn't have lied to you."

"It's okay."

"No, sweetheart, it isn't." He cupped her face in his hands. "I should have been honest with you from the start. I thought I was protecting you. And I was ashamed of the mess I'd made out of things."

"We all make mistakes."

He stroked her cheek with his thumb. "But I want you to know how deeply sorry I am. It's been just the two of us for a long time now. I would never do anything to intentionally hurt you."

"I know. It's all in the past now," she said. Hadn't losing the hotel been penalty enough? Was it fair to keep punishing him for his sins? And if she were the one who had made the mistake, wouldn't she want to be forgiven?

He was all she had left. They were a team. They had to stick together.

"What happened to you?" She sat on the edge of the bed and took one of his hands. It felt warm and strong. "Was it another attack?"

He shook his head, wearing a wry smile. "Acid reflux, the doctor said. Brought on by extreme stress. My cardiologist did a full workup just to be safe, and as far as they can tell I'm fit as a fiddle. They should be releasing me any time now."

She doubted *fit as a fiddle* was the term the doctor used. Probably more like *out of the woods*. "I'll wait around and take you home."

"Victoria, I also wanted to say I'm sorry that I was so rude to the duke. I guess I was just a little…surprised. He doesn't seem your type."

No kidding. It had been so long since she'd been in a relationship, she wasn't sure what her type was, anymore. And considering all her past disastrous relationships, maybe it was time to rethink exactly what her type should be.

"I wasn't sure about him at first," she told her father, "since he does have something of a reputation with women. But the truth is, he's not a bad guy. In fact, he's actually quite sweet. When he's not being arrogant and overbearing, that is."

"Is it…serious?"

She emphatically shook her head. "God, no. It's… *nothing.*"

He gave her that fatherly *you can't fool me* look. "It didn't look like nothing to me. The way he came to the door to see if you were okay. He has feelings for you."

Not in the way her father suspected. "It isn't like that. We're keeping it casual. *Very* casual."

He raised a brow at her. "Let's face it, Vicki, you don't do casual very well. When you fall, you fall hard."

That used to be true, but she'd changed. The past few years, she hadn't fallen at all. She hadn't given herself the opportunity. She had pretty much sworn off men after her last catastrophic split.

It had been inevitable she would eventually take a

tumble off the celibacy wagon. She just never suspected that it would be with a man like Charles.

"This is different," she told him. "*I'm* different."

"I hope so. I know you think you're tough, but I've seen your heart broken too many times before."

She had no intention of putting herself back in that kind of situation. "Would you mind if we don't have a discussion about my love life? Besides, *your* heart is the one we should be worrying about."

He gave her hand a squeeze. "I'm going to make this up to you, Vicki. All the trouble I caused. I'm not sure how yet, but I will."

"I can take care of myself, Daddy." And if not, it was time she learned how. She'd been relying on him for too long.

All that mattered now was that he was alive and well, and they were back to being happy.

Victoria didn't see Charles again until Sunday night, when he showed up unannounced at her door. He looked delicious in dark slacks, a warm, brown cashmere sweater and a black leather jacket.

Any thoughts she had of turning him away evaporated the instant he smiled. She did love that smile.

"Inviting yourself over again?" she asked, just to give him a hard time.

"I tried calling today, but you didn't answer," he said, as if that were a perfectly logical reason.

"My phone died. I just plugged it in a few minutes ago when I got home."

"Are you going to let me in?"

Like she had a choice. She stepped aside and gestured him in. "Just for a few minutes."

He stepped inside, bringing with him the scent of the brisk autumn air. He took his jacket off and hung it over the back of the couch, then sat down. She sat beside him. Something about him being there was very…comfortable.

Or it could all be an illusion.

"You look tired," he said.

"It's been an exhausting weekend. My father was admitted to the hospital with chest pains Friday night."

He sat forward slightly, and the depth of concern on his face surprised her. "Is he all right?"

"He's fine. It wound up being his stomach, not his heart, but I stayed with him last night and all day today, just to be safe." And while it was nice spending time with him, it made her realize just how comfortable she'd become living alone. It had been something of a relief to get back to her flat. To her home and her things.

"I guess this means things are okay with you two."

She nodded. "It's amazing how a scare like that can alter your perception. When I imagined losing him forever, the rest of it all seemed petty and insignificant."

"You should have called me," he said.

"What for?"

He shrugged. "Support. Someone to talk to."

"Come on, Charles. You and I both know that isn't the way this works. We don't have that kind of relationship. We have sex."

He grinned. "Really great sex."

"Yes," she agreed. "And in the end, that's all it will ever be."

She could swear he looked almost...hurt. "Would it be such a stretch to think of me as a friend?"

If he were anyone else, no. "Until tomorrow, or the day after, when the next woman catches your eye and I get tossed aside? That isn't friendship."

He frowned. "That's a little unfair, don't you think?"

"Not at all. It's quite realistic, in fact. I mean, can you blame me? It's not as if you don't have a reputation for that sort of thing."

"What if I said, for now, I only want to see you."

At first she thought he was joking. Then she realized he was actually serious. "I guess I would say that you're delusional. You're totally incapable of a monogamous relationship."

"Hey, I've had relationships."

"Name the longest one."

He paused, his brow furrowing.

"That's what I thought."

"Maybe I want to try."

In a monogamous relationship, she gave him a week, tops. And that was being generous. "I don't want to get involved. I don't want a commitment." Especially with a man like him.

"Neither do I," he said. "We'll keep it casual."

"Casually exclusive? That doesn't even make sense."

"Sure it does. You've never dated someone just to date them, with no expectations."

Not really. Like her father said, when she fell, she fell hard. That was the way it was supposed to happen, as it did with her parents. They met, they fell in love, they settled down and started a family. But it had never quite seemed to work that way for her. Perhaps she'd been expecting too much?

Maybe this time it would be different. In the past she had entered relationships with the understanding, the expectation, that it would be long-lasting. And when it didn't work out she'd felt like a failure. But this was different. She was entering this relationship with no expectations at all.

"We're attracted to each other," Charles said. "And you can't deny that we're hot in bed."

She wouldn't even try.

"So," he asked. "Why not?"

He made it sound so simple. "How long?"

He shrugged. "Until it's not fun anymore, I suppose."

"Who says I'm having fun now?"

He flashed her that sexy grin. "Oh, I know you are."

Yeah, she was. The sex alone was worth her while.

But what if the only thing keeping Charles interested was the challenge, the thrill of the chase? If she gave in too easily, would he lose interest?

"I'll think about it," she said, and enjoyed the look of surprise on his face when she didn't bend to his will.

He opened his mouth to say something—God only knew what—but the bell for the door chimed.

Before she could move, he rose to his feet. "That's for me."

For him? Who would he invite to her flat?

"Back in a sec." He walked to the door. She heard him open it and thank whoever it was, then he reappeared with a large white box in his arms. The name of an exclusive downtown boutique was emblazoned on the top. Exclusively women's clothing.

What had he done this time?

"What is that?" she asked.

"A gift," he said, setting the box in her lap. It was surprisingly heavy. "I saw it in the shop window and knew I had to see you in it."

What had he done?

"Open it," he said eagerly, grinning like a kid at Christmas.

She pulled off the top and dug through layers of gold tissue paper until she encountered something royal blue and shimmering. She pulled it from the box and found herself holding a strapless, floor-length, sequined evening gown. It was so beautiful it took her breath away.

"Do you like it?" he asked.

"Charles, it's amazing, but—"

"I know, I know. You can afford your own dress and all that." He sat down beside her. "When I saw it in the shop window, I knew it would be perfect for you. And I can see already that it is."

He was right. If she'd had every gown in the world to choose from, she probably would have picked this very one. He'd even gotten the size right.

The price tag was missing, but she was sure that from this particular boutique, it must have cost a bundle. More than she could afford to spend.

"It's too much," she said.

"Not for me, it isn't."

Maybe this was one of the perks of dating a multimillionaire. Even though they weren't technically dating.

Normally she wouldn't accept a gift like this. But it was just so beautiful. So elegant. The designer was one she had always admired and dreamed of wearing, but never could quite fit into her budget.

She considered offering to pay him back, but God only knew when she would have the money. As it was, she was barely making the rent.

Maybe she could say yes, just this once.

"I love it," she said. "Thank you."

"The manager said if it needs altering, bring it around Monday and they'll put a rush on it. I wasn't sure about jewelry or shoes."

"That part I have covered," she said.

She could tell just from looking at it that at least three inches would have to go from the hem. She folded it carefully and lay it back in the box.

"Aren't you going to model it for me?" he asked.

She shook her head and eased the top back in place. "It will just have to be a surprise."

Something told her that if she wore it for him before the party, the novelty might wear off.

See, she told herself, *this is what you would have to look forward to if you let yourself get involved with him.* She would always be fretting about how to keep him interested, worrying that any minute he would get tired of her.

"Could I at least get a thank-you kiss?" he asked, tapping an index finger to his lips. "Right here."

"Just a quick one," she said. Then she would kick him out so she could get to bed early for a change. She had a lot of sleep to catch up on.

She leaned in and pressed her lips to his, but before

she could back away, he cupped a hand behind her head and held her there. And it felt so good, she only put up the tiniest bit of resistance before she gave in and melted into his arms.

One kiss turned into two kisses, which then led to some touching. Then their clothes were getting in the way, so naturally they had to take them off.

When he picked her up and carried her to the bedroom, she had resigned herself to another sleepless but sinfully satisfying night.

Thirteen

Victoria sat with Charles in the back of the Bentley, her luggage for the weekend tucked beside his in the trunk. She had planned to drive herself to his parents's estate. But after a long week of Charles giving her every reason to make the hour-long drive with him—outrageous petrol prices, complicated directions, and who knew, maybe even highway robbery—she had finally relented and agreed to ride with him.

It wasn't as though she was concerned she wouldn't be welcomed. She and Charles's mother had practically become buddies over the past couple of weeks. Mrs. Mead had called every day as usual, but there were times when she called specifically to speak with Victoria, not Charles.

She wanted to know Victoria's preference for dinner

Friday night. Beef or fish? And which room would she prefer to stay in? One facing the ocean or the gardens? Did she prefer cotton sheets or silk, and were there any food allergies the cook should be aware of? Was there a special wine she would like ordered, or would she prefer cocktails? And the list went on. Victoria wondered if she was this attentive with all the guests who stayed with them.

With each call Mrs. Mead expressed how thrilled she and her husband were to be meeting Victoria. And even though Mrs. Mead never came right out and said it, Victoria couldn't escape the feeling that she was reading way more into Victoria and Charles's relationship than was really there. And Victoria was feeling as though she was being sucked into the family against her will. Which might not have been horrible if the man in question were anyone but Charles.

Yes, she and Charles had fun together—and not just the physical kind. He made her laugh, and she never failed to get that shimmy of excitement in her belly when he popped his head in her office or appeared unannounced at her door. But she still hadn't given him a definitive answer about the nature of their relationship.

And call her evil, but keeping him guessing gave her a perverse feeling of power. If she could just ignore the fact that she was coming dangerously close to falling for him. But she would never be that foolish. The instant she gave in, surrendered her will to him, the thrill of the chase would be gone, and Charles would lose interest.

Hopefully she would be long gone before then.

"By the way," she told him, "the employment agency

called just before we left. They have four more possible candidates for the assistant position."

"Splendid," he said. "Make interview appointments first thing next week."

"Why bother?" she asked wryly. "You haven't liked a single applicant yet."

They had all been perfectly capable. And not a gorgeous face or sexy figure in the lot of them. Which she suspected was the reason he'd dismissed them all without consideration.

"I'm sure the right one will come along," he said.

He or she would have to. Victoria's time was nearly up. At this rate she would have to stay longer to train whomever he hired, and she had other irons in the fire. In fact, she was expecting a very important phone call any day now that just might determine her immediate future plans. The opportunity of a lifetime, her father had said.

But she refused to let herself think about that and add even more nervous knots to the ones already twisting her stomach.

The hour-long drive seemed to fly by, and before she knew it they were pulling up to the gates of the estate. She noted it was not at all hard to find—one turn off the coastal highway and they were there.

And only then did she become truly nervous. What if they hated her? Made her feel like she was imposing? Would his parents smother Charles with affection and leave her feeling like the fourth wheel?

Things she maybe should have considered *before* she climbed into the damned car.

As they approached, the gates swung open. The car

followed the long, twisting drive, and she got her first view of his parents' estate. The home that she supposed would one day belong to Charles.

It was utterly breathtaking, and so enormous it made her father's estate look like a country cottage. Built sometime in the nineteenth century, the impressive structure sat on endless acres of rolling green lawns that tapered down to a stretch of private beach. The grounds were crawling with staff, all bustling with activity. To prepare for the party tomorrow night, she assumed.

"What do you think?" Charles asked.

"It's really something," she said, peering out her window. "Has it always been in the royal family?"

"Actually, this house comes from my mother's side. Her family originated on Thomas Isle, the sister island to Morgan Isle. They immigrated here in the late nineteenth century."

"I didn't realize you had ties to Thomas Isle," she said. Up until recently, their respective monarchies had ruled in bitter discord with the other. As few as ten years ago they weren't even on speaking terms.

"Have you ever been there?" he asked, and she shook her head. "It's very different from Morgan Isle. Farming community, mostly, and a little archaic by our standards. Although, in the last few years the entire island has gone with the recent green trend, and all the crops they export now are certified organic. We should go sometime, tour the island and the castle."

She wasn't sure how she felt about taking another trip with him, or the fact that he'd even suggested it. Here they were, going on four weeks of seeing each other, and he still wasn't making noise like he wanted out. The longer they dragged this out, the more attached they would become. Not to mention that if things worked out as she'd planned, she might not be on the island much longer.

The car slowed to a stop by the front entrance, and the driver got out to open the door for them.

As they stepped out into the brisk, salty ocean air, the front door opened and Charles's parents emerged. Victoria was struck instantly by what an attractive couple they made.

Mrs. Mead looked much younger than her husband, and that surprised Victoria. She'd imagined her older and more matronly. In reality Mrs. Mead looked youthful, chic, and stunningly beautiful. And though Mr. Mead was showing his age, he was brutally handsome and as physically fit as his wife. Nothing like the stodgy old man she's been picturing all this time. It was clear where Charles had gotten his good looks.

Talk about hitting the gene-pool jackpot! She could just imagine the gorgeous children she and Charles—

Whoa. Where had that errant and totally unrealistic thought come from? Talk about a cold-day-in-hell scenario. She didn't even know if Charles wanted children.

She didn't *want* to know. Because if the answer was yes, it would make him that much more appealing.

"Your parents are so handsome," she whispered to Charles. "I never imagined your mother would be so young."

"Don't let her face fool you," he whispered back. "She just has an exceptional plastic surgeon."

Victoria hung back a few steps as Mrs. Mead approached them, arms open, and folded her son into a crushing embrace. "It's so wonderful to see you, dear! Did you have a good trip?"

"Uneventful," he said, untangling himself from her arms so he could shake his father's hand. "Happy Birthday, Dad."

"Welcome home, son," his father said with a smile that lit his entire face. There was no doubt, they adored their child. Not that Victoria could blame them.

Charles gestured her closer. "Mum, Dad, this is my colleague, Victoria Houghton."

Victoria curtsied. "I'm so pleased to finally meet you both," she said, accepting Mr. Mead's outstretched hand, then his wife's.

"The pleasure is all ours, Victoria," his mother said, "And please, you must call us Grant and Pip."

Her name was *Pip?* Victoria bit her lip to hold back a nervous giggle.

"I know what you're thinking," Mrs. Mead, *Pip,* said. She looped an arm through Victoria's and led her toward the house. "What kind of a name is Pip?"

"It is unusual," she admitted.

"Well, my parent's weren't that eccentric. My given name is Persephone."

That wasn't exactly a name you heard every day, either.

"I don't know if Charles told you, but I used to be a runway model."

"No, he didn't." But that wasn't hard to believe. At least she hadn't put those looks and figure to waste.

"This was back in the sixties." She shot Victoria a wry smile. "I'm aging myself, I know. But anyway, those were the days of Twiggy. They liked them tall and ghostly thin. I was thin enough, but at five feet seven inches I wasn't exactly towering over the other models. So, because I was the shortest, everyone started calling me Pipsqueak. Then it was shortened to Pip. And that's what people have been calling me ever since. Isn't that right, Grant?"

"As long as I've known you," he agreed.

She didn't seem small, but then, with the exception of young children, everybody was taller than Victoria.

"My parents abhorred it, of course," Pip said, as they stepped through the door into the foyer, Charles and his father following silently behind. "But being something of a rebellious youngster, that only made the name more appealing."

The inside of their home was just as magnificent and breathtaking as the outside. Vaulted ceilings, antique furnishings, and oodles of rich, polished wood. So different from the modern furnishings in Charles's home. It was difficult to imagine him growing up here.

"I'll show you to your room so you can settle in," Pip said. "Then we can meet in the study for a drink before dinner. Grant, would you be a dear and check that Geoffery brought the correct wine up from the cellar?"

"Of course." He flashed Victoria a smile, then walked off in the opposite direction. If it bothered him being sent on errands, it didn't show.

"He's the wine connoisseur," Pip explained. "I'm more of a gin-and-tonic girl."

They climbed the stairs, Charles in tow, and Pip showed her to a room decorated in Victorian-era floral with what she assumed was authentic period furniture. A bit frilly for Victoria's taste, but beautiful.

A servant followed them in with Victoria's luggage.

"Would you like a maid to help you unpack?" Pip asked.

"No, thank you." She'd never been fond of total strangers rifling through her things—or even the maid who had been with her and her father for years.

"Well, then, is there anything you need? Anything I can get you?"

"I'm fine, thanks."

"Mum," Charles said, "why don't we leave Victoria to unpack? You can walk me to my room."

"If there's anything you need, anything at all, just buzz the staff." She gestured to the intercom panel by the door. "Twenty-four hours a day."

Jeez, talk about being smothered with kindness. "Thank you."

"Shall we meet in the study in an hour?"

"An hour is fine, Mum." Charles had to all but drag her from the room. And before he closed the door behind him, he told Victoria, "I'll be by to show you to the study, and later I'll take you on a tour."

The devilish look in his eyes said he had more than just a tour in mind.

"Charles, she's lovely!" his mother gushed the instant they were in his room. "So pretty and petite. Like a pixie."

"Don't let her size fool you. She can hold her own."

"Just the kind of woman you need," she said.

Could she be any *less* subtle?

He should have seen this coming. "Don't start, mother."

She shrugged innocently. She knew he meant business when he called her mother instead of Mum. "Start what, dear?"

"*Pushing* me."

She frowned. "Is it wrong to want to see my only son settle down? To hope for maybe a grandchild or two? I'm not getting any younger."

It was times like this he hated being an only child. "You're only fifty-eight."

She shot him a stern look. "Bite your tongue, young man."

So he added, "But you don't look a day over thirty-five."

She smiled and patted his cheek. "That's my sweet boy."

Ugh. He hated when she called him that. And she wondered why he didn't come around very often. He hoisted his suitcase up on the bed and unzipped it.

"Let a maid do that," she scolded.

"You know I prefer to do it myself."

She sighed dramatically, as though he was a lost cause, and sat on the bed to watch him. "You brought your tux?"

"Of course."

"And Victoria?"

"She would look terrible in a tux."

She gave him a playful shove. "You know what I mean."

"She's all set."

"I thought of offering her the use of one of my gowns, but she's at least two sizes smaller."

"I bought her a gown."

She raised a curious brow. "Oh, did you?"

"Don't go reading anything into it. I just wanted her to feel comfortable."

"It's been ages since you brought a date home."

"We're not dating," he said. Victoria's rules, not his. Although, if this wasn't dating, he wasn't sure what to call it. It was the longest exclusive relationship he'd ever had with a woman.

He'd kept waiting for it to lose its luster, to get bored with her. Instead, with every passing day, he seemed to care more for her. In a temporary way, that is.

"So what *are* you doing," she asked, and the instant the words were out, she held up a hand and shook her head. "On second thought, I don't want to know."

"She's a friend," he said, and realized it was true. A friend with benefits. The two roles had always been mutually exclusive in the past. He'd never even met a woman he would want to sleep with *and* call a friend. She was definitely unique.

And when the inevitable end came, he had the feeling he would miss Victoria.

After drinks in the study, Victoria, Charles, and his parents had a surprisingly pleasant dinner together. Victoria found Pip to be much less overbearing in person, and Grant was quiet but friendly. It was rare he got a word in edgewise, though.

Pip must have asked Victoria a hundred questions about her family and her career, despite the warning looks she kept getting from her husband and son.

"What?" she would ask them. "I'm just curious."

Victoria didn't mind too much, although around the time dessert was served, it was beginning to feel a little like the Spanish Inquisition. When the questions turned a little too personal, to the tune of "So, Victoria, do you think you'll want children someday?" Charles put the kabash on it by taking her on that tour he'd promised. Which ended—*surprise*—right back in her room between the covers. Which is where they stayed for the rest of the night.

They were up bright and early for breakfast at eight, then spent hours with his parents chatting and looking through family photos, taking a long walk through the gardens and along the shore. And Victoria couldn't have felt more welcome or accepted.

She had expected Pip to grow bored with her almost immediately and cast her aside in favor of spending time with her son. But Pip remained glued to Victoria's side right up until the moment everyone went upstairs to get dressed for the party.

Not that Victoria minded. She liked Pip. She was witty and bright. A lot like Charles, really. She could even imagine them becoming friends, but there wouldn't likely be a chance for that.

"My parents really like you," Charles said, as they walked up the stairs together.

"I like them, too. I never expected your mum to be so attentive, though. At least, not toward me. Shouldn't she be showering her son with affection?"

"When I'm not here, she's desperate to keep in touch. And when I'm here, we have a few hours to catch up, then we run out of things to say to each other. The novelty wears off, I guess."

That sounded like someone else she knew. Always wanting what he couldn't have. And once he got it, he grew easily bored.

He hadn't gotten bored with her yet. But he would. It was inevitable.

Or was it?

Given his pathetically short attention span when it came to women, if he was going to grow tired of her, wouldn't it have happened by now?

She shook the thought from her mind, and not for the first time. That was dangerous ground to wander into. A place where she would undeniably get her heart smashed to pieces.

God knew it had happened enough times before.

"The party starts in three hours," he said, when they reached the top of the stairs, where they would part ways and go to their own rooms. "How much time do you need to get ready?"

She didn't have to ask why he wanted to know. It was clear in his sinfully sexy smile. And she had to admit, making love in his parents' home in the middle of the afternoon did hold a certain naughty appeal.

She took his hand, weaving their fingers together. "Your place or mine?"

Fourteen

Victoria sat on the edge of the bed, her stomach twisted into nervous knots as she waited for Charles to fetch her from her room. They were already half an hour late, no thanks to Charles, who had finessed his way into her bed, then wouldn't get back out. She'd had to practically dress him herself and shove him out the door.

Now that she was ready, with nothing to do but sit and think, she couldn't keep her mind off of those one hundred or so guests she was going to have to meet. And the fact that she barely knew a single one of them. And how out of place she could potentially feel. Even when she and her father still had a thriving business, this echelon of society had been far out of their reach.

She was so edgy that when Charles rapped on the door, she nearly jumped out of her skin.

Here we go.

She shot to her feet, adjusting her dress, making sure she looked her best. She took a deep cleansing breath, then blew it out and called, "Come in!"

The door opened and Charles appeared, looking unbelievably handsome in his tux. "We're late—we have to…" He trailed off the instant he laid eyes on her, and for one very long moment he just stood there and stared. She was wearing the dress he had picked and had complemented it with the diamond jewelry she had inherited from her mother. Simple, but elegant.

But why didn't he say something? She swallowed hard and picked nervously at the skirt of her dress. "Well?"

"You look…" He shook his head, as though searching for the right words. He opened his mouth to say something, then closed it again. Then he shrugged and admitted, "I'm speechless."

She bit her lip. "Speechless good or speechless bad?"

He stepped closer. "Victoria, there are no words for how amazing you look in that dress." He lifted a hand to touch her cheek, then he leaned forward and brushed his lips across hers. So sweet and tender. And something happened just then. Something between them shifted. She could see in his eyes that he felt it too. Their relationship had…*evolved,* somehow. Moved to the next level.

"Victoria," he said, and she knew deep down in her heart what he was about to say. He was going to tell her that he was falling in love with her. She could just *feel* it. Her heart skipped a beat or two, then picked up double time.

He came so close, then at the last minute, chickened out. "We should get downstairs now."

She nodded, and let him lead her downstairs. She couldn't blame him for being afraid to say the words, to admit his feelings. This was new ground for him. And maybe he was afraid of rejection. But if he had gone out on a limb and said the words, she would have told him that she was falling in love with him, too.

Victoria found herself thrust amidst the upper crust of Morgan Isle society. The beautiful people. The weird thing was, despite any preconceived notion she may have had, that was really all they were. Just people. Not a single one treated her as though she were below them. And if deep down any thought so, they were kind enough to keep it to themselves.

Pip made sure that Victoria was introduced to all the right people and whispered to her juicy bits of gossip about them that Victoria found disturbingly entertaining. One by one she was reintroduced to the members of the royal family, and each took the chance to not so subtly try to convince her to stay with the Royal Inn. All she would say was that she was considering her options. She had to admit it was tempting, especially now that it was obvious they'd hired her on merit and not because of her father. But at the same time, she felt she needed a fresh start. Maybe, though, if the other position fell through, or if Charles asked her not to leave…

Which she was beginning to think was more and more likely. It seemed as though he hadn't taken his eyes off of her for a single minute all evening. Every time she turned he was there, watching her with that hungry look in his eyes. And she knew exactly what he was thinking.

He liked her in the dress, but he couldn't wait to get her out of it.

And people were noticing. Especially the women who were volleying for his attention.

"He can't keep his eyes off you," Pip told her, wearing the hopeful and conspiratorial smile of a mother who was ready to marry off her son.

"I noticed" was all Victoria said.

"He keeps insisting that you two are just friends, but I've never seen him look at a woman that way."

Her words sent an excited shiver through Victoria. Maybe Charles really did love her.

He saw the two of them talking and walked up to them. "Victoria, would you dance with me?"

"Go ahead," Pip said, eagerly waving them away. Whatever had happened between Victoria and Charles upstairs, Pip seemed to be sensing it, too. And no doubt loving every second.

Charles offered his arm and led Victoria out on the dance floor. The band was playing a slow, sultry number. Charles pulled her close to him, gazing down into her eyes. She felt mesmerized.

"Having a good time?" he asked, and she nodded. "Don't tell my mother I said this, but you're the most beautiful woman here."

Whether it was true or not, he made her believe it was. He made her *feel* beautiful. He was the only man she'd ever been with who made her feel good about herself.

His eyes searched her face, settled on her lips. "You wouldn't believe how badly I want to kiss you right now."

She grinned up at him. "And you wouldn't believe how badly I'd like you to." But they had always had an unspoken agreement. No physical affection when they were out in public together. He was hiding the relationship from his family, and she was protecting herself from everyone else. She didn't want to be labeled another one of his flings. Only this didn't feel like a fling any longer. This was real.

"Maybe I should then," he said.

It seemed to happen in slow motion. He lowered his head, one excruciating inch at a time, while Victoria's heart leapt up into her throat. Then his lips brushed hers, right there on the dance floor in front of everyone, softly at first. Then he leaned in deeper, catching the back of her head in his hand.

It was like their first kiss all over again. Sexy and exciting, and oh so good. And people were looking. She could feel their curious stares.

Their secret affair was officially out, and she didn't even care. She just wanted this night to last forever. She wanted *them* to last forever.

They parted slowly, hesitantly, and she rested her cheek against his chest, realizing, as they swayed to the music, that she had never been so happy in all her life.

Maybe he was afraid to say the words, but she wasn't. For the first time in a long time, she wasn't afraid of anything.

"Charles," she whispered.

"Hmm?"

"I think I'm falling in love with you."

She waited for him to squeeze her tighter, to gaze down at her with love and acceptance.

Instead he went cold and stiff in her arms. It was like dancing with a store mannequin.

You just surprised him, she told herself. *Any second now he's going to realize how happy he was to hear those words.*

Say something, she begged silently. *Anything.* But he didn't. It would seem she'd managed to stun him speechless again.

This time in a bad way.

Her knees felt unsteady and dread filled her heart. It was more than clear by his reaction that he didn't feel the same way. And he wasn't too thrilled to know that she did.

She had done it again. Despite going into this affair with no expectations whatsoever, she still managed to fall for Charles and get her heart filleted in the process. How could she have been so foolish to believe he actually cared about her? That he'd changed? That she was any different from the many others who came before her?

A person would think she'd have learned by now.

Tears of humiliation burned her eyes, but she swallowed them back. She wouldn't give anyone there the satisfaction of learning she was just one of many whose hearts he'd crushed.

She looked up at him with what she was sure was a strained smile. Her face felt like cold, hard plastic. "Thanks for the dance. Now, if you'll excuse me."

She broke away from him and walked blindly from the room, wanting only to get the hell out of there. She didn't even care that people were interrupting their conversations to stop and watch her pass. And she did her best to smile cordially, and nod in greeting.

So no one would realize she was dying inside.

"What did you do?" his mother hissed from behind him, as Charles helplessly watched Victoria walk away.

He turned to her, and under his breath said, "Stay out of this, Mother."

"Whatever you said to her, the poor girl went white as a sheet."

"I didn't say a thing." And that was the problem.

He shook his head and cursed under his breath. This was not his fault. Why did she have to go and say something like that? They had such a good thing. Why ruin it? And how in the hell had she gone from refusing to accept even a temporary exclusivity to falling in love with him? It made no sense.

Maybe she had just gotten caught up in the moment. That was probably it, he realized, feeling relieved. He needed to talk to her, before this thing was blown way out of proportion.

He started to walk away and his mother grabbed hold of his sleeve. "Sweetheart, everything inside me says she's the woman for you. And deep down I think you know it, too. *Why* won't you let yourself feel it?"

He pulled his arm free. "Excuse me, Mother."

He took the stairs two at a time. Her bedroom door was closed, so he knocked and called, "Victoria, I need to speak with you."

He didn't really expect a response, but he heard her call back, "Come in."

She was standing beside the bed, her suitcases open in front of her. She had changed out of her dress and it was draped across the footboard.

"What are you doing?" he asked.

"I thought I would get a head start on my packing," she said, but she wouldn't look him in the eye. She gestured to the dress. "You may as well take that. I'll never have a need for it again. Maybe someone else can get some use out of it."

He knew in that instant that she meant what she said, she was falling in love with him.

"Victoria, I'm sorry."

She bit her lip and shook her head. "No, it's my fault. I never should have said that to you. I don't know what I was thinking. Temporary insanity."

"You didn't give me a chance to say anything."

"Your silence said it all, believe me."

"I'm sorry. I'm just not—"

"In love with me? Yeah, I got that."

"We agreed this was temporary."

"You're absolutely right."

"It's not that I don't care for you."

She finally turned to him. "Look, this was bound to

happen, right? It's a miracle we lasted this long. It was going to end eventually."

"It doesn't have to," he said. They could just go back to the way things have been.

"Yes," she told him, "it does."

They were doing the right thing, so why did it feel like a mistake? "I feel…really bad."

She nodded sympathetically, but her eyes said she felt anything but. "That must be awful for you."

"You know that isn't what I mean."

"Look, I appreciate you coming after me and all. But honestly, you didn't do anything wrong. You did what you always do. And I should have expected that."

Maybe this wasn't her fault. Maybe he…led her on somehow. Made her believe he felt more that was really there.

She walked past him to the door and held it open. "Please leave."

"You're kicking me out?"

She nodded. "I created this mess. Now it's time I fixed it."

The drive back to the city the next morning was excruciatingly silent. Charles tried to talk to Victoria, to reason with her, but she refused to acknowledge him. The worst part wasn't even that she wasn't acting angry or wounded. She was just…cold.

He didn't follow her up to her flat when the car dropped her off, convinced that if he gave her time to cool off, she would see reason. But by eleven a.m. Monday he hadn't heard a word from her and she hadn't shown up at work. He checked her office to see if she'd slipped quietly in without him hearing her, and he realized all of her things were gone.

What the hell?

She was pissed at him. He got that. But that didn't mean she could just quit her job, just...*abandon* him.

He grabbed his jacket from his office and stormed out past Penelope, tossing over his shoulder, "Cancel all of my appointments."

Her car was parked out in front of her building, and he took the stairs two at a time up to her floor. He rapped hard on her door and barked, "Victoria!"

She opened the door, but left the security chain on. "What do you want?"

She looked tired, and the anger that had driven him there fizzled away.

"You didn't come to work," he said. "I was concerned."

"Technically, my three weeks are up. I don't work there anymore."

"But we haven't found a replacement yet. Who will do the training?"

"I'm sure you'll manage."

But that hadn't been the deal. And he didn't like being exiled in the hall. The least she could do was invite him in. She owed him that much. "Are you going to let me in?"

She hesitated, then she unlatched the chain and stepped aside to let him pass. "Only for a minute. I have a lot of packing to do."

"Packing? Are you going on a trip?"

"I'm moving."

She had said something about having to get a cheaper place. If she would just accept the damned job at the Royal Inn, she could stay right here. Or hell, she could probably afford to buy a house. "Where are you moving to?"

"London."

"England?"

"I was offered a position at a five-star hotel there. I start next Monday."

"You're leaving the country?"

"This Friday." She paused and said, "You could congratulate me."

Congratulate her? Wait. This was all wrong. She wasn't supposed to find a new job. She was supposed to change her mind and agree to work at the Royal Inn. "Whatever they're paying you, the Royal Inn will top it."

"I told you weeks ago, I don't want to work at the Royal Inn."

"But they want you. They're counting on me to convince you to stay."

"You'll just have to tell them you failed."

"It doesn't work that way. You can't leave."

She seemed to find his predicament amusing. "Look, I know you're used to getting your way, getting everything your heart desires, but this time you're just going to have to suck it up like the rest of us."

"It's not about that."

"Then what *is* it about, Charles? Because to me it sounds like you're just being a sore loser."

What was he trying to say? What did he really want from her?

He stepped toward her as though he could bully her to comply.

She didn't even flinch.

"You can't leave."

"Why? What can you offer me if I stay? A real relationship?"

"What we have is real."

"A commitment?"

He cringed. "Why do we have to do that? Why do we have to put a label on it? Why can't we just keep doing what we're doing?"

"Because that isn't what I want."

"It was a week ago. And why not? It was the perfect relationship. Totally uncomplicated."

Her expression darkened. "For you, maybe it was. But I'm tired of always being on edge. Waiting around for the other shoe to fall, for you to get bored and dump me. I just can't do it anymore."

"So you're dumping me first, is that it?"

She shrugged. "Welcome to the world of the dumpee. It's not fun, but trust me when I say you'll get over it."

She was right. He was usually the one to do the leaving. The one to walk away. So this was how it felt.

He knew that if he let her go, he would probably never see her again. But what choice did he have? She was right. It was very likely that in time he would grow tired of their relationship and need something else. He would feel trapped and stifled and get that burning need to move on. Then he would hurt her all over again.

It would be cruel and selfish to try to persuade her to stay. So he didn't.

He turned and left, walked away from her for the last time, an odd ache, like a spear thrust through his chest, making it hard to breath.

It's just that your pride has been slightly bruised, he assured himself. In a day or two he'd be fine. And when Victoria left, he wouldn't say a single damned thing to stop her.

Fifteen

When Charles's doorbell chimed late Thursday afternoon, he was sure it was Victoria, there to tell him that she'd changed her mind. But instead he found Ethan standing on his front porch.

Ethan looked Charles up and down, took in his disheveled hair, wrinkled clothes, and four days' growth of facial hair. "Christ almighty, you look like hell."

Appropriately so, considering that was how he felt.

He stepped aside so Ethan could come in, then shut the door behind him. "I think I caught some kind of bug."

"I hope it's nothing catching," Ethan said warily. "Lizzy will kill me if I bring germs home. She's due any minute now, you know."

Only if wounded pride had become contagious. "I think you're safe."

"Could this have something to do with Victoria? Word is she took a job in England." At Charles's surprised look, Ethan said, "Did you think we wouldn't hear? I guess you didn't manage to convince her to stay, huh? And the way you were locking lips at the party, I'm guessing you ignored our request that you not sleep with her."

"Are you angry?"

He shrugged. "Let's just say I'm not surprised."

"If it counts for anything, I don't think it would have made a difference. Victoria Houghton is the most stubborn woman alive."

He walked to the kitchen, where he'd left his drink, and Ethan followed him. "What are you doing here, anyway?"

"You missed our squash game, genius. I called your office and your secretary said you've been out since last Friday."

"Yeah." Charles sipped his scotch and gestured to the bottle. "Want one?"

Ethan shook his head. "So, what happened?"

"I told you, I caught a bug."

"She dumped you, didn't she?"

Charles opened his mouth to deny it, but he just didn't have the energy.

Ethan flashed him a cocky grin and gave him a slap across the back. "The notorious Charles Mead was finally set loose by a woman. I never thought I would see the day. And she's moving all the hell the way over to England to get the away from you."

Charles glared at him. "I'm glad I could be a source of amusement."

"Welcome to the real world, my friend."

"Go to hell."

Ethan laughed. "What I find even more amusing, is that you're in love with her, and you probably didn't have the guts to tell her."

"I don't do love."

"Everyone does eventually."

"I'm not looking for a commitment," he insisted, but the familiar mantra was beginning to lose its luster. And the idea of being with anyone but Victoria left a hollow feeling in his gut.

That would pass.

"I know you see marriage as some kind of prison sentence, and I find that tragic. My life didn't truly begin until I married Lizzy."

Charles wanted to believe that it might be that way for him, too. It just seemed so far out of the realm of reality.

"You want to reschedule our game?" Ethan asked. "Or do you plan to mope in here for the rest of your life?"

"I'm not moping." Maybe he was a little depressed. Maybe it had been a slight shock to his system. But in a few days he would be back on his game. Besides, Victoria could still change her mind. She could realize that he was right and accept their relationship on his terms.

You just keep telling yourself that, pal.

Ethan's cell phone rang. He unclipped it from his belt and checked the display. "It's Lizzy." He flipped it open and said, "Hey, babe." He was silent for several seconds, then his eyes lit. "Are you sure?" Another pause, then, "Okay, I'll be there as soon as I can. Ten minutes, tops. Just hold on." He snapped his phone shut, grinning like an idiot. "Lizzy is in labor. Her water just broke." He laughed and slapped Charles on the back. "I'm going to be a father."

"Congratulations," Charles said, practically knocked backward by the intensity of Ethan's joy. What would it feel like to be that happy?

But he already knew the answer to that. He'd been that happy for a while. With Victoria. Right up until the instant when he'd screwed it all up.

Maybe he did love her. Maybe this so-called bug he'd contracted was really just lovesickness. Maybe his mum was right, and Victoria was the woman for him. Was it possible?

"You okay?" Ethan asked, wearing a concerned look. "You just got the weirdest expression on your face."

"Yeah," Charles said, unable to stifle the smile itching at the corners of his mouth. The same kind of goofy, lovesick smile Ethan had been wearing seconds ago. And he liked it. It felt…good. "I'm okay. In fact, I think I'm pretty great right now."

"If I didn't know any better, I would say you just came to your senses."

Maybe he did. Instead of feeling trapped or stifled, he felt free.

"What are you still doing here," he said, giving Ethan a shove in the direction of the foyer. "Are you forgetting your wife is waiting for you? You're going to be a father!"

Ethan grinned and looked at his watch. "How fast do you think I can get from here to the palace?"

"It's a twenty-minute drive, so probably about five. Now get out of here."

"I'm already gone," Ethan said, and Charles thought, with a chuckle, *Me too*.

As she was emptying the drawer of her bedside table into a box, Victoria saw the corner of a sheet of paper wedged between the headboard and mattress.

Probably just a magazine insert or an old message slip. She almost left it there, figuring it would fall loose when the movers took her bed apart. Then something compelled her to wedge her hand into the tight space and catch the corner of the paper with the tips of her fingers. When she pulled it free, and saw what it was, she wished she had just left it the hell alone.

It was an old shopping list, but what stopped her heart for an instant is what she found scribbled on the opposite side; the note that Charles had left her that first night they spent together.

It must have slipped off the pillow and gotten caught. Reading it now, in Charles chicken-scratch scrawl, sent a sharp pain through her heart.

Victoria,
Have an early meeting but wanted to let you sleep. I had a great time last night. See you in the office.
XOXO
Charles
P.S. Dinner tonight?

She'd managed, up until just then, not to shed a single tear over him. But now she felt the beginnings of a precariously dammed flood welling up against the backs of her eyes.

Some silly part of her that still believed in fairy-tale endings actually thought he might come after her. That he might have a sudden epiphany, like a lightning bolt from the heavens, and realize that he was madly in love with her. That he couldn't live without her.

Well, that certainly hadn't happened. She hadn't seen or heard from him since Sunday when he walked out of her apartment without even saying goodbye.

"Victoria?"

She turned to see her dad standing in the bedroom doorway. "Yeah?"

His brow was wrinkled with concern. He'd been worried about her lately, claimed that she wasn't acting like herself. He even hinted that by taking this job she might be running away from her problems, rather than facing them. Sort of like he had done.

She was seriously wondering the same thing. But it was too late to back out now.

"Everything okay?" he asked.

She nodded, a little too enthusiastically, and stuffed the note in the pocket of her jeans. "Fine, Daddy."

"The movers called. They'll be here tomorrow at eight a.m."

"Great." But it wasn't great. She didn't want to move to England and leave the only home she'd ever known. But careerwise, there wasn't much left for her here. The Royal Inn was the biggest game on the island, and she definitely had no future there.

"Almost finished in here?" he asked, the worry still

set deeply in his face. She wished there was something she could do to ease his mind. This shouldn't have to be so hard on him. But she knew he felt responsible for sticking her in this position in the first place.

"I think I'll need one more box for the closet stuff," she said. "Other than that, it's pretty much packed."

The bell rang and her father gestured behind him. "You want me to get that?"

"Would you mind? And could you grab me a box while you're out there?"

"Sure thing, honey."

Her father had wanted to move to England with her right away, but she asked him to wait until she was settled and had her bearings. And she wanted time to find them a nice place. Preferably something close to the hotel. With her new salary, signing bonus and moving expense account, as long as she stayed out of Central London, money wasn't going to a problem. It was her chance to finally take care of him. And he deserved it.

She dumped the rest of the drawer contents into the box, then carried it over to the closet. She still had room for a few pairs of shoes.

She heard a noise in the bedroom doorway, and turned to her father, asking, "Did you get me a b—" Then she realized that it wasn't her father standing there.

It was Charles.

Her knees went instantly soft, and her heart surged up and lodged somewhere near her vocal chords.

He looked so good, so casually sexy it made her chest sting. And what was he doing here?

"I don't have a *buh*. But I do have a *box*," he said, holding it out to her. "Your father asked me to bring it in."

Her father actually let him into the apartment? Couldn't he have asked first? What if she didn't want to talk to him?

But you do, a little voice in her head taunted. *You're dying to know why he's here.*

He probably just came to say goodbye. To wish her the best of luck in her new life.

When she didn't step forward and take the box from him, he dropped it on the floor. "Your dad told me to tell you that he was heading home for the night, and he would be back tomorrow around seven."

Great, he left her to deal with this alone. Way to be supportive, Dad.

"I'm a little busy right now," she said.

He nodded, hands wedged in the pockets of his slacks, gazing casually around the naked room. "I can see that. It looks as though you're all ready to go."

"The movers will be here tomorrow morning at eight." Why had she told him that? So he could show up at the last minute and beg her not to go? Like *that* would ever happen.

"So, you're really going?" he said.

Did he think this was all for show? An elaborate hoax to throw him off her scent? "Yes, I'm *really* going."

The jerk had the gall to look relieved! Like her leaving was the best thing that had ever happened to him.

"I'm glad my eminent departure is such a source of happiness for you," she snapped, when on the inside her heart was breaking all over again. Why couldn't he just leave her alone?

"I am happy," he admitted. "But not for the reason you think."

Getting rid of her wasn't reason enough? "Let me guess, you have a new girlfriend. Or six?" *Way to go, Ace, make him think you're jealous.* She needed to keep her mouth shut.

"I'm happy," he said, walking toward her, "because for some reason I can't even begin to understand, knowing that you're really leaving makes me realize how damned much I love you, Victoria."

He said it so earnestly, that for a second she almost believed him. But this had nothing to do with love. Real or imagined. "You only want me because you can't have me. Give it time. You'll find someone to fill the void, then you'll forget all about me."

"Forget you?" he said with a wry laugh. "I can't even fathom the idea of being with another woman."

"For now, maybe."

He shook his head. "No, this is not a temporary state of mind. This is it. You're stuck with me, until death do us part."

Death do us part? Was he talking *marriage?* Charles? Who spent his life bucking the very thought of the institution?

She narrowed her eyes at him, unable to let herself believe it. Yet there was a tiny kernel of hope forming inside of her, that made her think, *Maybe, just maybe…*

She folded her arms across her chest, eyed him suspiciously. "Who are you, and what have you done with Charles?"

"This is your fault," he said. "If you weren't everything I could possibly want in a woman, we wouldn't even be having this conversation. I would still be living happily oblivious and totally unaware of how freaking fantastic it feels to realize you've met the person you want to spend the rest of your life with."

"I don't believe you," she said, although with a pathetic lack of conviction.

He just smiled. "Yes you do. Because you know I would never lie to you. And I would never say something like this if I didn't mean it."

She swallowed hard, those damned tears welling in her eyes again. But at least this time they were happy. "Does this mean I don't have to go to England?"

"I was really hoping you wouldn't."

"Thank God!" she said, throwing herself into his open arms. And she had that same feeling, the one she'd had the first time she kissed him.

He was the one.

She was exactly where she was supposed to be.

His whole body seemed to sigh with relief, and he rested his chin on the top of her head. "I love you, Victoria."

She squeezed him, thinking, you are not going to cry, you big dope. But a tear rolled down her cheek anyway. "I love you, too."

"I'm sorry it took me so long to come to my senses."

"You know what they say. The things we have to work hardest for, we end up appreciating more." It sure made her appreciate him.

"Since you're not going to London, how would you feel about that position at the Royal Inn."

She looked up at him and grinned. "When do I start?"

"I'll talk to Ethan tomorrow." He lowered his head, rubbed his nose against hers. "You realize this means you'll have to deal with my mother a lot more now. She's going to go into anaphylactic shock when she hears I'm finally settling down. Which reminds me…" He rifled around in his pocket. "You want to give me a little room, so I can do this right?"

She backed away from him, wondering what he was up to now, then she saw the small velvet box resting in his palm. Then he actually lowered himself down on *one knee*.

Oh, my God.

He flipped the box open and in a bed of royal blue velvet sat a diamond ring that made her gasp. Not only was the stone enormous, but it sparkled like a star in the northern sky.

"It's beautiful."

"It was my grandmother's," he said. "Given to me when she died, to give to the woman I chose to be my wife. And until I met you, I didn't think there was a finger in the world I would ever want to place it."

That was, by far, the sweetest thing anyone had ever said to her. And she was pathetically close to a complete emotional meltdown. Her head was spinning and her hands were trembling and she had a lump in her throat the size of small continent.

"Victoria, will you marry me?"

She knew if she dared utter a sound she would dissolve into tears, so she did the next best thing.

She dropped to her knees, threw her arms around Charles and hugged him.

He laughed and held her tight. "I'll take that as a yes."

*****

CONVENIENT MARRIAGE, INCONVENIENT HUSBAND

BY
YVONNE LINDSAY

New Zealand born to Dutch immigrant parents, **Yvonne Lindsay** became an avid romance reader at the age of thirteen. Now, married to her "blind date" and with two surprisingly amenable teenagers, she remains a firm believer in the power of romance. Yvonne feels privileged to be able to bring to her readers the stories of her heart. In her spare time, when not writing, she can be found with her nose firmly in a book, reliving the power of love in all walks of life. She can be contacted via her website, www.yvonnelindsay.com.

Dear Reader,

Love. Acceptance. Security.

When these have been a constant in your life, too often, you can take them for granted. And that's something that neither Brent Colby nor Amira Forsythe will ever do.

Sometimes I think it's very easy to look at people who "have it all" and to feel envy – even when we're very happy in our world with family and life and work. Amira Forsythe is one of those women it's probably easy to envy. Beautiful, elegant, from a wealthy family – what on earth could she want for?

In *Convenient Marriage, Inconvenient Husband*, Brent and Amira have to overcome the bitterness of their past and forge a new alliance. But how can that be successful when one of them isn't telling the full truth?

I'll leave that to you to find out in coming pages.

With warmest wishes,

Yvonne Lindsay

To Bron and to Trish, my wipit buddies.
Thanks for your cheerleading and your constant
support. You guys keep me sane...well, mostly! PTB.

One

"Marry me. I'll make it worth your while."

What the hell was *she* doing here? Amira Forsythe—more frequently known as the Forsythe Princess—was as out of place here in the Ashurst Collegiate Chapel men's room as she was in his life, period. He didn't know which he found more startling. Her demand or the fact she'd actually followed him in here. Brent Colby straightened from the basin and casually reached for a fresh towel. He painstakingly dried his hands and dropped the towel in the deep wicker basket before turning to face her.

His eyes raked over the expensively styled, natural honey-blond hair that tumbled over her shoulders, the immaculate makeup, the exquisitely tailored black suit that hugged her generous curves and threw her luscious creamy skin into sharp relief against its unrelenting somberness. Her fragrance—an intriguing combination of flowers and spice—reached across the sterile atmosphere of the tiled room to infiltrate his senses. Against his better judgment, he inhaled. Stupid mistake, he silently rebuked himself as his blood thickened and heated, pooling low in his groin.

At her throat, her pulse beat rapidly against the single strand of pearls that shimmered in their priceless perfection against the nacre of her skin. A dead giveaway. Beneath that well-groomed exterior, she was scared.

Scared of him? She ought to be. Since she'd left him at the altar eight years ago, he'd had a wealth of anger simmering silently inside. When she'd made it absolutely clear she wouldn't be providing any excuses for her behaviour, he'd rebuilt his world without her in it. For the better.

Brent allowed his gaze to meet and clash with hers, took satisfaction in the way her pupils dilated, almost consuming the icy-blue irises—the distinctively chilling Forsythe stare. Marry her? She had to be kidding.

"No," he replied.

He started to walk past her. Even going back into the chapel where the throng of mourners exchanged platitudes after Professor Woodley's wife's memorial service would be preferable to this. Her hand on his arm halted him in his tracks.

"Please. Brent, I *need* you to marry me."

He stopped and looked pointedly at her ringless

fingers on his arm, not betraying for a second what her touch did to him. How his nerves tautened and his heart rate increased. How he'd like nothing better than to push his fingers through the thick silk of her hair and bend his mouth to the smooth column of her throat. Even after all this time, she still had this effect.

Rather than let go immediately, her grip tightened on his forearm before she eased her hold and contradictorily he wished she hadn't. He didn't know what she had in mind, but one thing, at least, was certain. He didn't want a bar of it.

"Amira, even if I was open to discussion on the matter, this is neither the time nor the place."

"Look, Brent, I know we have some bitterness between us—"

Some bitterness? The woman had left him standing at the front of the church swelled with a couple of hundred guests with little more than a text message to his best man. Yeah, there was "some bitterness" between them, all right. Brent had to fight to hold back the derisive bark of laughter that rose in his throat.

"Please. Won't you hear me out?"

Amira's voice had a tiny wobble in it. Another betrayal of the inimitable Forsythe calm. If her grandmother were alive today, no doubt she'd be deeply disappointed in her only granddaughter, and sole remaining direct descendant, for exhibiting such weakness.

"As I recall, you had your shot at marrying me. You blew it. We have nothing to say to one another." Brent bit the words out through a jaw clenched on all the things he'd like to say. In two long strides he was at the men's room door.

"You're the only man I can trust to do this."

He halted in his tracks, his hand resting on the metal push plate on the door. Trust? That was laughable coming from her.

"I think you'll find you're mistaken. If I were you, I wouldn't trust me not to take you for every last red cent. After all, money is the issue here, isn't it?"

"How…how did you know?"

Brent sighed inwardly before meeting her strained gaze. "Because with your kind it always is."

He should have kept on walking. Engaging in conversation with Amira was the last thing he needed.

"Wait. At least give me an opportunity to explain why. Honestly, I *will* make it worth your while. I promise."

"Like your word is worth anything?"

"I need you."

There was a time he'd have walked through a burning building to hear her say that again, but that time was long past. The Forsythes of this world didn't need anyone. Period. They used people. And when they were done using, they discarded. But there was something in the tone of her voice and the fine lines of strain around her eyes that piqued his interest. That she had a problem on her hands was evident. That she thought he could solve that problem, equally so.

"All right, but not now. I'm working from home tomorrow. Meet me there. Nine thirty."

"Nine thirty? I have—"

"Or not at all." He'd be damned if he'd cater to her social schedule. She'd see him on his turf, on his terms, or not at all.

"Yes, nine thirty's fine."

Amira turned to go. Typical, Brent thought. She got what she thought she wanted. Now he was summarily dismissed. But then she halted in her tracks and turned around.

"Brent?"

"What?"

"Thank you."

Don't thank me yet, Brent added silently. He followed her outside through the chapel and into the adjoining Jubilee Hall of Ashurst Collegiate where, as he watched, she disappeared into the throng. It occurred to him that she must have been the woman his assistant said had been persistently phoning his inner-city office each day and refusing to leave a message when told he was still overseas on business. How on earth had she tracked him down here? He'd only returned late last night in a mad dash attempt to make the service. Attending Mrs. Woodley's memorial was a deeply personal matter, one of respect. It rankled him that Amira had soured what was already a difficult day.

He scanned the hall. He didn't even need to close his eyes to still see the rows of impeccably uniformed boys lined up for assembly each morning, hear the sonorous tones of the headmaster—experience again that sensation of not truly belonging.

He hadn't wanted to come to Ashurst, one of New Zealand's most prestigious private boys' schools, but his uncle, his mother's brother, had insisted, saying even though he didn't bear the Palmer name, he still deserved the education that came with his familial lineage.

That was the trouble with old money. Everyone thought they called the shots, knew what was best for you, if only because it was the way things were "done."

Brent hadn't wanted any handouts. He'd seen what having the Palmers pay his fees had done to his father's pride. Zack Colby might never have had the wealth of his wife's family but he'd taught Brent the benefit of working for his place in the world. As a result Brent had worked his backside off to be awarded one of the rarely bestowed Ashurst Scholarships for Academic Excellence—and he'd repaid every cent to his uncle before he'd left school.

But he hadn't been so perfect a student that there weren't some rough patches. He and his two best friends had excelled at their share of mischief as well. He glanced across the milling crowd of past and present students and faculty members, searching for the faces of his cohorts—his cousin, Adam Palmer, and their friend, Draco Sandrelli. He wasn't disappointed; they were making their way over to him already. Adam was first at his side.

"Hey, cuz. Was that who I thought it was coming out of the men's room a minute ago?"

"What? You need glasses now?" Brent responded with a smile that didn't quite make it to his eyes. He lifted a glass of mineral water from the tray being circulated by one of the waitstaff and took a long quenching gulp.

"Very funny. So what did her highness want?" Adam persisted.

Brent weighed up telling them the truth. There had never been any secrets between them before. Now wasn't the time to start holding back.

"She asked me to marry her."

"You're kidding us, right?" Draco laughed, his faint Italian accent betraying his origins despite the number of years he'd spent living and working around the world.

"I wish I was. Anyway, I'll find out more tomorrow."

"What? You're considering seeing her again? After what she did?" Adam shook his head.

"Yeah. I am. But don't worry. I don't plan on saying yes anytime soon."

Brent looked around the room, scanning for a golden-blond head, but she was nowhere to be seen.

"Do you know why she asked you?" Draco asked, his voice threaded with disbelief and a healthy dose of mistrust.

"Last time I heard from her was that bloody text she sent when we were at the church waiting for her to turn up," Adam added.

Brent clenched his jaw at the memory. They'd been at the altar, the three of them lined up and good-naturedly joking about the lateness of his bride and Brent's soon-to-be married status when Adam's cell phone, nestled in his breast pocket, had discreetly vibrated several times in succession. They'd ignored it. Time had continued to tick past with no sign of Amira. Eventually Adam had checked his phone, his face turning gray at the message.

Tell Brent I can't go through with it. Amira.

Initially Brent had wondered whether it would have made any difference if they'd gotten the message sooner—if he'd been able to get to her house before she'd disappeared with her grandmother—but he'd long discounted that as a waste of energy. And once the shock had diminished into cold, hard anger, he'd cursed himself for a fool for having believed her when she'd said she was different from the mold her grandmother had cast her in.

Back then she'd told him money didn't matter to her, and he'd believed her. In the lead-up to their wedding, though, disaster had struck his business. The container load of imported products, with which he'd swept the young adult games market and seen his fortunes soar, had been faulty. To save Amira from anxiety he'd delayed telling her his first million dollars was slowly being filtered down the drain as he recalled stock and personally backed each and every warranty claim. He'd managed to keep the news quiet for days, but somehow it had broken in the national papers as front page news the morning of their wedding.

It turned out that money mattered to her a whole lot more than she'd admitted. He'd learned that the hard way when she'd sent that text, not even having the guts to face him in person and call things off. Brent always made certain he learned his lessons the first time around. The Forsythe Princess wouldn't get another shot at screwing with his life—or his head—again.

"I have no idea what she's up to, but I'll find out

eventually," Brent replied. "C'mon, let's go and pay our respects to Professor Woodley, then get out of here."

Suddenly all he wanted was the open road and the powerful roar of his Moto Guzzi taking him away from his demons. Together the three men shouldered their way through the throng, oblivious to the admiring glances of many of the women there—young and old—to where a small group spoke with the professor. One by one, the members of the group disappeared, leaving them alone with their favorite tutor from their school days.

"Ah, my rogues. Thank you for coming, boys."

Brent stiffened. He hadn't been called a rogue since the day the professor had caught the three of them demon riding on the dark and winding coast road five miles from school. He could still hear the professor's words of censure when they'd arrived back at their hall of residence, and the disappointment in his voice that they'd taken such crazy risks with their lives.

"All of the students in your year are diamonds... some polished, some still a little rough. All, except you three. You, sirs, are rogues!"

They'd escaped with four weeks of detention and loss of privileges, but none of them had ever lived down the regret that they'd caused the older man such pain with their actions. Especially when they later learned his only son had died on the stretch of road they'd been riding. They'd spent the rest of their final year at Ashurst making it up to him.

"So, how are you all? Married, I hope. There's nothing quite like the love of a good woman, or the constancy of having her at your side." The older man's eyes filmed over. "It's times like this that I realize just how much I'm going to miss her."

"Sir, we're really sorry for your loss." Ever the group spokesman, Adam's voice rang with sincerity.

"As am I, my boy, as am I. But don't think you can dodge me that easily." A faint twinkle appeared in the old man's eyes. "Are you married or not?"

One by one each of them shifted under his penetrating gaze, until he hooted with laughter, drawing the attention of the people around them.

"I take it, not, then. Never mind. I have a good feeling about you boys. It'll happen when the time is right."

"Perhaps marriage isn't for all of us," Brent replied, which only opened up the professor to one of his famous lectures on the sanctity of marriage.

But Brent stopped listening, his attention suddenly caught by Draco's expression. The man looked as if he'd seen a ghost. In the next instant Draco had excused himself and hightailed it across the room, toward the catering staff.

"What was that about?" Adam asked as the professor's attention was taken by another group stopping to give their condolences.

"Don't know, but it looks interesting," Brent answered, his eyes locked on the body language of the tall slender woman with short spiky dark hair, who appeared to be in charge of the catering.

Judging by the stiffness in her pose, she wasn't too pleased to be bailed up by Draco. He smiled at her, turning on the infamous Sandrelli charm; but the woman turned up her nose at him and spun on her heel to stalk away, summarily dismissing him by the looks of things.

"He won't like that," Adam said, and sure enough, after the briefest of hesitations, Draco followed hard on her heels, his face set in a determined mask of intent.

"Looks like he won't be coming on that ride with us after all," Brent noted reluctantly. These days the three of them managed little enough time together. "C'mon. I've had enough of this place. Let's go."

Outside they were treated to the sight of Draco standing in the large circular driveway that opened out at the entrance to Jubilee Hall, clearly trying to persuade the catering manager not to leave. But the woman wasn't having any of it. She put her older model station wagon into gear and spun up a rooster tail of gravel from beneath her tires as she drove away. Draco jogged over to them.

"Don't even ask," he warned, his dark features like a thundercloud as he reached for the helmet on the seat of his bike.

With nothing more than a nod of acknowledgment, Brent and Adam did the same, and before long, the matching high performance bikes were gunning it out of the gates and onto the private road that led to the motorway and back to Auckland City.

From her car, parked beneath the heavy branches of an ancient oak tree, Amira watched as Brent came out of the hall. A tremor shot through her, leaving her hands trembling on the steering wheel of her BMW Z4

Coupe. Damn, just when she'd managed to get her nerves back under control.

The distance between the men's room in the chapel and where she'd parked her car had disappeared into a fugue of disbelief at what she'd actually done. She'd been planning this ever since she'd seen the funeral notice for Professor Woodley's wife. Brent had always spoken so highly of the professor; his respect for the old man was an integral part of him. There was no way he'd miss the funeral. It was the only way she'd be able to see him, to surprise him. She'd visualized how she would meet him, what she would say. She just never believed she'd have either the courage, or the gall, to confront him in the men's room.

Her eyes had eaten up the sight of him. Of the breadth of his shoulders, the green glint in his hazel eyes, the expert cut and fall of his glossy hair that she'd fought not to push back across his forehead the way she always used to.

The past eight years had been kind to him, despite his financial difficulties when they'd parted ways. But then, if the latest New Zealand Rich List was anything to go by, the years had been more than kind. He featured strongly in the top twenty now. She wondered if he still cared about things like that. That kind of recognition had driven him in the past, but there was one thing that had always eluded him—acceptance by the old school, especially when their marriage had not taken place.

Her gaze remained fixed on him as he shrugged into a well-worn leather jacket and pulled his dark helmet on, the darkened visor flipping down to obscure his sharply chiseled features. She'd know him anywhere. The way he moved. The way he held his head.

He was slightly heavier set than he'd been at twenty-five, but it looked good on his frame. There was an aura of strength and power about him that spoke to her on a physical level she hadn't experienced since she'd last been in his presence. Or maybe it was just that. Her own very personal and intimate reaction to his nearness. To his masculinity.

Even now she couldn't believe how she'd managed to pluck up the courage to follow him into the men's room and make her demand. But she'd never before been on the verge of destitution. Need had a way of making you do things that you wouldn't normally do, she thought with a bitter grimace. And she'd do whatever it took to get Brent to agree to her terms.

Amira gripped her fingers around the steering wheel in an attempt to control their shaking. She was going to have to do a whole lot better than this tomorrow if she was going to succeed. She'd crossed the first hurdle; the next stage couldn't be that difficult, could it? She refused to believe otherwise. Brent Colby might be hugely successful but he'd always be the new boy on the block unless he could find favor with the old boys' network that governed the movers and shakers of New Zealand business—favor that had been solidly blocked by her late grandmother at every turn. Now, Amira could give him entrée into that rarefied world. She only hoped he still wanted it as much as he'd once wanted her.

Her future, everything that was important to her, depended on him.

No one could understand how deeply important this was to her. No one. For once in her life she wanted to be taken seriously. To be recognized as having a value to society higher than just being some figurehead or spokesperson—the face behind the people who did all the real work. She could live with the loneliness that engendered—she was used to being put on a pedestal, being isolated. But she could not live with failure. It was too important to her that she succeed this time without her grandmother's influence hanging over her like Damocles' sword.

Isobel Forsythe's death had been the catalyst that had really shaken her up—and not just her death but the draconian terms of the old woman's last will and testament. Amira knew her grandmother had done her best to put a stick in the spokes of this particular dream, but it had only served to make her all the more determined to succeed. Contrary to her grandmother's beliefs, Amira did not hold with the thought that it was unreasonable to promise happiness to those less fortunate. It was her personal mission to see this through. To make something worthwhile of her existence.

She jumped at the roar of the three motorcycles as they swept past where her car was parked. Her eyes inexorably drawn to Brent's form hunched over the powerful bike, taking the lead with the kind of effortless precision with which he approached everything.

He'd been so cold and aloof when she'd tried to talk

to him. Not too surprising given where they were, but he was so distant. Not even betraying so much as a hint of anger for what she'd done to him in the past. And she'd known he was angry—bitterly so. She'd heard of Brent's reaction from her grandmother's solicitor, Gerald Stein, who'd been in the vestibule at the church, awaiting her arrival so he could walk her down the aisle.

Deep inside, her heart gave a painful twist. There'd been no wedding then, but she had to make sure that one went ahead now or her promise to little Casey—and more than a dozen other underprivileged or seriously ill kids—would be broken forever.

He had to agree. He just had to.

Two

Amira hesitated at the gate to the long sweeping driveway she knew led to Brent's home. All she had to do was lower her window and press the button on the intercom; then the gate would be opened. It was all very civilized, so why did she feel as if she was entering a panther's lair?

Clipped hedges lined the sides of the drive toward his riverside property. There were only six houses on this exclusive lane leading to the tidal Tamaki Estuary. He'd really come up in the world. It was a far cry from the inner-city apartment he'd had when he met her.

Time was ticking past and she wouldn't discount him turning her away if she was late. She pressed her window control and reached out to activate the talk button on the intercom.

"It's Amira Forsythe."

Should she say anything else? Did he retain staff at the house, or would he answer the intercom himself?

There was no answer but for the smooth electric hum of the imposing black iron gates gliding apart, admitting her to his private corner of the world. Her hands were slippery on the leather steering wheel as she swept down the driveway.

The front of the house was no less imposing than the gated entrance. Amira pulled her car up in front of a four car garage and made her way toward the entrance of the French Provincial style home. Her practiced eye swept the inviting lines of the house. No expense had been spared on this baby, all the way up to the wooden shingle roof. Her heels clipped over the smooth-honed natural stone pathway leading to the front door.

A shiver of anticipation ricocheted through her as she lifted her hand to the intercom beside the door. Her hand was still in the air as the door suddenly swung open.

Amira's breath caught in her throat at the sight of him. Dressed in Armani, he was a sight to behold. Even her late grandmother couldn't have disapproved of him dressed like this. His dark brown hair was swept back off a wide forehead, not a hair daring to slide out of place today. His shirt remained unbuttoned at the neck, exposing a triangle of warm tanned skin. Had their circumstances been different, she'd be in his arms already. Perhaps even with her lips against that tantalizing triangle, tracing the indent at the base of his throat with her tongue. Her inner muscles clenched on a rising heat that threatened to swamp her.

She forced herself to quell her instinctive reaction to him. To focus on the reason she was here.

"You're on time. Good. Come in."

"I make it a habit to be on time. Especially when it's something as important as this."

Amira stepped over the threshold and into the black-marble-lined foyer.

"Really, Amira? I can remember at least one occasion where you were late. Very late, in fact. But then maybe *that* particular occasion wasn't important to you."

Her cheeks flooded with color. It hadn't taken long for him to refer to their wedding day. It was only to be expected.

"I wanted to explain to you, Brent—afterward. But I knew you wouldn't listen to me."

"You're right. I wouldn't. Which begs the question, why should I listen to you today?"

He stood opposite her—his arms crossed in front of him, his feet shoulder width apart—not inviting her any farther into his home. His body language couldn't be any more defensive than if he'd donned armor and guarded his inner sanctum with a broadsword. One look at the firm set of his sensually chiseled lips reminded her she was not here to fantasize.

"Perhaps I still have something to offer you. Could we—" Amira made a helpless gesture with her hand "—could we sit down?"

"Come up to my office."

Brent spun on a well-polished heel and headed up a wide sweeping staircase leading to the upper level of the house. Opposite the top of the stairs he showed her into a large airy office. The dove-gray carpet muffled their footsteps as they entered the room. Amira looked around—the room was a reflection of the man he'd become since she knew him last.

There was no doubting his success and wealth in the choice of state-of-the-art office equipment, quality furnishings and window treatments—no expense had been spared here, either—but one thing about him, at least, hadn't changed. Built-in glass-fronted bookcases lined the walls. He'd always been an avid reader, and judging by the appearance of many of the book spines, these were not here simply for show.

"You always did love your books," she commented as she perched on the edge of a wing-backed leather chair, her mind suddenly inundated with memories of lying in the sunshine in the park, or at the beach, dozing with her head in his lap, while he read his latest acquisition.

"Among other things less enduring," Brent responded enigmatically as he took his seat behind his desk.

She fought not to flinch as he scored another direct hit. This was going to be more difficult than she'd anticipated. His antipathy toward her filled the air, beating against her as if it had its own life force.

Amira blinked at the light streaming in through the dormer windows behind him. He had her at a distinct disadvantage, purposely she realized. Seated where he was, she couldn't discern his expression or read his eyes like she always used to. She angled her head so she avoided the worst of the morning glare. She'd concede this tactic to him but she'd be damned if she'd concede anymore. Too much rode on the outcome of today, even—as dramatic as it sounded—her very life as she knew it.

"Nice place you have," Amira commented conversationally.

She wasn't about to let him know how nervous she was about this meeting, nor how uncomfortable she felt right now. The contrast between the old memories she'd fought so hard to suppress was at total odds with the distinctly chilly reception she was now subject to.

"Cut to the chase, Amira. We both know this isn't a social visit. What's behind your absurd proposal?"

Amira swallowed and took a deep breath. She had to be honest about it and cut straight to the chase as he demanded. He wouldn't accept anything less.

"Money. As you guessed so astutely yesterday."

Brent laughed, a harsh short sound totally lacking in humor.

"Why doesn't that surprise me? If there's one thing that drives you Forsythes, it's money. At least you're honest about it this time." His tone was scathing.

Amira stiffened in her chair, her back impossibly straight.

"And money doesn't drive you?" she asked pointedly.

"Not anymore," came his succinct reply.

"Somehow I find that difficult to believe."

"Believe what you will. It means nothing to me."

And nor did *she* anymore, she reminded herself. There'd been a time when they meant the world to each other. But that had been torn to pieces on the shattered remnants of their dreams when she'd publicly humiliated him. She couldn't let what she'd done to him that awful day hold her back now. Somehow she had to convince him that marrying could prove beneficial to him too. On the surface of things, she could see that money wasn't a major motivator for him anymore. She had to hope that, on top of the financial benefit she planned to propose, the promise of inclusion into the exclusive old boys' network would be sufficient inducement.

"Fine." She drew in a calming breath. It wouldn't help her cause if she lost her temper now. "As you probably heard, my grandmother passed away recently."

"Yes, go on."

No condolences from him then, she thought bitterly. Mind you, it really was no surprise when her grandmother had barely tolerated him at best—and at worst she'd forced Amira to give him up completely.

"She put certain…conditions on my right to inherit under her will."

"What sort of conditions?" Brent leaned back in his chair.

Although his body appeared totally relaxed, she knew he was alert and listening carefully. Every muscle in that well-toned body was attuned to her, whether he liked it or not. It had always been that way between them. Visceral. Instant. Unquenchable. Even now she felt the electric tingle through her veins that being around him had always brought. It was a distraction she could well do without and one look in his hazel eyes and the remoteness within them forced her back on track.

"Restrictive ones, unfortunately. I must be married before I turn thirty to inherit."

"So you have just under eighteen months to find some poor fool to be your husband." Brent leaned forward on his desk. He flicked his gaze over her body. "With your obvious attributes, that shouldn't be difficult," he concluded dismissively.

"I don't want just some poor fool. I want you." *Oh hell,* that didn't come out right, she thought frantically. An obvious sign of her distress. Normally she was as diplomatic and serene as the media portrayed her.

A small smile played around Brent's lips. "A rich fool like me, perhaps? Sorry to disappoint you but I'm not in the market for marriage to anyone—and certainly not to you."

"No! That's not what I meant at all." Amira hurriedly searched her mind for the words she desperately needed to persuade him to agree to her plan. "Basically, I need a husband. And that's it. I'm not interested in all the accoutrements that come with marriage, or the complications of a relationship. I have more than enough on my plate right now without that. With you, I know I'm safe. There's no one else I can ask who wouldn't expect more from a marriage than what I'm prepared to give. I think I'd be safe to say you have no desire for me anymore so we could agree that it would be purely a business arrangement."

"A business arrangement?"

Finally she'd knocked that reserve from his expression, although she couldn't be sure if what he now exhibited was interest or well concealed mockery.

"Yes, an agreement, between old friends."

His lips firmed into a straight line and he eyed her speculatively.

"And exactly what are you prepared to give to this *old friend?*"

"Ten percent of the value of my inheritance," she named a sum that made Brent's eyebrows raise slightly before she continued, "together with platinum level entry to the Auckland Branch of the New Zealand League of Businessmen."

"All that just for the pleasure of being your husband—on paper?"

There was no doubting the sarcasm in his voice now. Once again color flooded her cheeks.

"I realize you think I'm not exactly a prize, Brent, but even you haven't been able to buy your way into the NZLB. I can ensure that your application is approved. Just think of the contacts it will bring you. I know you have a new project underway in the city and that you've been stonewalled on consents for some time. Delays are costly, especially with the type of waterfront expansion you're planning. A word in the ear of the right people and those problems will disappear.

"I'm sure your lawyer will be happy to draw up some kind of prenuptial agreement that will include the money I'm prepared to give you and the introduction to the NZLB as part of the schedule of what I promise you on marriage."

"What about my money? I assume you want your slice of that too?" His voice remained neutral, as if they weren't talking millions of dollars here.

"Not at all! I don't want a bar of your wealth. That's not what this is all about. You'll be bringing me everything I need by being my husband. You're the one man who can do this for me."

"The only one?"

The way he said it made it like an insult. Amira stood. She refused to be drawn into debate over it. She'd made her pitch. Now the ball was firmly in his court.

"I'll leave you to think my offer over." She delved in her Hermès bag to withdraw a card, which she deposited on the polished mahogany desk. "Here, call me when you've made your decision. I'll see myself out."

Brent watched in silence as Amira left his office. He didn't bother to pick up her card. He knew her number. Had always known it and, try as he might, he'd been unable to scourge it from his memory.

So, she thought she'd be "safe" with him. She had no idea. Safe certainly wasn't the first word that sprang to mind when he saw her. Even the severe gray businesslike pinstripe suit she'd worn today did little to hide the tempting shape of her, or the allure of ruffling that touch-me-not aura she projected to the world.

Her belief that he needed her help to gain access to the old boys' network to see him complete his latest development opposite the passenger wharves in downtown Auckland needled him though. He thought she'd have done her homework a little better than that.

Brent Colby needed no one to be a success in his world. The consents were slow coming through, granted, but they would come through in the end. It was all part of the game of showing who held power in the city, and he was prepared to play that game if it got him to his goal in the end. Since he'd made and lost his first million dollars, he'd learned patience— the hard way. He certainly didn't need Amira Forsythe's influence.

He should have turned her down flat. Her crazy idea wasn't even worth thinking over. The fact that she'd walked away from him when he'd needed her most should have convinced him of that. That she'd walked away from him because of money, even more so.

He thought of the figure she'd named as a settlement if they married. While it was no small sum, it was a drop in the ocean compared to his current wealth.

But then Amira's grandmother had always coached her well on the importance of financial security. So what if she had to shell out a few million to access many more. He could just imagine what lengths someone like Amira would go to, to get her hands on his bank balance now. Even go so far as proposing marriage, perhaps?

And that's where something didn't ring true. Amira had her own wealth. The Forsythe family were among the founding fathers of New Zealand, with business interests that were as far reaching as their reported philanthropy was widespread. And Amira was the end of the line. The approved line, that was. Brent had heard rumors of an Australian-based distant cousin who'd long since worn out his welcome, his credit and his word on the strength of the Forsythe name.

Brent's inner warning system told him there was more to her request than met the eye. Yes, she'd changed in the eight years since he'd last seen her, but she hadn't changed so much that he couldn't tell when she was hiding something from him. And that something piqued his interest.

Brent leaned back in his chair and swiveled it to the window so he could look out over the immaculately manicured lawn leading beyond the tennis court and down to the Tamaki Estuary. He loved this view. The contrast between where he was now and where he'd grown up in a council housing estate across the river was never more prominently displayed than when he looked across the water.

The Amira Forsythes of this world could never understand what it was like to work hard for everything in your life rather than be born into inestimable wealth and privilege by a fluke of nature. He thought back to Amira's grandmother, Isobel. The harridan had barely tolerated him when he and Amira had started going out—and then only because he'd been featured in the nationwide business papers as New Zealand's next up-and-coming entrepreneur.

But that had all changed when the imported products upon which he'd started to build his fledgling empire had turned out to be faulty; and in honoring the warranty requirements, he'd cleaned out every last cent he'd made, and then some. Sure, he could have declared bankruptcy. Reneged on the good faith with which his clients had distributed his stock. But he wasn't that kind of man.

He'd held on to the title to his apartment by the skin of his teeth. With that security he had started the long, soulless road to rebuild his wealth. Bigger than before. Better than before. He knew the value of hard work all right. Over and over again. And that was something that Amira could never understand with her background.

No doubt old Isobel would be turning in the family vault right now if she knew what her precious only granddaughter had proposed. If she'd thought for one minute that her name would be sullied by association with him.

Man, he'd thought he'd struck the jackpot when he'd first met Amira. The Forsythe Princess. With her almost royal demeanor and wealth, and the well-known and much documented disapproval of her grandmother, not many men had dared ask her out. But he had.

Amira hadn't bothered to hide her surprise when he'd approached her at the Ellerslie race track during Auckland Cup Week. She'd been judged overall winner of the fashion parade and had finally extricated herself from the phalanx of photographers when he'd stepped up, tucked her arm in his and led her away from the intrusive glare of flashbulbs. In lieu of a formal introduction, he'd promised her lunch well away from the seething mass of racegoers and the thunder of hooves on the track. To his surprise and delight, she'd accepted.

Their romance had made headlines for weeks as they indulged in the flush of first love. Sometimes dodging the media, others making the most of the publicity to let the world know how lucky they were to be together.

He'd hardly been able to believe his good fortune. He was brash and raw and everything her family wasn't. And yet she'd loved him as passionately as if he were her equal. At least he'd thought she did. But Amira had shown her true Forsythe colors when she'd jilted him hard on the news of his financial failure. Just when he'd needed her support and love the most.

He swallowed against the acidic acrimony of the past. Better he'd discovered it then rather than later, his friends and family had pointed out. But hindsight was no salve to his wounded heart or his tattered pride. She'd hurt him. Cut him far deeper than he wanted to admit—then, or now.

He'd never before considered himself a vengeful man, but as Brent studied the fast-moving flow of the outgoing tide on the estuary it occurred to him that in coming to him Amira had handed him the means to a satisfying stroke of revenge on a gold-edged platter.

His pulse quickened as he thought the matter through. She'd made it clear she didn't want the physical aspects of a relationship, but he doubted she'd resist him forever. Seducing her again would certainly be no hardship. They'd been electric together. Yes, it would give the cutting edge to his plan.

How sweet would it be to stand her up this time, to give her a taste of her own bitter medicine? And how appropriate when she was now the one who stood to lose everything she held dear—the power, the prestige and, most of all, the fortune behind the Forsythe name.

Brent spun his chair back to the desk and reached for his phone, flicking it to speaker and punching in the numbers to Amira's mobile phone.

"This is Amira Forsythe." Her voice filled his office again, and deep inside of him something clenched tight.

"I'll marry you."

"Brent?" she sounded unsure.

"You were expecting it to be someone else?"

"No. I just didn't think you'd make up your mind so soon."

"Afraid you're losing your appeal, Amira?"

"No, not at all. I'm just…surprised, is all, but pleasantly so. Obviously we'll need to meet to sort out a few things. How are you placed tonight? Shall we say dinner at eight thirty?"

She mentioned the name of the waterfront restaurant that had been their favorite haunt so long ago.

"If you're happy to be in the public eye together so soon. It'll raise questions you might not want to answer just yet."

"Rather sooner than later, don't you think?" she replied, totally matter-of-fact. "What time can you pick me up? It's better that we arrive together."

Brent confirmed a time with her that would allow them ample time to get to the restaurant from her place.

"Great. I'll see you then. And Brent? Thank you for doing this. You won't regret it."

The relief in her voice was palpable, making his internal warning system go to high alert and making him even more certain she was hiding more than she was letting on. As he said goodbye and disconnected the call, Brent smiled grimly.

Regret was for fools, and no one had ever accused Brent Colby of being a fool.

Three

Amira let herself into her suite of rooms later that afternoon. She'd managed to finish earlier than expected at the Fulfillment Foundation's office and looked forward to a little down time before going back on show tonight with Brent.

She'd long been thankful she had her own entrance to her rooms at the Forsythe Mansion in Auckland's premier suburb of Remuera. The privacy it gave her had negated the supercilious once-over from her grandmother every time she came and went during the day. It never mattered how immaculate her outfit, how perfect her grooming, Isobel had always managed to convey that she found fault somewhere.

Most people would probably have thumbed their

noses at the matriarch. But Amira wasn't most people. She knew how lucky she was to have been given a home and a future by her grandmother after her parents' untimely deaths in a yachting accident on the Waitemata Harbour. She'd been given every opportunity to get ahead. So, she wasn't the academic genius her grandmother had hoped for, and she took after her mother more in looks than Isobel's own son, Amira's father. But despite her shortcomings, Amira had her strengths and her grandmother hadn't been averse to using them in the course of running the many charities whose boards she sat on. And it had been rewarding work—always. Not least of which because finally there was something Amira was darned good at.

Even now, although she had no need to slip in unnoticed, old habits died hard. She preferred her own small apartment anyway. The sheer size and age of the main part of the house, more like a museum than a home, was overwhelming to most visitors and she'd been no different. Amira had never quite shaken that first impression she'd gained when, after a vicious and public court battle between Isobel and her parents' chosen guardians, she'd arrived to live here. It was more than her bereaved ten-year-old mind could take in.

Isobel had kept an iron grip on all Forsythe affairs up until the last six months before her death, when a series of strokes rendered her incapable of holding the reins any longer. Not a single word had passed the old woman's lips in those last months, but every last glare had been a criticism. For Amira, trying to juggle her grandmother's home care as well as her charity commitments had been wearing in the extreme.

She noticed the message light was flashing on her machine as she kicked off her heels. Amira reached across the table to press the play button. A vaguely familiar male voice oozed from the speaker, making her skin crawl.

"Amira, dar-ling. I've just received the written confirmation of the terms of dear Aunt Izzy's will and couldn't wait to tell you how much I'm looking forward to moving in. Perhaps we can come to an arrangement— a mutually *satisfying* arrangement—about your accommodations. Eighteen months seems so long to wait."

She hit the erase button with a shudder, wishing she could clear the memory from her mind as easily. Roland Douglas, her second cousin on Isobel's side of the family, had about as much presence as a cockroach— and he was just as hard to get rid of. Isobel had long since cut ties from that side of the family, but for some reason, prior to the stroke that had robbed her of her speech, she'd made a codicil to her will naming Roland as default beneficiary should Amira not be married or have "borne live issue" by the time she turned thirty.

Whether Isobel had intended it to be a catalyst, to get Amira to hurry up and find the right kind of man to be her consort as she assumed the Forsythe mantle, no one would ever know. But one thing was certain—without marriage Amira would lose everything, even the annuity that she received to cover her living costs.

When Amira had questioned if her grandmother had

been of sound mind at the time of drawing up the codicil, she'd been assured that a neurologist had sworn an affidavit to the effect that while Isobel was physically impaired her mind remained as sharp as her legendary tongue. She didn't stand a chance of appealing against the will's terms.

Amira stepped through to her bathroom, eager to wash away the taint of Roland's words. He really took sleaze to new heights, and his unsettling phone calls bordered on harassment. If worse came to worse and he inherited, there was no way they'd be coming to any arrangements, satisfying or not.

A shudder ran through her body. Too much rode on her ability to come into her inheritance. Too many hopes and dreams. If marriage was what it took, then marriage it would be.

As she removed her clothes and stepped under the pounding shower, she let the heated water sluice away the tension of the day. Seeing Brent again had been difficult enough, although the stress of that meeting had dissipated somewhat when he'd agreed to marry her. No, the thing that worried her most was the Fulfillment Foundation—the charity she herself had established for the purpose of fulfilling the dreams of sick and dying children and their families. They were running on an absolute shoestring, and her administration staff's wages were now nearly a month overdue.

It said a lot for their belief in her and in the charity that they hadn't up and left by now. But the length of time it was taking to get serious financial backing in a world continually hungry for sponsorship dollars had begun to put the mission of the foundation in jeopardy. Somehow she had to get those wages paid—soon, before her staff were forced to leave and seek other employment.

Going out with Brent tonight was a stroke of brilliance. It would pique public interest in their reunion, and she had every intention of selling their story to the highest bidder. The more conjecture and speculation she could drum up in the short time they had available before announcing their engagement, the better.

Amira closed her eyes and sighed as the shower spray drenched her hair and she lathered up her shampoo. She'd stopped by Auckland's children's hospital, Starship, on her way home from the city and could still see little Casey McLauchlan's face now. All the orphaned five-year-old wanted was the chance to see Disneyland with her new adoptive family. Something that might never happen if her leukemia, now hopefully in remission, came back before the foundation was firmly on its financial feet. Amira had promised the little girl, who'd already lost so much in her short life, she'd have her wish, but the reality of being able to make that happen became more remote by the day.

Brent had said yes, she reminded herself, and if everything went to plan she'd come into her inheritance on the day of the wedding and everything would be all right. She just had to grasp hold of that and make sure it happened.

She'd almost convinced herself of it by the time she'd completed her shower and dressed in a pair of lightweight track pants and a tank top. She had a couple of hours before she had to get ready for dinner with Brent so she might as well make the most of the time, she thought, and indulge in some much missed reading time. She stretched out on her sitting room couch, a towel across the arm of the chair where her hair spread to air dry into lush natural curls, and tried to focus on the words that danced across the page of the novel she'd been trying to read for the past few weeks.

Amira woke with a start to a darkened room and the echo of her doorbell still ringing in her ears. She bolted upright from the couch and took a swift look at the antique carriage clock on the mantelpiece as she stumbled to the door. Damn! It was a quarter past eight already. How on earth had she allowed herself to fall asleep like that?

Brent tapped his foot impatiently as he waited for someone to open up. Just as he reached to press the doorbell again, the door suddenly swung open. His eyes narrowed in appreciation at the sight of Amira, her hair a sexy disheveled mass of curls. One thin shoulder strap of her tank top slid down her arm, and the lack of awareness left by deep sleep remained prominent in her pale blue eyes. As she identified him, the thin fabric of her top peaked around her nipples. She really needed to work on that Forsythe cool.

"Brent! I'm so sorry. I fell asleep. If you can give me ten minutes I'll be ready. Please, come in and pour yourself a drink or something—" She fluttered her hand in the direction of her sitting room. "I'm sure you remember where everything is."

"I'll let the restaurant know we'll be a little delayed."

Brent gave her a pointed look and was amused to see a flush of color steal across the sweep of her cheeks.

"Of course. Look, I'm really sorry about this."

"Don't worry. Just get ready."

Brent silently doubted she'd be finished in the ten minutes she'd said, but she must have moved like the wind because in no time she was back in the sitting room wearing a wraparound gown, in a deep red-wine color, teamed with a set of heels that almost brought her eye to eye with him. She'd tangled her hair up with a bunch of clips on her head, and her makeup, as ever, was immaculate. The Forsythe Princess was very firmly back in residence—a total contrast to the enticing creature who'd met him at the door.

He recognized her shield, for want of a better word, for what it was. He'd identified it early on in their previous relationship. Any time she felt insecure about a situation, she became even more impossibly regal and untouchable than ever. He'd started to gauge how comfortable she was by the height of her heels, and if tonight's ice picks were anything to go by she was battling for supremacy.

"Okay, I'm ready. Let's go," she said, slightly breathless.

"Just one thing."

He might not be able to get her to change her shoes but he could do this. Brent stepped close to her and reached to slide out the pins holding her hair. He let them fall to the floor as he extracted each one then, with both hands, he ran his fingers through the honey-blond tresses.

"There, that's better."

Damn, he shouldn't have touched her. His fingers tingled from the silky contact of her hair, and his body had reacted with a burning awareness that was destined to make their evening very uncomfortable.

Amira gave him an icy glare. "If you say so," she answered before turning a cold shoulder to him and stalking out the door.

Brent held the door of his Porsche 911 open for her, catching a glimpse of her legs as she lowered herself into her seat. He waited a moment, counting slowly to ten, as she scooped up the fabric and arranged it to hide the tempting golden tanned curve of her thighs. He should have brought one of his other cars, something that would have afforded them both some distance between them, rather than this—his latest toy.

As he settled into the driver's seat and fired up the engine, he was too wound up to appreciate the roar of the six-cylinder turbo, and it bothered him that he'd let Amira get under his skin like that. Thankfully the journey from her home on the northern slopes of Remuera to the restaurant on the waterfront was only a short one. Inside of fifteen minutes they were walking along the sidewalk toward the Italian place that had been the scene of so many of their secrets and shared whispers so long ago.

They stepped inside to a bustling and busy atmosphere. The maître d' led them toward the cozily lit table for two in the back corner. Brent rested his hand at the small of Amira's back, smiling slightly to himself as he felt her flinch, then relax, beneath his touch. Well, she'd have to get used to it if she wanted to carry this off. No one would believe an engagement between a couple who never touched.

Heads turned and conversation stopped as they settled at their table, before resuming again more audibly than before. He heard their names being whispered, heard the questions hanging in the air. The rumor mills would be working overtime by morning.

While he was no stranger to the press, he loathed this kind of publicity—being under the microscope for others' entertainment. He'd had enough of that when his first business venture had collapsed, and with Amira's simultaneous abandonment of him it had reached fever pitch. Nowadays he only dealt with the press on his terms and when it would benefit his business.

He was glad that despite the surrounding noise and diners they were afforded some privacy by the partial screening of a large potted palm. As they accepted menus, Brent leaned forward.

"Seems we're already the topic of discussion here. You okay with that?"

Amira looked surprised. "Of course," she replied. "Did you expect I'd cut and run at the first sign of interest? You forget; I'm quite used to it."

Brent shifted back in his seat. Used to it? If anything she looked bored by it. "So it won't bother you that we're going to be the focus of gossip tomorrow."

"It will only be gossip. You know that. I know that. It's all that matters. Besides, when we announce our engagement the forerunning publicity will have been good."

"Good? Why so?"

"Well, we'll be able to get a far higher price for our story if there's been enough speculation about our romance being rekindled, don't you think?"

"Oh, definitely," he said before picking up his menu and studying it carefully.

A cold ball of lead solidified in the pit of Brent's stomach. There it was again. Money. He knew he shouldn't be surprised, but it angered him that her unabashed focus remained the same. For a moment when he'd arrived at her place this evening he'd caught a glimpse of the Amira he'd fallen in love with the first time. The unguarded, private version. But, as she'd just proven with her comment, the real Amira Forsythe sat before him now. The woman who'd greeted him in disarray at her front door was no more real than a chimera.

It wasn't too late to pull out of this charade. He could get up from this table and leave right now. If he did that though, he'd be denied the satisfaction of seeing through his own agenda, and he'd thought about that a lot today. About how he could show her what she'd really said no to when she'd chosen not to fulfill her promise to marry him. By the time she realized what she'd missed out on, he would have his reward. And hopefully, he'd have managed to rid his system of the ghost of her memory for good.

"So when do you think we should make the engagement announcement? Is a week too soon?" She interrupted his thoughts.

"A week?" Brent was surprised she wanted to move this all so quickly. "Don't you think that's a little too soon after your grandmother's death. After all, it's only been what? Six weeks?"

"Hmm." Amira tore a piece off the garlic pizza bread that had been delivered in a basket to their table while they pondered their order. A worried little frown appeared between her brows. "Well, it isn't as if we don't already know one another, is it? A month would be too long so why don't we compromise with a fortnight?"

"A fortnight?" Brent took a sip of the excellent red wine their waiter had poured at his request, then nodded. "Yeah, I think that would be okay."

Amira continued. "And what about the wedding, we're in mid-March now. The soonest I could fit it in would be late May or early June—Queen's birthday weekend probably. Are you free then?"

"Queen's birthday? Yeah, why not?" Since the wedding wasn't going to happen, he really didn't give a toss. He continued. "If you can get it all sorted by then, that'll be fine. I have business commitments after that which would make a wedding impossible before Christmas, and I'm sure you don't want to wait that long to access your inheritance."

While it wasn't strictly true, he saw no reason not to apply his own timeline to her plans.

Amira toyed with the stem of her wineglass, attracting his attention to her long slender fingers, the tips manicured within an inch of perfection. Not so much as a chip of nail polish to mar the facade she presented to the world. He wondered briefly if she'd remain this immaculate when her world fell apart.

"Of course, we won't be able to book anything decent at such short notice." She worried at her lower lip with her teeth before speaking again. "We could always do it at the mansion. There's enough room, and we don't need as many guests as last time. I'll get some publicity people to organize it as soon as possible."

"Publicity people?" This whole situation was crazy enough as it was without turning it into a three-ring circus.

"Well, there's a great deal to juggle between your commitments and mine. I want everything to have the greatest impact." She hesitated and looked at him. "This is a business arrangement after all. We can't leave anything to chance."

"No. We can't."

He shouldn't have been all that surprised, though, he reminded himself. She was brilliant at playing the media. In her token position as glamour spokesperson for the numerous charities her grandmother had favored, she'd perfected her role. It was only to be expected that he, and their wedding, would be given the same polished treatment.

Besides, this time around it was as different from their last wedding plan as chalk was from cheese. They'd made all their plans together—and look at how that had all turned out, he reminded himself ironically.

She was right. It was better to leave this in the hands of a neutral third party.

"How about someone who can handle the organization and publicity releases together? Can you think of anyone who could handle both? The less people involved in this the better. Less room for the truth to come out," he suggested.

"I'll go through a few names I have and compile a short list to discuss with you. We can interview them together if you like. No point in choosing someone you're not at ease with."

"Good of you to realize that," he answered drily. "Are you ready to order?"

"Yes, but there's just one more thing."

"What's that?"

Amira drew in a deep breath before continuing. "How we present ourselves in public. I know I said I wasn't interested in the—" She suddenly looked uncomfortable, a blush coloring her cheeks. "You know. The physical side of things, but I've been thinking it would probably be best if we were to act like any normal couple in love."

Brent reached across the table and uncurled her fisted fingers from where they lay on the tablecloth. His thumb stroked over her knuckles, back and forth. Her eyes flew open and her mouth formed a small O of surprise.

"Like this, you mean?"

She moistened her lips, and he found himself watching the pink tip of her tongue with intense interest.

"Yes, exactly like that," she eventually managed.

He let her hand go and sat up straight. "Sure, no problem. I think I can convince anyone watching that we struggle to keep our hands off one another. How about you?"

"I…I'll manage," Amira said, hiding behind the large menu, effectively ending the conversation before he could provoke her further.

The rest of their evening passed comfortably enough and they coordinated their coming week as to when they could be seen going out together. Amira had a full schedule of engagements for various charity functions, and she'd made it clear she needed him to escort her.

It was as Brent signed for the bill that a bustle of activity drew his attention to the entrance of the restaurant. The maître d' rushed over to him, a worried look on his face.

"I'm sorry, Mr. Colby. I can assure you that none of my staff made the call that brought those people here."

A small, but growing, collection of paparazzi now jostled for position on the pavement, held back by three of the waitstaff from the restaurant.

"Can we use the back entrance?" Brent asked.

"No. Don't worry. We'll go through the front," Amira interrupted before the maître d' could reply. "Perhaps it might be an idea to get someone to bring your car around, though. Save us being hounded all the way to the car park."

There was something in Amira's tone that made Brent assess her carefully after he handed his keys to one of the waitstaff and gave instructions on where his car was parked.

"You don't sound surprised that this is happening."

"I'm not. I made a few calls this afternoon."

"You organized this to happen?"

"Of course. Is that a problem?"

She sat there, as serene as a swan on a smooth lake. The engineer of the bedlam they would be subjected to on leaving the restaurant. He had to hand it to her. She was playing this for all it was worth.

The roar of his car as it was brought to the front, followed by a cacophony of protest from drivers restricted from passing the vehicle where it was double parked on the busy road, drew him to his feet.

"No. Come on, then," he said, determinedly taking Amira's hand in his. "Let's get this over with."

The maître d' walked in front of them, hands raised as if he could ward off the intrusive flash of the cameras and the volley of questions that filled the air. Brent held the passenger door of the Porsche open for Amira and gritted his teeth as she took her time settling into the car. She acted as if she was oblivious to the craziness around them, but he knew she was angling for the best shots as she smiled up at him, the expression on her face luminescent. Finally she was finished, her profile a perfect cameo of disinterest in the paparazzi. Brent strode around to the other side of the car and slid in behind the wheel.

He gunned the engine to a squeal of protest from the tires and pulled out into Tamaki Drive and away from the chaos he loathed. If tonight was a sign of things to come, this was going to be one of the hardest projects he'd ever undertaken. As a fire lit deep in his belly, he acknowledged that there was nothing he liked better than a challenge.

Four

"Did you want to come in for a nightcap?" Amira asked, breaking the strained silence that had stretched out in the car during their journey back to her place.

"Yeah, why not?" Brent agreed, much to her surprise.

He'd been bristling with frustration since they'd left the restaurant. The square line of his jaw tense, his eyes fixed on the road ahead of them—never once making an attempt at conversation.

Inside her suite, she could feel the tension coming off him in waves. She decided to take the bull by the horns.

"You're angry with me," she stated, sliding out of her Jimmy Choos and wiggling her toes in the carpet before crossing to the antique drink cabinet and opening it.

"What makes you say that?" Brent hedged.

"Brent, we might not have spent any time together in the past eight years, but I still know you. You're mad as hell. Why?"

"I don't like being used."

"Used?" She sloshed a measure of his preferred brandy into a handblown balloon and passed it over to him, before dropping a few ice cubes in a tumbler over a Baileys Irish Cream for herself.

"I hate being a public spectacle."

"That was nothing, and you know it. It's the fact it took you by surprise that's made you so mad. So, for that I apologize. In the future I'll keep you in the loop."

"The loop."

Amira hesitated, her glass poised halfway to her lips. There was an undercurrent in his voice that shrieked a warning. She placed the glass down on the coffee table and sank down onto her couch.

"What's wrong?" she asked.

"You make it sound like I'm just a player in this, Amira. A chess piece to be moved around the board at your discretion. We're both in this. We both have something to gain. If you don't include me and if I don't have some input into what is going to happen, you can count on not having my support. I can far more easily withdraw from our agreement than you can."

So there it was: his first threat. Amira thought again of the overdue wages, of the families who needed her help. Of the promise she'd made to Casey. A desperate sigh built up deep inside, a sign of all she couldn't afford to let out, couldn't succumb to. She drew herself up straight, as if she was on an upright high-backed chair rather than the deeply comfortable three-seater designed for sprawling in front of TV.

"I'm well aware of that, and I have apologized. It won't happen again. You know I have too much riding on this to want to jeopardize your commitment."

She allowed herself to relax a little as Brent sat down next to her and took a sip of his brandy.

"To be honest, what you did reminded me a lot of your grandmother. She always did like to be the one pulling the strings."

Amira felt as if she'd been slapped. She lifted her chin in response to the carefully aimed hit. He'd never know how much it had stung. Let him score his point.

"I'll take that as a compliment," she responded.

"Believe me. It wasn't."

He reached over and cupped her chin with one hand, forcing her to look straight into his eyes. She could see the gold rim of color around his pupils and the striations of green and brown that tinted his irises. Her breath hitched as she allowed herself to fall a little into the past—to a time when they'd maintain eye contact across a crowded room as a silent form of communication to express their love. Then suddenly he let her go, breaking the spell that wound about her, reminding her of the gulf that yawned between them.

Reminding her of what she had to do.

If there was one thing she excelled at it was maintaining appearances. She'd never let him know how much he'd rattled her just now. She knew there had been no love lost between Brent and Isobel, and as emotionally cold as her grandmother was she had firmly believed she was acting in Amira's best interests. Besides, despite her enemies, her grandmother had been an incredibly powerful woman.

"Compliment or not, Isobel was highly regarded by the very men you need to get your waterfront project off the ground. Knowing how to pull strings, and which ones to pull, can be a very valuable tool, wouldn't you say?" Amira managed to utter the words with a casualness she was far from feeling.

"Speaking of which, when do you propose to sponsor my admission to the league?"

"I can start tomorrow. Processing can take a while."

"Any chance you can speed it up."

"I'll do what I can. It certainly won't hurt for our new relationship to be in the papers tomorrow. The timing will be perfect. The league is a closed bunch, but they keep their eye on the pulse of what's happening around town."

She might be Isobel Forsythe's granddaughter but she lacked the kudos to make the same kind of demands her grandmother had been famous for—she only hoped that this time they would listen to her. They'd see Brent as an asset to the organization once they looked past his lineage and reputation, she was sure of it. A shiver ran down her spine.

Everything hinged on making this marriage happen—even the roof over her head. The thought was daunting and reminded her of the fine line she had to tread. One misstep and Roland would inherit it all and then she, and her foundation, would be out in the cold. Literally.

Later, after Brent had gone home, Amira let herself into the main part of the house. The air was still, almost as if it was waiting for the mistress of the house to assert her wishes.

Her eyes flicked up to the life-sized oil portrait of Isobel, where it presided over the landing halfway up the staircase. As much as she'd learned to respect her grandmother, theirs had never been a loving relationship. The mere thought that she'd become, or even *could* become, like the old woman was terrifying.

Would she too push everyone away until she died— old and virtually alone? Distanced from those she could have drawn close to her if she'd only shown a modicum of affection? With Amira's current situation she could begin to understand what had driven her grandmother to be the way she was, even if she could never condone it.

Isobel had married into the Forsythe family as a young woman with no more than a nouveau riche background and a fine arts degree to her name. Her union with Dominic Forsythe, the heir to the then-flagging Forsythe fortune, had to all accounts and purposes been a loveless match. Designed more to bolster the coffers of her husband's family and to give Isobel's father acceptance in the marketplace, she had made the best of a bad situation.

It was ironic that Amira was putting herself in a similar position, albeit reversed.

Dominic had swiftly handed over the reins of control

to his new wife when her astute mind and business acumen had proven to be far stronger than his own. Amira wondered if her grandfather had ever felt emasculated by Isobel's strength, or whether their marriage had eventually slid into one of comfortable companionship rather than one embroidered with passion and color. Her own father had been born late into the marriage, when Isobel had been in her mid-forties. He'd been doted on by both his parents, and when Dominic had passed away shortly after his son's birth, Isobel had become even more possessive and controlling than before.

Amira started up the stairs, her hand trailing on the polished wooden balustrade, aware with every step of the cold look of disapproval on her grandmother's features. She passed the landing and continued up the stairs to where her father's portrait was hung.

As a child she'd often slipped out of bed to sit in front of the picture—wondering what her life would have been like if he and her mother hadn't taken their yacht out that fatal stormy winter's day. Her grandmother had, to all intents and purposes, cut her son from her life when he'd eloped with Camille du Toit, the French au pair Isobel had employed to assist the housekeeper at the mansion. Clearly she hadn't wanted to share him with anyone who took his focus away from the fortune she'd amassed, but it had been a harsh shock to her system when he hadn't come to heel when faced with the threat of financial abandonment.

By the time she'd fought the courts for guardianship of Amira, who had been cared for since her parents' deaths by family friends, Isobel had obviously decided she had loved her son too much—given him too much leeway. Amira's upbringing was austere by comparison. Gone was the spontaneous affection she'd been unstintingly shown by her parents. In its place was a disciplined regimen of social and scholastic expectations.

Unfortunately, she hadn't exhibited strong academic tendencies, and it hadn't taken long before it was instilled in her that if she didn't marry well she would never amount to much of anything in her grandmother's eyes. The full weight of trying to earn Isobel's approval had weighed heavily on Amira's teenage shoulders and she'd been massively relieved when she'd shown a forte for the charity work for which Isobel was renowned.

When, about a year ago, she'd pitched her idea for the Fulfillment Foundation to Isobel she'd been crushed to be told she'd receive no support from any of the numerous benefactors that Isobel had on her leash. Besides, Isobel had starkly informed Amira it was creating unreasonable expectations in "people like that."

But Amira remembered what it was like as a child to dream and to wish for things. Things she could never have. And the children she wanted to help had so much less than she'd had in her lifetime. She'd vowed to make the Fulfillment Foundation a success, no matter what her grandmother said. While donations were slowly beginning to trickle in, the foundation still needed operating capital of almost ten million dollars a year.

And so, even in death and with her final flick of the

reins on Amira's life, Isobel had forced her to this—to a marriage of convenience for monetary gain.

Amira looked at the portrait of her father, her eyes swimming with tears.

"It's got to be worth it, Dad. It just has to be."

"Here's the short list of publicity agents who would also be happy to handle event organization for us."

Amira dropped the file onto Brent's desk and sat down in the visitor's chair opposite him. She'd come here this morning to drag a decision out of him come hell or high water. They'd been out numerous times over the past two weeks to a variety of high profile functions, and the number of messages now stacked up on her message service was beginning to make her head ache.

On top of everything, her PA at the foundation had handed in her notice, doubling Amira's workload. It wasn't Caroline's fault. No one could work forever for the sheer love of it. If she'd thought she could have gotten away with it, Amira would have sold off some of the antiques in her suite, but everything was entailed by the Forsythe Trust. She was completely hamstrung.

"Are you sure you wouldn't prefer to handle this on your own?" His voice was a deep rumble from behind the laptop screen, which shielded him from her view.

"Brent, I don't have the time and nor do you. We agreed this had to be done perfectly. It's something we have to delegate."

He swiveled away from the computer and leaned on the desk.

"Fine. Who do you think is best?"

Amira reached over to flip open the file. She spread the photo resumes with one hand; then with her fore-finger she stabbed at one in particular.

"This one. Marie Burbank."

"Why?"

"She has some experience in corporate publicity, but her strength lies in non-profit organizations—which I'm hoping will segue into the charity work I'm in-volved in if we can work well together. Plus, she's worked in event management prior to setting up her own agency."

Brent picked up the resume. "She looks young."

"Which means she wasn't on the circuit last time we were going to get married—she won't be influenced by all the horrid publicity that generated. She's young and she's eager, and because her agency is still new she also has the time to devote to us exclusively. I think that makes her a clear winner, don't you?"

"Bring her on board."

"You don't want to meet with her first?"

"Have you met her?"

"Yes, I thought she came across extremely well. I liked her, and I think we can trust her."

"Good, then if you're ready, let's go."

"Go? Where?" Amira flicked a look at her Rolex. "It's nine now, I have a meeting at eleven in the city. Will that leave us enough time?"

"Depends on how long it takes you to choose."

Brent shut down his computer and tucked it neatly

into its case. Then he shrugged into his suit jacket. He still took her breath away with his dark good looks and impressive build. Her hands itched to reach out and straighten his tie, to flick that tiny speck of lint from his shoulder. Just to touch him for once and know it wasn't staged for other people's benefit.

Amira curled her fingers into a tight fist. She had to stop thinking like that. This was a business arrangement only. There was no room for emotion or need.

For the first time in her life she was grateful for her grandmother's discipline, and she drew on every last ounce of composure as she smoothly rose from her seat and tidied the file back into her slim leather briefcase.

"Choose what?" she asked absently, snapping the case closed.

"Your rings."

"My…? Surely that won't be necessary."

"Everyone is going to expect it. Appearances, Amira. Isn't that what's important? I think Isobel's legal advisers would be pretty suspicious of a wedding with no rings, don't you?"

"Well, what about my old rings. Don't you still have those?"

Brent halted in his tracks. "No. They were among the first things I sold. As you'll remember, I had to liquidate my assets rather quickly at the time."

A surprising pang of loss caught in Amira's chest. Of course he'd sold them. A man like Brent wouldn't hold on to the trappings of the past—especially ones with such a negative connotation. She didn't even know what she'd been thinking when she'd said what she had. She drew in a calming breath.

"Yes, I'm sorry. That was insensitive of me. But really, Brent, I'd prefer not to go ring shopping. After all, it's not as if we're in love or anything. I'll be happy with whatever you choose."

"No. We'll do this together. It might have escaped your notice, but stock in my companies has been steadily climbing since we've started being seen together. I hate to admit it, but you're actually good for me."

He took a step closer to her, close enough that she caught a hint of his cologne. It was still the same one he'd worn all those years ago. The one she'd given him.

"So, what do you say?"

His voice dropped an octave and Amira swallowed. She ached to lean forward just a little more, to press her lips to his and say yes. It shook her to realize, though, that what she wanted to say yes to was more than just his request to choose rings together. She wanted to say yes to him, the man.

Every minute they spent together reminded her, painfully, of what they'd shared before. Of what she'd thrown away. Of what her grandmother had made her do and of how she'd discovered, too late, that she'd been masterfully manipulated into doing exactly what Isobel had wanted all along. All at the expense of her and Brent's happiness. And she'd been foolish enough, naive enough, to let it happen.

"Amira?" Brent prompted.

"Okay. Let's get it over with. I really don't have much time."

Thankfully, he stepped away and gestured to the door. As Amira preceded him down the stairs she began to wonder what toll this was going to take on her. This forced ambivalence to their proximity.

From the dark days after her parents had died she'd craved a sense of true belonging—of being loved and wanted just for herself. She'd had that fleetingly with Brent, but she'd thrown it away. She had believed she'd inured herself to that need. Learned to cope without it. Being with Brent like this just proved the opposite. She needed love, needed him, more than ever before, and it was killing her inside to realize she would never again have his heart.

Five

Brent flicked a glance in his rearview mirror. Amira still followed behind in that cute little BMW of hers. Her reaction back at the house had taken him off balance. He'd have expected her to jump at the chance of a new piece of bling. Okay, well not bling exactly. Something tasteful and understated—and outrageously expensive. Just like her.

He thought about what she'd said—about her old rings. Had she really expected him to hold on to them? He shook his head slightly. As if. He pretty much couldn't wait to rid himself of everything he'd ever associated with her, although holding on to his apartment—the place he'd become her first lover—had been out of necessity rather than for sentimental reasons.

The rent he'd gathered from leasing it had helped him repay his final creditors, and its eventual sale five years later had put him another few rungs back up his ladder. Now here he was. Successful. Strong. Financially secure no matter what might happen in the future.

He wondered briefly, whether they'd have made it—him and Amira—if they'd gone ahead with the wedding. If her highness would have been able to tolerate the cheap and close conditions of the tiny apartment he'd rented after leasing his apartment. If she could have stood the endless tins of baked beans on toast instead of four-star luxury dining, while he made certain every last penny of his debt was repaid.

He flicked another glance in the rearview mirror. It was doubtful. Oh sure, she probably would've given it a shot. Until the first time a cockroach crawled across the bench of the poky kitchenette. She'd have been "her not-so-serene-highness" then.

Anyway, all this conjecture was irrelevant. What was important now was that he carry this thing through to its bitter end. And it would be bitter. Bittersweet for him, at least. It hadn't been easy to forget the effect she'd had on him all that time ago and was even less easy to forget the devastating blow her rejection of his love had wreaked upon him. God, he could still remember that awful cold mummified feeling that had encased his body as Adam had shown him the text message on his phone. Somehow he'd managed to enunciate the announcement that there would be no wedding that day. Hell, he could still count every step he'd taken to the front door of the church, to where she wasn't waiting to walk down the aisle.

From there it was all a bit of a blur. Draco and Adam had caught up with him on the pavement as he stepped forward to hail a taxi, instead turning him around and shepherding him to the car Adam had brought them in to the church. People had begun to spill down the front steps by that stage. Bewilderment painted on many faces. Even the magazine reporters and photographers had milled about in confusion, their attempts to get the first pictures of the happy couple suddenly thwarted.

She'd stood him up with a bloody text message. He still couldn't believe it. He'd made Adam drive him to the Forsythe mansion where the housekeeper very coolly informed him that Mrs. and Miss Forsythe were both not at home and were not expected back for some time. He'd returned to his apartment at that point— certain he never wanted to see or hear from her again.

It had been a disastrous end to the week from hell. His entire world had crumbled. First the initial trickle of product returns followed by the flood of faulty merchandise coming back into his warehouse. Calls to the overseas manufacturer had proven futile, and to avoid destroying the name he'd worked so hard to build for himself he had to personally stand behind every last guarantee.

He'd stayed up late every night, going over flowcharts and budgets—seeing where he could cobble together the money needed to meet the demands of his unhappy customers. He hadn't wanted to worry Amira over it at the time, and he'd hoped he could cap the problem before it became overwhelming. Of course he hadn't counted on the newspaper spread announcing the recall of the product and his fall in fortune hitting the stands on the morning of the wedding. Nor had he counted on Amira reading the paper and deciding she didn't want to marry someone on the verge of bankruptcy after all.

Brent eased his foot off the accelerator and indicated to take a turn into a restricted parking area. She'd learn that you couldn't get away with treating other people like that. She wouldn't get to fool him again.

At the jewelers they were shown straight to a private room where the owner himself placed a series of small black velvet cases on the table between them. Brent watched Amira's face as one by one the owner opened each case and presented them to her for approval. He wasn't sure what he'd expected to see—some gleam of avarice, perhaps? But no, Amira remained as cool and composed as if she was presiding at a charity fund-raiser.

"What do you think, Brent? There are so many beautiful rings here. I'm finding it hard to choose."

She turned and gave him one of those serene smiles he recognized as the one she reserved for when she wasn't mentally engaged in what she was doing. The smile she'd perfected for the times when she was expected to front as her grandmother's puppet. And now she was his.

"What about this one?" he replied.

Brent deliberately reached over and picked the largest solitaire from its nest of velvet. Myriad sparks of color flew from it as the overhead lights refracted through the multiple facets. He took Amira's hand and slid the ring onto her finger. Her swiftly indrawn breath was the only indicator of her discomfort before she gracefully removed the ring and laid it back in its case.

"No, I don't think so."

"Perhaps something a little less overwhelming?" the jeweler suggested, sliding another case forward.

Inside was a princess cut diamond with tapered baguette diamonds set in the shoulders on each side. It was a beautiful piece.

Brent took the ring from the box and again put it on her finger. It was a perfect fit. The gold band hugged her finger, complementing the warm tone of her skin and the stones sparkled, showcased to their absolute brilliance in the setting.

"Yes, we'll take this one," he said without looking at Amira again. He couldn't when all he could remember right now was the night he'd given her first engagement ring to her. He'd planned every aspect of the evening in painstaking detail. He'd opted for simple and romantic over extravagance and had organized a picnic on a point of land overlooking Auckland City's inner harbor. As the sun had begun to set, he'd bent down on one knee and bared his heart and his love to her. He'd never believed he could be so happy when she said yes. Then again, he'd never believed she hadn't meant it.

"No!"

Her sharp denial dragged his attention back from the past.

"Why, what's wrong with it? It's a beautiful piece. Worth more than many people earn in a year."

"That's exactly what *is* wrong with it. You know the people I work with, the charities I serve. This…it's just too much. Too ostentatious. Do you have something simpler, with a colored stone perhaps?" She directed her question to the jeweler who, with a rueful look, unlocked a large wooden sliding drawer behind him and lifted a tray of rings from within.

"Perhaps one of these is more to your liking?" he inquired.

Brent sat back in his chair and watched Amira scan the assorted rings. Her eyes hovered over a section of aquamarines.

"Take those ones out," Brent instructed. "We'll look at them."

The jeweler lifted the section from the tray and returned the rest of the rings to the drawer, methodically locking it again.

"This one, I think," Amira said quietly as she picked up a smallish square-shaped aquamarine, with a sprinkling of tiny diamonds edging it.

"No," Brent interrupted her before she could try the ring on. "This one."

He reached across and lifted another ring, one with a much larger stone of the same cut and rimmed by white diamonds. He slid it on her finger and, holding her hand, turned it this way and that so the light caught on the stones.

"Sir, you've made a wonderful choice. It's a cushion

cut, just over five carats with excellent clarity, and the twenty-four surrounding stones—"

"It's too much," Amira protested.

"Look, you can tell your people it's fake for all I care," Brent said in a measured tone, totally ignoring the jeweler whose face had blanched at his words, "but you're my fiancée. You're wearing my ring. You think I want the world to see you wear something like this when you're going to be my wife?"

He gestured to the ring she'd selected, then picked up the obscenely large solitaire he'd chosen first and held it in front of Amira's face.

"This one?"

He lifted her hand to the same level.

"Or this. It's your choice."

Fake. The word rippled through her. Fake like their engagement. Fake like their marriage would be. Suddenly Amira felt as if she couldn't go through with this. It was all too much. It was one thing putting on a public face to the world but quite another when she'd have to maintain the same thing at home as well once they were married. There'd be no respite.

A stab of pain hit her square in the chest, and her fingers curled involuntarily around Brent's.

"Well? What's it going to be?" he demanded, not letting up an inch.

Amira wondered what the jeweler thought of their behavior. Hardly the usual thing one would expect from a newly engaged couple.

"This one. I'll take this one."

She pulled her hand from Brent's and stood, going to slide the ring from her finger.

"No, leave it. You may as well start wearing it straight away. We've got that charity ball to attend tonight, haven't we? Someone's bound to notice and set tongues wagging. Who knows, I might even manage to raise a couple more points on the exchange by morning."

There was an edge to his voice that sent a cold chill down Amira's spine. He flipped his platinum card from his wallet with a casualness that went a long way toward telling her how much he cared about what the ring had cost. His action would probably have been the same if she'd chosen the solitaire. Either way, price wasn't an issue for him.

She thought about how adamant he'd been that she select something showy and clearly expensive. Had he forgotten her so completely—forgotten that the trappings of wealth had never been what drove her?

After he'd completed the transaction, they walked out to their cars together.

"I'll see you tonight then," Amira said, depressing the electronic lock on her car key.

"Yes, I'll have my driver pick you up at eight."

"Your driver?"

Wasn't he coming to collect her himself? She had no wish to arrive at the hotel on her own. Certainly not with this pale-blue skating rink on her finger. It would be a struggle to maintain her poise when faced with the inevitable questions that would come her way.

"I'll meet you there. I have business in the city until about six so I've taken a room at the hotel to prepare."

"All right then. That will have to do."

As she drove away to her eleven o'clock appointment, she took a look in her rearview mirror. Brent stood there in the parking lot, dark sunglasses obscuring his eyes, which were undoubtedly still watching her.

A sensation of free-falling swept through her with stomach-lurching suddenness. This had all been her idea, but suddenly she didn't feel as though she was in control anymore. And control was vital to carry this through effectively. Otherwise, everything would have been in vain.

The black Mercedes-Benz E-Class V8 purred to a halt at the entrance to the hotel on Symonds Street, and Amira waited patiently for her door to be opened. As the door was held wide she swung her legs out and stood, allowing the sensuously soft fabric of her floor-length white silk gown to fall into its perfect lines. Elbow length white gloves had offered her the perfect foil for hiding her engagement ring, and she tugged them into place before adjusting the white faux fur stole she'd added to the ensemble at the last minute. She looked up as a large warm hand clasped hers.

"You're here," she remarked with a smile.

"I told you I'd be here," Brent said, drawing her closer. "Let's give them something to photograph, hmm?"

And just like that his lips were on hers. Amira's body surged to instant awareness as every nerve in her body jumped to attention. His lips were cool and soft as they pressed against hers. She leaned in toward him—drawn to his heat and strength like a bee to nectar—lost in the mastery of his lips.

It was over before it had begun, but it was no less devastating for all its brevity. Tiny tremors rocked her body as their vision was obscured by a mass of flashbulbs.

"Miss Forsythe, so it's true that your romance with Brent Colby has been rekindled?"

"How long have you been back together?"

"Amira! What would your grandmother think of your reunion?"

Questions flew from every direction—loud, confusing. Brent suavely directed Amira toward the front door and past the liveried doorman.

"Let's go inside. I think we've given them enough for one night, don't you?"

"Yes, definitely," Amira said, fighting to maintain her composure in the face of the barrage of questions.

With a smile painted firmly on her face she fought to keep her breathing even—a task harder than she anticipated as, with her hand firmly in the crook of Brent's arm, she and Brent entered the hotel lobby. She concentrated on the strength of the muscles in his forearm, on the fine cloth of his suit, on the enticing hint of his cologne that wafted by her as they stepped in unison toward the main ballroom.

"Pity we couldn't have timed the engagement announcement for tonight," Brent commented, bending his dark head to hers.

"No, we wouldn't have been able to sell the story if we made a public announcement at something like this. Not for as much anyway," Amira replied. "Marie said we should make the announcement next week, and I agreed."

Beneath her fingers she felt the muscles in his arm clench.

"I bow to your superior event management skills," he replied silkily, but Amira could tell her response had needled him.

So why not tell him the full story, she argued silently. What was stopping her from giving him the truth, lock, stock and two smoking barrels, about the foundation and what her grandmother had done to throw every obstacle in its way? About her promises to the children?

She swallowed against the lump in her throat. The lump that was pride and fear of failure blended with a burning desire to create a success in her life. Something that wasn't manufactured by her grandmother's influence. Something that was more than a tax break and could give hope to families from all over the country.

Something that, for the first time since she was ten years old, she could call her own.

Amira flicked a glance at his stern features. His dark brows were drawn in a straight line across his eyes— eyes that were more green than brown tonight as anger shone from them in unmistakable terms.

She quietly sighed. She'd made this rod for her back and she'd bear it. Brent was the only man she wanted at her side. Sure, she had considered other men for the role of her husband but she'd been telling Brent the truth when she'd said she didn't want any part of the accoutrements of marriage.

A coil of something undefined tightened deep inside her, giving the lie to her words. The truth was as startling to her as it was unexpected. The tension eased up a little, only to squeeze a tight band around her heart. Was it possible that she still hoped they could actually make a go of this fake marriage? That Brent could come to love her again? The thought rushed through her on a wave of exhilaration, only to be solidly dashed against the brick wall of the past. No, he'd never forgive her for what she did to him on their wedding day. Ever. He'd only entered into this sham relationship so he could further his already massive business enterprises. Expand his empire.

She'd entered this with her eyes and ears wide open. It would be tilting at windmills if she dared hope or dream for anything else. For once, Amira welcomed the pragmatism of her grandmother's influence and drew on every last ounce of it that she had in her personal armory.

If Brent caught so much as an inkling that she had entertained the thought of them creating a true marriage again she had no doubt he'd be laughing himself as far away from her as possible. Better that this should remain a charade, she consoled herself. That way no one would be hurt.

Six

As they drifted through the ballroom, Amira took the opportunity to introduce Brent to several members of the NZLB. As far as he was aware, his application to join was still under consideration, which basically meant he had to jump through these social hoops to move from consideration to the platinum level of membership she'd recommended. Would they make their decision tonight? He certainly hoped so.

Either way, it was worth the wait compared to how long he'd been stonewalled by all other aspects of his latest waterfront development. With the advent of the new performance arena, the scope for further business and parking in the surrounding area was huge. The sooner he could get his expansion project off the ground the better.

The band started to play, and several couples drifted onto the native timber parquet dance floor.

"Care to dance?" he murmured in Amira's ear.

She stiffened slightly, and for a moment he thought she'd refuse. But then with a regal incline of her head she accepted his request.

"Just give me a moment to put these down," she said, gesturing with her small silver clutch to her stole.

"Sure, would you like me to check them in or leave them at our table?"

"The table is fine. They're nothing of value."

Nothing of value? He'd lay odds each item had cost several hundred dollars. Her flippancy rankled. He pushed the irritation from his mind as he lifted the stole from her shoulders, inhaling a hint of her perfume as he did so. There it was again—that intriguing blend of spice and flowers. It hit him straight in the gut, sending all his instincts on full alert.

"I'll be just a minute," he said, taking her evening bag from her also.

The short respite of traveling the distance to their table and back to the edge of the dance floor allowed him to drag his wayward hormones under control. Business. He reminded himself. It was purely business. With a healthy dose of revenge, a little voice reminded him as he stepped up to Amira and took her hand, leading her to the dance floor.

She flowed into his arms as easily as if they did this sort of thing together every night. And in the old days they had, pretty much. When she'd come to visit him at his apartment he'd always had music playing in the background. Sometimes soft jazz, similar to what the band was playing tonight. Other times the gentle strains of a classical interlude. He loved music of any sort, but away from his office, or his social scene, he preferred to keep the sounds gentle and flowing. It helped to unwind at the end of a stressful day. All the easier when she'd been in his arms as well.

As far as female company was concerned, he'd been careful in the past years not to associate with any one woman more than twice in the public arena. He had no desire to be paired with someone in any shape or form for some time. Oh sure, one day he expected to marry and have a family. But he had a lot of work to do first.

And he had other matters to occupy his relaxation time these days, with the lap pool at his house he could enter into a punishing physical routine that scraped away every last vestige of a tough day at the office. Or he could get Draco or Adam for a vigorous game of tennis on his full-sized court.

He didn't need Amira and music in their subtle blend of seduction to calm him anymore. Although, as they swayed and moved to the music he felt his pulse kick up a beat, recognized the stirring in his loins that her proximity provoked.

She looked beautiful tonight. Every inch the consummate princess of style and charm. Her hair was twisted up tightly at the back of her head, exposing the graceful lines of her neck and the diamond drop earrings that fell from her earlobes. The tiny diamante straps that held her dress up appeared impossibly fragile, showcasing the curve of her shoulders with a feminine elegance that teased him to push them aside. To replace their caress with one of his own.

Brent reined in his thoughts, shifting his hips slightly away from Amira's. Before long he would lose control over his wayward flesh. Would show her exactly how much she attracted and tormented him still—and then who would have the edge?

Business. He reminded himself once more. Strictly business.

"Looks like the leaders of the NZLB are having a discussion together. Hopefully it's about your application," Amira said in a low voice, her breath a soft brush against his ear.

He turned his head slightly so he could see Auckland's most powerful collection of businessmen with their heads together over what looked like a bottle of fifty-year-old Chivas. One of the men laughingly gestured toward Amira and himself, and he carefully averted his gaze—but not before he'd seen the nods of approval from around the table.

"Looks promising, if they are indeed discussing my application," Brent replied.

"I think you have Uncle Don on your side. With his approval the others will soon follow suit."

"Uncle Don? I thought you didn't have any surviving family?"

He felt her stiffen in his arms and realised too late how painful his comment might have been.

"He's my godfather. His parents and my grandparents used to socialize together all the time, and he and my father were schoolmates. They lost touch when Mum and Dad married, and I haven't really seen him much over the years. But if he thinks that admitting you to the league will please me he'll lend his weight behind your application."

The music began to wind down and the emcee for the evening took the podium, inviting the guests to take their seats.

Brent fought the unexpected pang of physical loss as Amira peeled away from his side and led their return to their table. Their table partners were a mix of couples, one or two he'd met before, one he hadn't but was keen to foster a business relationship with.

As the evening drew on, Brent came to realize that Amira had probably planned it this way. She had, after all, been the one who directed the seating arrangements for the function and was due to assume the podium to make a short speech of thanks on behalf of the research charity the evening was a benefit for.

She managed everything with a finesse he reluctantly admired. No one would have realized how much work she'd put into the function from the way she laughed and conversed with their fellow guests—then maybe she hadn't done it all after all. Her type rarely did, he'd found over the years. With the backing of a strong support team they could still make their daily latte and air kiss sessions with their cronies at whichever Auckland café was the place of the week.

When it came time for Amira to make her speech, he watched as she rose and glided to the main stage. The deep low V of her gown showed a tantalizing glimpse of the soft curve of her lower back. She'd finally removed her gloves, and her long slender arms were bare. The overhead lighting on the stage caught the glint of her ring, and he smiled in satisfaction.

Brent flicked his gaze around the room. Yes, every man's eyes were on her. He tried to convince himself that he didn't feel the heated streak of possession that made him want to cover her body from their gaze, but he failed miserably.

It was ridiculous, he told himself. But then again, his reaction would certainly be expected if theirs was a real engagement, and to all intents and purposes it had to appear that way. To that end, he took delight when he caught the eye of one particularly lecherous watcher and gave him a narrow-eyed glare that clearly said "back off." He was deeply satisfied when the man gave him a nod of acknowledgment and then had the good grace to look away from Amira's tantalizing form.

This engagement might be business, Brent reminded himself, but there was a fair amount of game playing as well. And he was a consummate sportsman, no matter what the code. He sat back and listened as Amira thanked the sponsors for the evening and introduced the directors of the research charity, who she then called to the stage. Once everyone was lined up, she announced the total sum the evening had raised and presented a check to the directors.

As she came back and settled at the table, Brent leaned a little closer.

"You do that very well," he commented. "Even I was convinced you meant it."

"Of course I meant it. I'm not just a figurehead for these things you know. Whatever reasons Grandmother had for her involvement in her charities mine have never been in question."

"Helping those less fortunate than yourself?" Brent couldn't keep the edge of skepticism from his voice.

Amira's lips firmed in a straight line before she parted them to speak. "Yes, actually. Although that's no concern of yours."

He leaned closer. To anyone watching them it would look like a lover's private exchange.

"And all those millions you'll have at your disposal when you inherit? What do you plan to do with those? Come on, Amira. You don't expect me to believe this philanthropy is real—it's really just a game to you, isn't it? Something to fill your days. I bet you're looking forward to a *really* good time with all that money," he murmured.

Amira caught her breath at the veiled insult. She knew there were many people who only saw her for what she was—Isobel Forsythe's granddaughter—and not for who she was or how hard she worked behind the scenes. It had never really mattered to her before what others thought, so long as she did her job well.

Brent's comment, however, cut her deeply. His opinion of her must really be appallingly low. If that's how he felt, she was glad their marriage would be nothing but make-believe. It would be easier to hide her renascent feelings knowing he held her in such contempt.

"Well, you can never have enough, you know. Money, that is," she replied, even though the words felt like dry cereal in her mouth.

"Hear, hear." Brent lifted his champagne glass in a silent toast. "Thank you for being honest with me."

Honest? She'd always been honest with him. The only trouble was the one time she'd doubted her feelings for him, doubted her heart, it had turned out to be the biggest mistake of her life.

The rest of the evening passed successfully enough, rounding off with an invitation from the NZLB table inviting Brent and Amira to join them. With a raised brow, Brent accepted. Once Amira had introduced him to the men she made her apologies and withdrew. She'd done her part by sponsoring his application and by making the necessary introductions. Now it was up to him.

She checked with the hotel staff to make sure everything was progressing as it should for the evening and, with her back to the shadows, let her shoulders relax just a little. Only another hour and it would all be over tonight. Then she could put away her polished persona and relax in a warm bath before collapsing into bed.

She fingered the ring Brent had given her earlier today. How different it was from the simple diamond he'd given her the first time. How different their circumstances now. A pang of loss pulled at her heart. She'd been a fool to listen to Isobel that morning. A complete and utter fool. She should have known that Brent would have had his reasons for not telling her of the collapse of his business and finances. She should have trusted her instincts that his attraction to her had never been about her own perceived wealth.

If only he'd known, she thought bitterly. She was entitled to nothing on her own apart from the payment her parents' insurance policies had made available to her on their deaths. A payment Isobel had topped up and set instructions in place for it to end on Amira's thirtieth birthday. Oh, sure, Isobel had imagined that Amira would be well married by now, to some scion of New Zealand business with a bank balance to match. But in that, as in so many other things, Amira had failed her grandmother again.

Sure she lived in the Forsythe Mansion and materially she wanted for nothing. However, nothing was actually hers. The token stipends she was paid for her work on the various charities Isobel had spearheaded had been poured into the Fulfillment Foundation. If the truth be known, she was probably in worse financial position than Brent had been eight years ago.

Like him, she had her pride, if nothing else. She had to succeed at this or acknowledge failure in every area of her life. And, as far as she was concerned, that was not an option.

The next morning the papers were live with speculation about the revival of Brent and Amira's romance. As she sipped her morning cup of Earl Grey tea and nibbled at her toast, Amira let a smile of satisfaction spread across her face. In no time the calls would flood in from the women's magazines—each one wanting an exclusive. Maybe she'd even be able to forestall Caroline's departure if she could cover back pay and at least the next couple of months' wages.

For a moment she wished they'd brought the wedding closer but then quickly discarded the idea out of hand. They couldn't be seen rushing things or it would arouse suspicion. Certainly the few short months they'd agreed upon could be seen to be acceptable. And then there'd be the wedding pictures to sell as well.

A warm glow started deep inside at the thought of being able to tell Casey and her new family when they'd be going to Disneyland. It would make everything worthwhile. Even the pain of being in a loveless marriage to a man who despised her.

With the anticipated calls of the magazines in mind, Amira changed her voice mail message on her machine, directing all inquiries to her publicist. That itself would confirm the rumors of an engagement she'd seen in one of the papers.

She wondered how Brent was faring this morning. It would probably pay to have him put the same message on his voice mail as well. She picked up the phone and dialed his number.

"Colby," he answered, his tone clipped.

"Brent, good morning. I trust you slept well now that your development will be going ahead sooner than you anticipated?"

Before they'd left last night he'd told her that the league had accepted him into their exalted establishment and had assured him of their support with his current venture.

"Yes, thank you. I did sleep well, although I could have done without the string of photographers along the estuary walkway when I went for my morning run." He sounded rueful. "I think until things die down a bit I'll stick to my home gym. It was time I updated the treadmill anyway. How about you? Pleased with how last night went?"

As she replied in the affirmative, it struck her how empty their conversation was. As if between colleagues, not people who the world would soon believe were lovers. Their engagement was a hollow victory but a victory nonetheless she reminded herself.

"You might want to put a message on your voice mail directing everyone to Marie. As our publicist she'll relish handling all that side of things."

"Good idea."

"By the way, I don't have any official functions on my calendar for this week. I was thinking it might whet people's appetites for news if we're not seen together quite as much. What do you think?"

He hesitated a while before answering. Amira had no trouble imagining the expression on his face as he pondered her suggestion. No doubt he'd be thinking she had a hidden agenda. And maybe she did. A part of her wondered if it would simply be easier not to be reminded daily of what she'd thrown away when she stood him up—be easier not to be reminded of how artificial her life had become.

"Sure, that works for me. With the waterfront job coming together I'll be pretty full on this week anyway."

Amira regretted her suggestion the moment they said goodbye and she hung up her phone. She'd thought it would be easier. In reality she welcomed any excuse to see him, to touch him—even if it was only for show. Now she had no excuse to see him during the week, and by his own admission he was busy.

She'd just have to fill her time with other matters, she decided. By the end of the week, Marie had been approached by the major weekly glossy magazines for the rights to an exclusive interview with Brent and Amira. The staggering sums they offered were all much the same with various additional incentives thrown in to sweeten the individual pots.

"So what do you two think? Which magazine do you want to go with?" Marie asked as she stepped back from Brent's desk where she'd laid out the different offers they'd received.

"Who has the highest circulation?" Brent asked, his face a noncommittal mask.

"This one," Marie pointed to one of the offers.

"Then we should go with them," he replied.

"No," Amira interjected as Marie started to gather up the papers.

"You'd rather go with someone else?" Marie asked.

Amira straightened in her seat, avoiding Brent's gaze as she chose her words carefully. No matter what she said, no matter how this came out, he'd still think badly of her. She thought about those wages, about the strain her staff was under.

"I'm not satisfied they're offering enough. Why don't we play them off one another, like an auction?" she asked.

"An auction—I haven't coordinated one of those before." Marie paced back and forth a few times, her brow furrowed in concentration. "I think you're right, Miss Forsythe. We could definitely lever this higher. I know you vetoed mentioning your past engagement, but I'm thinking we might need to offer them more, perhaps something about why you two split in the first place…?"

Brent rose from his chair in a flood of movement. He gave Amira a cold, hard look.

"Is that what you want? To rake over old coals to get more money?"

His voice could freeze Lake Taupo solid, Amira thought as she gathered her strength to her.

"If that's what it takes to drive up the price, yes."

A light seemed to die in Brent's eyes.

"Then do what you must."

Marie looked from one to the other. "Oh-kay, I'll get onto this right away then and get back to you as soon as I have a plan together."

"Thank you, Marie," Amira said, her gaze not moving from Brent's set features.

"I'll let myself out."

When Marie had gone Amira spoke.

"I hope this change in plans doesn't make you want to pull out of the interview."

"I'll show up for the interview no matter what you've arranged. Just know that I don't believe you need to do this, Amira."

"Believe me, I do."

His expression said it all. He thought she was nothing more than a money-hungry greed machine. He sighed and wiped his hand across his eyes.

"When will it be enough?"

"Don't you know? It's never enough. Not for people like me." She managed a brittle laugh to cover the hurt she felt inside at the disgust on his face. She could never tell him the truth of her grandmother's hold over her. That even as Isobel's closest blood relative she'd never been good enough to win the old lady's heart, nor the unstinting support that should have been hers by right. That she'd always been held up as an example of her parents' failures to provide for her properly.

"You know, I'd actually feel sorry for you if I didn't think it was a total waste of time."

"I've never asked anyone to feel sorry for me," Amira replied, injecting steel into her tone. "I do what I have to do, when I have to do it."

"That you do." Brent turned away from her, his hands clasped at his back as he faced out the window to the estuary beyond. "Is that all for today? I think you should go."

"Fine, I'll be in touch after I've heard from Marie."

He didn't so much as nod in acknowledgment as she left the room, and inside she felt as if another piece of her soul had been shaved away.

Seven

The interview with the women's magazine went extremely well, and the photo spread showed exactly what it should—a couple in love, with a second chance at happiness.

Amira dropped her copy of the magazine on her coffee table. So why didn't she feel happy? The publication had sold out within hours of reaching the newsstands and supermarket stands, and Marie had fielded offers from Australia to feature their article there also.

She should be dancing for joy. The money from the interview had already been deposited in the foundation's account, and the staff's wages had been paid, together with a generous bonus for their loyalty. Amira pressed a knotted fist against her chest. The hollow ache inside never went away; instead it grew ever more painful.

The smiling couple on the front cover of the glossy magazine didn't seem real. Maybe that's because they weren't real, she reminded herself.

And maybe how she was feeling was due in part to the legal envelope that had been delivered by courier to her here at home the other day. The prenuptial agreement she'd suggested Brent have his lawyer draw up. She'd skimmed through it, then signed and returned it. Oh sure, she knew she should have had her own lawyers give independent legal advice on the document before signing, but it was pretty basic really.

The terms had been set out in black and white. In return for agreeing to marry her, Amira would see to it that Brent received the platinum level entry into the NZLB as she'd promised, together with a sum of money being not less than ten percent of the amount she would inherit under her grandmother's estate upon marriage. She didn't see how it could be any simpler. Gerald Stein, the family lawyer, would probably have a heart attack if he knew what she'd just done, but he'd still been away on a much-needed extended vacation, touring the cathedrals of Europe. Besides, she had taken control of her life.

She had offered those very things, Brent had agreed, and now their engagement was out there for all the world to see. Of course all the world also meant that no doubt Roland would soon know that his plans to move into the Forsythe mansion were in imminent danger of being thwarted. She wondered what type of message he'd take to leaving on her machine then. Thank heavens for caller ID.

As if the mere thought of the phone triggered it to ring, it suddenly shrilled in the quiet of her apartment. Despite herself, Amira jumped, her heart racing in her chest. A quick check of the screen confirmed it wasn't Roland, and with a brief sigh of relief she recognized Gerald Stein's private number.

"Gerald, how are you? How was your holiday?"

"Wonderful, thank you. But tell me, child, what on earth have you been up to? We must talk—urgently."

There was a note to Gerald's voice that instantly set Amira's nerves on edge. She drew a deep breath before answering.

"Up to, Gerald? Why, fulfilling the terms of grandmother's will. I suppose you've seen the news."

"Exactly. Look, it's vital I talk to you before you do anything else, and please, give no more interviews or statements to the press until we've spoken. I'll have Cynthia clear a spot for you at three thirty. See you then."

Without even waiting for her affirmative he hung up, leaving Amira with a disconnected beep in her ear and a puzzled frown on her face. She'd never known Gerald to be so abrupt, nor to sound quite so harried. Not even when Isobel had passed away, and the two of them had gone way back. In fact, Amira had often wondered if their relationship had ever proceeded beyond the professional boundaries of lawyer and client.

Whatever had happened in the past, it was her future that needed her full attention right now. Amira checked her PDA and made a few quick phone calls to rearrange things so she could make her meeting with Gerald.

She dressed conservatively for the meeting, wearing a pale pink silk blouse under a black suit with a knee-length pencil skirt. Patent black leather high-heeled pumps matched her slim bag to complete the ensemble. She tied her hair back in a long braid that fell down her back in a straight line, bumping against her spine as she walked.

The offices of Stein, Stein & Stein were located in the heart of Auckland City, in one of the few remaining heritage buildings on Queen Street, which resisted full modernization and clung tenaciously to its splendor of yesteryear. As a child she'd always been fascinated by the old wooden paneling that lined the corridors leading to the partners' offices. On those rare occasions that Isobel had brought her into town, it had always been a treat of magnificent dimensions to take tea with Gerald in his office. Now, of course, Amira realized how narrow her world had been. Her every step guided by her grandmother, her every behavior constantly monitored. Still, as structured as her life had been, it had stood her in good stead. Now she could face down a battalion of New Zealand's elite and coax sponsorship from them. For all but the Fulfillment Foundation, anyway.

She wondered whether Gerald's call was related to the problems she'd had with paying the staff. His firm handled the legal issues on behalf of the foundation and had seen to its registration as a charitable trust. But what if someone had brought a grievance against her or the foundation? A deep sense of misgiving plucked at the back of Amira's mind.

Gerald didn't waste time getting to the point of their meeting. He was blunt and to the point.

"You have to call off your engagement."

"Call off my engagement? But why? Gerald, you know I have to marry to inherit. Brent and I have come to an arrangement with which we're both extremely comfortable."

Okay, so maybe that was a slight exaggeration, she admitted silently. But they had made an arrangement. An arrangement she would abide by no matter how much it played on her mind, and no matter how much she now wished it could have been based on mutual respect and even love.

"It's impossible. I'm sorry, my dear, but you have no choice." A worried frown settled over his watery blue eyes, and he adjusted his glasses on his nose as he reached for the papers lying in front of him on the desk.

"But I don't understand. You told me that I had to marry to inherit under grandmother's will. That's exactly what I'm doing, in," she said while mentally counting off the calendar, "eight weeks' time."

"I can assure you, if you're going to inherit you will not be marrying Brent Colby in eight weeks' time." He swiped his glasses off his nose and cleaned them with a tissue before settling them back on. "Your grandmother was quite explicit. I never saw the need to tell you about her proviso because I never dreamed you and Colby would get back together. You know how Isobel felt about him. And, of course, after your failed wedding…well, enough said about that. Suffice to say I chose not to inform you of these terms because I didn't believe in waking sleeping dogs. Especially not hard on the heels of your bereavement. That said, I've done you a great disservice. I'm terribly sorry, my dear."

A disservice? He'd withheld a vital piece of her grandmother's will from her. And all because he hadn't wanted to upset her? An icy trickle of dread ran down Amira's spine. What had Isobel put in place that meant she had to break off her engagement with Brent?

"What proviso?" she said quietly.

"Now, you know your grandmother only had your best interests at heart."

"Tell me about the proviso," she insisted in a voice that brooked no further argument.

"Right. Yes. Of course." The elderly solicitor shuffled the papers before him and lifted one page. He cleared his throat then began to read. "And I furthermore direct that under no circumstances will my granddaughter, Amira Camille Forsythe, inherit if she should resume her previous relationship with the said Brent Colby, or if she should marry him."

Amira's heart twisted painfully. This was unbelievable. Her mind struggled to comprehend the ramifications of Gerald's words even as the sound of his voice died on the air. How could Isobel have made such an outrageous demand? Wasn't it bad enough that she'd used emotional blackmail to force Amira to withdraw from marrying him eight years ago? And that now, from her grave, she was forcing Amira to marry *anyone* else?

"Surely that won't withstand a challenge." Amira finally managed through lips that felt stiff and frozen.

"It may, and it may not. Either way, do you really have the time to devote to a challenge through the court? And, my dear, while I hate to remind you of this, do you really have the funds at your disposal to mount such a challenge?"

She hadn't believed it could get much worse, but Gerald's words were the death knell to her plans. There was no way she'd be able to fund such a legal challenge even if it could be pushed through the court system with any haste. Her body slumped in the deep leather wing chair where she'd perched so many times, legs swinging happily, as a child. The contrast between then and now had never been so evident.

Who would have thought her life would come to this? A marionette still being manipulated by a domineering old woman. Her breath shuddered in her lungs as the enormity of her grandmother's reach clutched deathly fingers around her dream and wrenched it from the realms of possibility.

"Amira?" Gerald interrupted her thoughts. "I know this has come as a shock to you, but may I remind you of the alternative?"

A cynical laugh fought its way past the lump in her throat.

"What? Bankruptcy? Living on the streets?"

She couldn't help it, but right now no other solution

presented itself. It wasn't just about the money, no matter what Brent thought of her in that regard, although without the money from her inheritance the foundation would be lost forever—closed due to mismanagement and insufficient funds. And it would be all her fault. All those lost dreams, not to mention the loss of employment for her staff.

How would she explain it to the children and their parents? How would she break the news to Casey? A sob rose in her throat, but she swallowed against it, instead closing her eyes for a moment and pushing down the urge to cry out in desperation. Why was it that as soon as one door opened in her life another slammed viciously shut just as quickly?

And how was she to break the news to Brent? Would he ever understand or forgive her now that she was forced to jilt him again? Tears burned harshly at the back of her eyes, and she closed them again, determined not to let go.

Gerald cleared his throat uncomfortably. For a man who'd just come back from a lengthy holiday, he already looked strained and gray with stress.

"I don't wish to be indelicate, but do you recall the other part to this inheritance clause in Isobel's will?"

"Other part?" Amira's mind refused to budge from the death of her hopes for the future.

Gerald shuffled through the copy of the will on his desk and stabbed a stubby finger at the paper. "Yes, this one. This subclause relating to having borne live issue before your thirtieth birthday." Gerald sounded as uncomfortable suggesting it as he obviously felt if the way he ducked his head and fidgeted with his papers was anything to go by.

A child? How on earth would she find someone to father a child when all she wanted was what was right-fully hers? And how did one go about that sort of thing anyway? Brent was out of the question. Once he knew she had to break off their engagement again there was no way on this earth he'd touch her, let alone give her a child, even if they hadn't agreed to keep their relation-ship purely on a business footing.

Which left what? A sperm donor? A one-night stand and hope for a hit? Her mind instantly rejected both options as impossible. She could no more submit to a coldly clinical procedure using donor sperm to bring a baby into the world, for the sheer purpose of inheriting, than she could fly off the Auckland Sky Tower. Nor could she subject herself, or her theoretical child, to the dangers of a one-night stand.

No. If she was to have any man's child, by choice, it would be Brent's. Which left only one option.

One man.

Could she carry it off? Could she withhold the truth from him that she was going to jilt him again for long enough to get him to father a child with her?

Amira's stomach churned at the thought of using him so cold-bloodedly. But would it be cold-blooded? They'd had a passionate relationship before. Could she hope to stoke that fire of attraction between them again to trick him into impregnating her?

She thought of little Casey—a child to whom life had already dealt too many blows with the loss of her family and her leukemia. She thought of the many other children being added to the register of the Fulfillment Foundation. Of the families desperate for some respite or hope—families who deserved so much more than the months and years of unhappiness they'd been dealt through circumstance.

A picture of Roland's dissolute features swam into her mind, together with the latest gossip headlines from Australia, which speculated over the size of his gambling debt, his hard drinking and loose women. And she knew she had to do it. She had to seduce Brent to have his baby.

Eight

"Two to one odds. Not bad," Adam commented over the rim of his brandy balloon as he watched Brent line up a shot on the billiard table. "But I like your odds better. I'm thinking I might place a bet. What do you reckon?"

Despite Adam's attempt to distract him, Brent pocketed the brown and set up his next shot. The wide-screen LCD TV mounted on the wall opposite them droned on. Not satisfied with touting two to one odds that Amira wouldn't show up on the day, the cohost on the late night show that was screening had offered ten to one odds that it would be Brent who'd fail to show.

"I reckon you should keep your money in your pocket," Brent answered, hoping his cousin would drop the subject. He should be so lucky. "Or at least place a decent bet on this game."

Adam just laughed. "C'mon, Brent. You know you have no intention of going through with this. Can't a man have a little fun along the way? It's not as if I'm likely to make any money off you tonight any other way, what with Draco AWOL and—"

"It's not a joke, Adam," Brent said quietly.

"Yeah, I know. She cut you up pretty bad last time. So, how's it going anyway? You guys are spending a lot of time together. Mending any bridges?"

Brent chalked the tip of his cue. Mending bridges? No. Not a chance. But he was making some inroads at getting under her skin. He thought back to the brief montage of clips they'd shown on the late night talk show. One in particular had shown Amira in an unguarded moment, and the hunger on her face as she'd looked at him had been unmistakable.

"I don't know about bridges, but she's asked me to Windsong this weekend."

Adam sat up in his chair. "*The* Windsong? The Forsythe private hideaway? My, my, things are looking up."

Brent laughed. Looking up or not, he planned to have Amira in his bed by the end of the weekend. He wanted her bound to him in every way possible. That way, when he cut her loose, she'd get a taste of what he'd gone through eight years ago.

"Well," Adam said as Brent finished off the table, "as scintillating as your company is, I'd better be on my way. Have a few problems of my own to sort out."

"Anything I can help you with?"

"No, I can handle it. This one's right up my alley. Or at least she will be, eventually." He gave Brent a wink and grabbed his car keys from the coffee table. "Thanks for dinner. We'll have to try and track down Draco and pin the next meal on him. It's not like him to miss these nights when he's back in New Zealand. Do you think it has anything to do with that woman at the memorial service?"

"Who knows, but if it is, I can't wait to hear why. If he calls, I'll let you know."

"Same," Adam agreed.

After he'd seen Adam off, Brent wandered back in to the game room. The late show was still going on about him and Amira. He flicked a finger on the remote to turn off the TV. Couldn't anyone talk about anything these days but the upcoming nuptials of the Forsythe Princess and the Midas Man, as they'd dubbed him in the national papers during recent years?

He took a sip of his brandy, but the entertainment slot had soured his taste buds. The Midas Man. They trotted out nicknames with unerring frequency and with no small amount of irritation to the recipient. There was nothing golden in his touch. Everything he'd gained he'd achieved through sheer bullheadedness and damn hard work. And he'd done it alone.

Alone. The word echoed through his mind. How different would their life have been had she gone through with their first planned wedding? Would she still be at his side? Would they have started a family by now, the halls of the house echoing with the sounds of children at play?

He pushed the thoughts from his mind. It was time wasted dwelling on an impossible past. He hadn't made his fortune by looking back.

He thought ahead to tomorrow's meeting with Amira and Marie and of the matters they needed to discuss. Topping the list was some way of getting Marie to generate counterpublicity to the current reign of conjecture as to whether or not Amira would actually make it to the altar this time. For his own satisfaction he wanted to put a lid on any comment that she might not make it.

Above all, the last thing he needed was some magazine to run a story expounding on the theory he might be the one to pull out this time. He didn't need her to be spooked at this stage of things. Mind you, with the carrot of her inheritance dangling juicily in front of her he'd wager the better part of his fortune that there was no way she'd be standing him up this time.

It niggled at him constantly, this avaricious need of hers to gather more and more funds. The subsidiary rights to their engagement and reunion story had sold for an exorbitant sum, a sum he had no doubt that she'd drummed up as high as she could get it.

She'd never been this focused on money before, never been this…greedy. The word had a nasty sound to it, one totally at odds with the Amira he'd fallen in love with the first time around. But that woman had been phony, he reminded himself—as phony as his intention to follow through with their wedding now. It occurred to him that when he didn't turn up at the wedding she'd no doubt sell that story to the highest bidder too.

It was an irony that wasn't entirely wasted on him, and a smile curled his lips as he switched off the downstairs lights and made his way upstairs to the master suite.

Her uncharacteristic grasping need for disposable income had sent up a few flags in his mind, and he had called in one of his handpicked private investigators to do some digging to find out what lay behind the apparent change in Amira's fortune. With her father having been the only, and much beloved, child of the old dragon and her husband, Amira stood to gain a lot from Isobel's passing. Unless there was more to it than Amira had said. If that was the case, he'd soon know all there was to know.

He thought about her elegant beauty at the charity function the other week—the night he'd received his formal invitation to the league. She'd carried the whole evening off with a sophistication totally at odds with her current financial obsession.

When the car had pulled up in the forecourt of the hotel and he'd stepped forward to assist her from her seat, his heart had slammed against his chest at the sight of her. Every instinct in him had fought, with untamed need, to sweep her past the ballroom entrance and instead to the suite he'd used to prepare for the evening. And there he wanted to slake the simmering lust for her that glowed, silent and hungry, beneath the surface of his composure.

Damned if she didn't still push all his buttons to high alert every time he saw her. It was a situation he'd expected to have mastered by now, to have wrestled under control. But instead it only seemed to gather strength. To burn hotter, harder.

He should never have agreed to her terms of a strict business arrangement. He'd entered into this too lightly—too intent on extracting his own revenge against the only woman he had ever loved. He hadn't stopped to weigh the cost, physical or mental. And right now that physical cost was tying him in knots. There hadn't been a single night in this past week where he hadn't woken, sheets tangled about him, his body raging with a fever only Amira could assuage. Tonight would be no different. It augured badly for the next couple of months, but he could and would tolerate it if it meant he'd get to teach her that overdue lesson. To show her you couldn't walk all over people the way she'd walked all over him.

The next morning an e-mail from his private investigator awaited him. He was surprised to get a response so swiftly, but the content of the e-mail surprised him more. Surprised and concerned him.

Amira Forsythe was, to date, the sole donor to and benefactor of the Fulfilment Foundation. He'd heard of the foundation and of Amira's work with it. He'd assumed that, as usual, she was a figurehead—no more than an attractive spokesperson whose primary function was to attract sponsorship and public interest with her already high profile. Further details followed on the mission statement of the foundation and its charter. Brent found himself agreeing to its core structure and overall purpose, but he was horrified when he saw the projected costs to run the foundation and its current financial position.

Where was the money Amira's family were famous for bestowing on the charities of their choice? He could name at least ten charities, without even straining his memory, the Forsythes publicly supported in varying degrees. So why not this one?

By the looks of things, it was Amira's baby.

He poured himself a fresh cup of coffee and continued reading the report. Further digging had shown that Isobel had been outspoken amongst her peers about the infeasibility of the foundation—a fact that puzzled Brent. Why this one? Was the old lady so determined to control everything Amira did that she'd quashed her granddaughter's ideas? The fact Amira had gone ahead and set up the foundation and put things in motion to implement its plans showed backbone he'd never witnessed in her before.

The next paragraph had him replace his mug carefully on his desk and whistle long and low. How his PI had garnered this particular snippet of information he really didn't want to know. It went deeper into the Forsythe financial structure than Brent would have imagined possible, even with the exorbitant sum he paid the PI. The guy had definitely earned himself a generous bonus.

Apparently Amira had no personal income—only a small annuity from her parents' life insurance. An annuity that her grandmother had topped up in keeping with inflation—a fact her parents had sadly neglected to consider, obviously, when they'd taken out their policies. Worse, the annuity, which appeared to be channeled directly into the foundation, was due to cease on Amira's thirtieth birthday.

How on earth did the foundation function? The donations from the general public were abysmally low. Without major sponsorship or generosity from a clutch of private donors, the entire thing would collapse around her ears. How could she play with people's lives like that? To all accounts and purposes she was virtually promising these children and their families the moon; yet all she could deliver was a handful of space dust.

A slow burning anger rose from Brent's gut, making his vision blur and his hands clench into fists on the desktop. Just how irresponsible could Amira be? He knew what it was like to do without and what it was like to have to accept financial aid to achieve his potential.

Sure, he'd paid back every penny his uncle had put forward, but without that money in the first place, he'd never have had the opportunity to attend Ashurst and even earn the scholarship that had made repayment possible. Whatever people said, money moved mountains. Not having it made people vulnerable and the Fulfillment Foundation was there for the most vulnerable of all.

The foundation promised scholarships, family holidays—all manner of things that any child or family could wish for. Hadn't these people suffered enough without added disappointment? Did Amira have no idea of the amount of pride it took to accept a handout, or any inkling as to what it would feel like to see that pride trodden upon when the promise was broken?

Amira had been given opportunities galore in her life and yet she was still as flippant with others as she'd been with her promise to marry him—to love him. Obviously the foundation was nothing more than a passing interest to her. A game. It made him feel ill to see how she had trivialized something so important.

He could make a difference to this charity. He could help these people reach for their dreams, see the children involved know happiness where before they'd only known illness and hardship. His mind began ticking off the possibilities and he opened a new e-mail, to both his accountant and his lawyer, listing a series of instructions.

The Fulfillment Foundation would reach its potential, eventually. But one thing was certain. Amira Forsythe would not be at its helm when it did so.

Amira paced the confines of her sitting room. A baby. She had to have a baby with Brent. She laid her hand on her stomach. What would it be like to bring his child into the world? A flush of heat spread through her body. What would it be like to be back in his arms—in his bed? Her womb tightened, sending a spiral of longing through her body. Her breasts suddenly heavy, sensitive to the softness of her silk bra, the tease of lace across the demi cup.

She remembered the touch of his hands, the taste of his skin, the heat of his possession with a primitive longing that made her groan out loud in the pristine silence of the room. She fisted her hand to her mouth. God, how on earth would she get through this?

She had eight weeks—only eight weeks—to pull it off. A quick check last night of her last menstrual cycle, thankfully always as regular as clockwork, showed her prime time to conceive would probably fall over the coming weekend. If that didn't work out she had one more chance and then, if that failed also, nothing.

Would she be lucky enough to get pregnant right away? She'd heard so many stories of women who'd struggled for years to become pregnant.

This was monumental. The decision to make a child, to bring a helpless baby into the world for any reason other than out of love went against everything she'd ever believed in. Everything she'd ever hoped for. But the thought of holding her child in her arms. Someone who was hers. Someone who didn't judge, didn't find fault, didn't find her wanting. The concept was almost overwhelming.

She was getting ahead of herself. First she had to swing it. She had to coerce Brent into her bed and convince him to have unprotected sex with her. She had to ruthlessly lie and use him—seduce him into making love with her, sharing breath, sharing each other's bodies.

Again her body tightened, thrummed in anticipation. It would take some planning, but planning was what she was good at. And she had the means and the motivation to get him there; all it would take was a little subtlety, some nuance. She could do this. She had to.

He'd never forgive her when he found out. A fine tremor ran through her body. He'd be angry. Far more angry than when she'd left him standing at the altar. But she'd gladly bear his anger to honor her promise to the children. Gladly bear his child.

It all seemed so clinical. So unfair. What had her grandmother been thinking when she'd inserted that wretched clause in her will? Not of Amira's happiness, certainly. But then had her happiness ever been Isobel's primary focus? Amira scoured her memories.

She had grown up desperate for some measure of affection from Isobel, always striving for her approval—almost trying to make up to her grandmother for her parent's failings. With the charity work she'd begun to believe she'd finally achieved that goal, until Isobel had dismissed her plans with the Fulfillment Foundation.

What made a woman so bitter that she didn't want to invoke hope in others? Was duty everything?

Right now it was. It was Amira's duty to the beneficiaries of the foundation to have that baby, no matter how cold-blooded its need for conception.

Her heart turned over in her chest. How could she do this? After her own upbringing she'd made a fervent promise to any future child of hers that they would know the joy of being loved by two parents, as she had even if it was short-lived.

But then the question raised itself in her mind. How could she not? Once she inherited and the foundation was set up in perpetuity she could manage quite nicely on a small but solid base of investment income. Even after she paid Brent what she'd promised, her baby would want for nothing.

Nothing but parents who loved each other.

Children all over the world were brought up in single parent families, she argued with herself. And it wasn't as if she knew for certain that Brent would reject their baby, in fact she very much doubted he would. She could even end up with a major battle on her hands for custody if truth be told.

Well, she'd cross that bridge if and when she came to it, she decided. Right now, the most important thing was getting pregnant.

Nine

On Saturday morning Amira stood at the end of the jetty and tried to breathe evenly. Anything to settle the butterflies that lurched about like crazed winged beasts in her stomach. She still couldn't believe he'd agreed to this respite weekend at Windsong.

The private cove and beach had been in the family for generations. One rustic dwelling replaced by another until the current two-storied plantation-style home was constructed during Isobel's reign. With access only by air or by sea, the property was intensely private, and the small staff employed to keep the house and grounds in pristine condition lived on the outskirts of its expansive boundaries.

The wind rustled through the phoenix palms that

lined the front of the house where it faced the sea, the sound reaching out to where Amira waited. Warm air circulated around her, caressing her bare midriff beneath the knotted white muslin blouse she wore above an ankle length cotton skirt. The well-worn fabrics pressed against the outline of her body in the breeze, and she was forced to hold on to the cowboy-style sun hat she'd perched on her head when she'd received the radio call from the launch's skipper to say they were ten minutes away from docking.

Clouds gathered in the sky, beginning to chase away the glorious sunshine that had bathed the island since sunrise this morning. The rain, when it came, would force them indoors.

A shiver of anticipation rolled through Amira's body, echoed by a thrill of excitement as the launch cleared the point and swooped in a semicircle toward the jetty. This was it. He was here. Everything now hinged on the success of today, and tonight. Just one night, but oh, the possibilities were endless.

She'd panicked a little when he'd called off from coming over to the island yesterday, being Friday, saying a problem at work would keep him late. But she consoled herself that she still had tonight and even all day tomorrow if everything went to plan. It had to be enough.

She could see him now, on the flying bridge next to the skipper, his short dark hair ruffling in the breeze. Dark sunglasses shaded his eyes, and his face was an unreadable mask from this distance.

Suddenly she couldn't wait for him to disembark. To be able to reach out, to touch him.

But she couldn't rush things. With the way they'd structured their arrangement, physical contact had been limited. The kiss he'd given her at the hotel a couple of weeks ago had been the only public display of affection to date, although he'd made a habit of using a proprietary touch when they were out. As if he was staking a silent claim. That said, to rush things now might throw her plans into total disarray.

She swept her hat off her head and her fingers clenched into the straw brim. It was too important that everything go off perfectly. She had to stick to her plans. To tantalize. To tease. Until falling into one another's arms was the most natural thing in the world, and the chasm of the past that lay between them could cease to exist for awhile.

Brent felt an all too familiar clutch in his gut when he saw Amira standing on the jetty waiting for the launch to dock. There was a casual relaxed air about her, as if here she was a different person to the one he'd squired around to Auckland's major functions in the past few weeks. Even what she was wearing was more like the old Amira. Just how many faces did she have? Once, a long time ago, he'd thought he knew her. The only thing he was certain of now was that he most certainly didn't.

Nor did he trust her. Not after discovering the financial mess that was the background of the foundation.

Her invitation to come out to Windsong for the week-end had intrigued him, even though she'd made the suggestion on the pretext of finalizing their wedding plans and guest list without interruption or distraction from their work. There were no paparazzi here, no gossip columnists. Altogether no financial advantage to them being together, aside from the fact that it was the kind of thing a normal engaged couple might do.

Except they weren't that kind of normal.

His mouth twisted in a wry smile. She was up to something again. Maybe it was the late night talk show earlier this week that had headlined the odds of their wedding going ahead that had spooked her. Perhaps it had been enough to make her want to assure Brent of her intention to follow through on the day, or even assure herself of his.

His gaze swept up past the palm trees and the immaculately manicured lawns preceding the pillared front of the house. He'd never been invited here before but he'd heard a great deal about the place. Why anyone needed a weekend retreat with nine bedrooms and six bathrooms, not to mention two offices, was beyond him. But then old Isobel had always known how to make an impression.

The launch bumped gently against the rubber bumpers on the jetty and, with a quiet word of thanks to the skipper, Brent skimmed down the stairs from the flying bridge. He collected his overnight bag from in the main cabin then stepped off the transom at the rear and onto the jetty where Amira waited.

Instantly every cell in his body went on full alert. Her skin still carried the golden blush of summer, and he couldn't help but let his eyes skim over her—from the deep exposed V of her blouse to where it knotted beneath her full breasts and then below to her bare midriff. Instinctively, he reached out, traced a finger across the soft curve of her belly.

He pulled his hand away, but not before he felt the answering quiver across her skin.

"Shall we go to the house? I've prepared some breakfast. You haven't eaten already, have you?"

"No. Sure, lead the way."

Amira prepared breakfast? Didn't she have staff here, he wondered. He stayed slightly behind her as she walked along the narrow jetty, her bare feet making next to no sound on the smooth weathered boards. Her hips swayed slightly as she took each step, and he felt heat rise under the collar of his shirt. Damn, if he didn't know better he would think she was deliberately enticing him. He drew level to her as they crossed the lawn to the house.

"Would you like to put your things away first?" Amira asked as they entered the spacious front foyer.

"Yeah, that'd be great."

Her warm friendliness had him on the back foot. He'd grown used to her being the cool ice princess she was renowned for. Cool, icy and avaricious.

Upstairs, the room she showed him was huge. A super-king-sized bed, clad in coffee-colored linens that matched the walls and contrasted perfectly with the creamy colored carpet, took pride of place against one wall in the room. Opposite, French doors opened out onto a wide balcony with a view of the bay.

"Nice room," he commented.

"It's the master. I thought you'd be comfortable here."

"You don't use this room yourself?"

"I have my own room just down the hall," Amira answered, bending forward to smooth an imaginary ripple out of the bed covering.

He hadn't been certain she wasn't wearing a bra beneath her blouse before, but now he was. Painfully certain. She bent forward a little farther, unwittingly exposing another inch of sun-gilded skin and just a hint of a dusky pink nipple. His body went rock hard. He dropped his weekend bag on a large chest at the foot of the bed and grabbed his toilet bag from inside. Determined to put some space between them, he strode through to the ensuite bathroom she'd shown him and put his things on the cream-colored marble vanity.

Coming over for this weekend worked in well with his plans. When he dashed her hopes of marriage he wanted her in his thrall. Physically and emotionally. While she'd strived to maintain an emotional distance since they'd been back together, he'd sensed that under the surface she wasn't quite as cool as she portrayed. No matter how he'd orchestrated her comeuppance, she was still a mightily attractive woman. A fact his libido had taken note of more than once. This craving for her had become a constant. Taking it to the next level would be no hardship.

A small sound from behind made him look up in the mirror. Amira stood in the doorway—the light from behind making her clothing translucent and haloing her blond hair. He clenched his hands on the edge of the basin. She was beautiful—a pity that it only went skin deep. Knowing that made it easier to do what he had to eventually do. Women like Amira had to learn that with wealth, came privilege—and with privilege, responsibility to others less fortunate.

"If you've forgotten anything, there should be toiletries in the drawers and cupboard. Help yourself, won't you."

He watched as her fingers played with the knot of her blouse. Pleating the short tail of fabric over and over. A sure sign she was nervous. Help himself? He knew where he wanted to start. With her. Here. Now. He swallowed and turned to face her.

"I'm sure I'll be fine."

"Good, well, I'll go downstairs and put on the coffee. Turn left at the bottom of the stairs when you're ready to come down and then left again to the back of the house."

Brent hung up the two changes of clothing he'd brought for the weekend. It didn't take long; after all, they weren't here for a fashion shoot. Which begged the question, what exactly were they here for? There was a skittishness about Amira he couldn't quite put his finger on. He'd lay odds she didn't only want to discuss wedding arrangements.

He had no trouble finding the kitchen. All he'd needed to do when he got downstairs was follow the delicious aroma. Fresh waffles steamed on a plate in the center of a scarred pine table and coffee percolated noisily on the stove top.

"I wasn't sure how you liked your waffles," Amira said as she gestured for him to sit down at the table, "so there's cream, fresh fruit and syrup. Whatever takes your fancy, really."

There was enough food here to feed an army. As he loaded his plate Brent couldn't help feeling that she was in some way overcompensating—the question was, for what?

"What did you have planned for today? Shall we start with the guest list?" he said as he helped himself to a second cup of coffee.

"We've got plenty of time to get that finalized. I was thinking, while the weather's still good, how about we head to the beach? There's a Jet Ski in the boatshed. I can take you for a tour around this end of the island if you like, while our breakfast settles. Then maybe we can have a swim?"

"Sure, sounds like a plan." So already she was putting off finalizing the wedding arrangements. Interesting, considering it was the reason behind her insistence he come over to Windsong for the weekend.

They changed after breakfast. Amira into a bikini top and shorts, Brent into a T-shirt and swim trunks. He couldn't tear his eyes away from her tanned belly. It tantalized and teased, drawing his attention to the slenderness of her waist and the rounded curve of her hips, the cradle of her pelvis. It was all too easy to imagine her wearing nothing at all.

As they climbed on board the Jet Ski, Amira turned her head back to him.

"You might want to slide a bit closer to me and put your arms around my waist. It gets a bit choppy in the channel."

In any other circumstances he wouldn't have hesitated, but even the thought of sliding forward so his thighs cradled the soft roundness of her buttocks, had him already half-erect. His hesitation was almost his undoing as he slid back a bit on the seat when she opened up the throttle and headed out into the bay. Holding on to her was the only sensible option, but he'd be damned if he was going to pull himself hard up against her while he did so. He wanted to drive her crazy, not the other way around.

She was an excellent guide, pointing out several properties owned by various members of New Zealand's elite, as well as some areas of historical significance. As they headed back to their bay he even started to feel himself relax. Then, suddenly, somehow in their sweep into the bay and toward the boathouse he managed to end up ignominiously in the water. As he sputtered to the surface, the air rang with Amira's laughter.

"Wretch. You'll pay for that," Brent warned with a determined smile on his face as he struck out toward the Jet Ski.

She may have taken him by surprise this time, but she wouldn't get away with that again. He latched on to Amira's foot before she could maneuver away, and suddenly she was there, in his arms, her full breasts hard against his chest, her legs swirling in the water around his. His blood pressure instantly ratchetted up a notch, his breathing quickened. His arms tightened around her, his legs entwined with hers. She couldn't mistake the strength of his reaction to her.

His eyes locked with hers, and he saw something change in her expression. All humor died, to be replaced with something else. Something elemental—hungry. He stopped treading water, and they slowly began to slide beneath the surface. Instantly he let her go and felt her push toward the surface. As he kicked back up and broke the surface himself, he saw Amira pulling herself back up onto the Jet Ski.

"I—I'll put this away, okay? Did you want to come in now or stay in the water a bit longer?"

She didn't make eye contact, instead lifting her arms to wring out her hair. The movement made her breasts lift, exposing the underside of each lush globe beneath the bottom edge of her bikini bra. That did it. Brent ripped off his T-shirt and bunching it up into a ball, threw it toward her, where it landed on the running board with a slap.

"Take that in for me would you? I think I'll swim for a bit. Work off some of that breakfast." And not a little bit of the sexual frustration that held him in its grip.

With a nod she turned the Jet Ski and returned it to the boatshed. Brent couldn't help but watch her as she made her way back down the jetty, stopping only for a moment to slip off her wet shorts and carry them together with his T-shirt to the beach where she laid them over the branches of a nearby pohutukawa tree. Swim, he told himself. Swim hard.

Despite it being early April, the water temperature in the sea was still bearable. Brent swam the width of the cove with punishing strokes and then turned to swim back again. Eventually, he slowed his pace slightly and turned toward the beach, to where Amira lay on the lounger on the sand. She was watching him, he could feel it, and it did nothing to ease the ache building up inside of him. As he rose from the water he heard her laugh.

"You're supposed to be here to relax, not exhaust yourself." She smiled as she rose from the lounger and picked up his towel.

She sauntered over to him and shook out the towel. He went to take it, but she ignored him, instead, beginning to dry him herself. Trails of fire followed her touch as she dragged the terry cloth over his arms and then across his chest. His nipples contracted into tight beads as she stroked across his rib cage and then drew the towel lower, to his abdomen, his waist.

"Thanks," he said, grabbing the towel from her and turning slightly away so she couldn't see the havoc her touch had wreaked.

"No problem."

He could hear the amusement in her voice. Amusement blended with something else. He flicked a glance at her. Oh yes, it was definitely arousal. Beneath the white triangles of her bikini top her nipples were equally as hard as his own, and her chest rose and fell as if she was the one who'd just completed a marathon swim. What was going on? She'd been so cool and remote these past two weeks, and now it was as if she was a smoldering ember, ready to light up at any time.

Had their proximity been as difficult for her as it had been for him? Another thought occurred to him. Or was this her secret agenda? Did she plan to seduce him into going through with the wedding? Had that article rattled her Forsythe cool so much that she was willing to sully herself with him one more time?

As he balanced the idea in his head, his all-too-eager flesh reminded him of how her touch had ignited his desire. If seduction was her intention, he certainly didn't plan on putting any roadblocks in her way. Oh no. If anything, he wished she'd make her intentions clear so he could rid himself of some of this tension that had been building up since the day she'd cornered him in the chapel men's room.

Amira watched as Brent finished drying himself, threw his towel down on the sand and then himself facedown after it. Had she gone too far, drying him like that? She didn't want to scare him off. She smiled ruefully. Scare off someone like Brent Colby? Now there was the definition of impossible. But getting back to her goal, she had to be careful. She needed to woo him, to slowly seduce him, not to rush at him like a bull at a gate no matter what her hormones were begging her to do.

She stretched out languorously on the lounger and sighed. Who'd have thought this would be so difficult? It wasn't as if they were strangers to one another physically, and the past few weeks had proven they could work well together—paint a believable facade.

"That's the third time you've sighed in the past couple of minutes. What's up?" Brent interrupted her thoughts.

Amira forced a laugh. "I think I'm finding this relax and chill out time more difficult to get into than I thought," she covered quickly.

"Maybe you're trying too hard," Brent said as he rolled halfway over to face her. "We should probably head back to the house and get this wedding stuff out of the way. Then maybe you'll be able to relax."

"Yeah, I think you're right." Because God only knew she was struggling right now.

Just as she straightened to sit up in her chair and gather her things from beside her, a huge wet drop of rain landed smack between her shoulder blades. She squealed in shock.

"We'd better hurry," Brent said, leaping to his feet in one sensuous glide of man and muscle. "That cloud's about to burst."

He'd no sooner spoken than the cloud did just that, drenching them and their gear within seconds with pelting drops of rain. Brent bent and dragged his towel up off the wet sand and grabbed Amira's hand, tugging her back toward the house. Caught off balance she stumbled, landing heavily in the soft sand and pulling him after her.

"Look at us, full of sand. We'll need to go around the back." She laughed breathlessly as they got back up and scrambled across the beach, kicking up more sand as they went. "There's an outdoor shower near the pool. We can wash the sand off before we go inside."

"What about our stuff?"

"Hey, it's soaked now. A bit more water isn't going to hurt it. We can pick it up later."

They ran across the lawn, and she gestured to the right-hand side of the house.

"That way. There's cover."

They skittered to a halt just inside the portico that housed the outdoor shower. An intricate latticework of trellis between narrow pillars provided a measure of privacy from the poolside. Not that anyone was there to watch them.

"Here, you go first, I'll grab some fresh towels from the pool house," she said after reaching over and turning on the shower faucet.

She was back in a moment. She ducked under the roof and put the towels she'd collected on the shelves just inside the door. Outside, the rain continued to bucket down. She turned to face Brent and almost wished she'd waited outside in the rain until he was done.

He stood beneath the showerhead, his arms up against the wall above him, the long deep triangular shape of his shoulders and tapered muscled back bared for her scrutiny. His trunks clung to the outline of his backside—hugging the gentle curve of his butt cheeks. Rivulets of water ran over him, and she wished she had the courage to reach out and track their path as they wended their way down to his waistband.

"I— Ah, I've brought the towels."

"You want to get under the shower with me?"

Amira swallowed. Did she? Oh Lord, yes—more than anything. But would she be moving too fast again? Before she could overthink the situation, he put out his hand to her and she moved forward, sliding under the showerhead and letting the warm water pour over her scalp and through her hair. Brent filled his hand with soap from the soft soap dispenser on the wall and smoothed the slightly spice-scented liquid across her back and down to her waist before sliding around to the front and moving back up to her shoulders again.

She closed her eyes as the water ran over her face, but they flew open again just as quickly as Brent loosened the ties of her bikini bra.

"What are you doing?"

"You're bound to have sand stuck in there. You want to be comfortable when you dry yourself, don't you?"

Words failed her as his fingers completed their task, and her bikini top fell on the tiled floor beneath them.

Ten

"Amira, turn around."

His voice was low and deep, and without thought she slowly turned to face him. Her breath hitched again at the expression on his face.

"You always were too beautiful for words," he said softly, before reaching out a finger to trace the areola of one nipple with a featherlight caress.

Her skin tightened at his touch, an almost unbearable wave of need swamping through her body—wishing him to touch her again.

"Brent?"

The sound that escaped on his name was both a plea and a question. In answer he bent his dark head to her breast and caught her nipple between his lips. As he

stroked his tongue around the hardened peak, her legs
threatened to buckle. His strong arm slid around her
waist, pulling her to him, holding her against that part
of his body that left her in no doubt as to how much he
wanted her right this minute. And, oh, did she want
him. It felt so right to be in his arms, to feel the power
of his muscles beneath her fingertips. They fit together
as if they'd never been apart, her body clamoring for his
touch, her mouth watering for the taste of him.

He transferred his attention to her other breast, his
tongue darting over the surface, lapping at the water that
ran over her skin, sending sensation spiraling through
her body.

She had to touch him, feel him. She slid her fingers
beneath the waistband of his trunks and eased them
away, far enough so she could push her hands inside to
caress the hot hard shaft of his passion for her. He
flinched slightly at her touch, a low growl sounding
deep in his throat.

He pulled away from her slightly, meeting her gaze
with a heated stare.

"Are you sure you want to do this?"

"Ye—"

"Before you answer," he interrupted, placing his lips
against hers and stealing her response before she could
finish, "be very sure of what you're going to say,
because if you say yes, I won't be able to stop."

A thrill of excitement rippled through her. Stop? Oh
no, she didn't ever want him to stop.

"Yes," she whispered against his lips, flicking her

tongue across the seam of his mouth for emphasis. "Yes, I want this. Yes, I want you. Yes, I don't want you to stop."

Brent's body shuddered in response to her reply, and he took her lips with his in a kiss that was as fierce as it was mind-numbingly intense. He pressed her against the tiled wall of the shower and swiftly undid the side ties on her bikini. She parted her legs slightly to let the wet fabric fall away, to expose herself to him, to his touch.

His fingers danced over her curls, softly, gently. So gently she wanted to scream at him to take her. But then she felt his hand cup her and a shimmer of pleasure made her groan out loud.

"How long? How long since you've felt like this?" His hand shifted, his fingers parting her, stroking at the entrance to her inner heat.

"Forever." She could barely enunciate the word.

She hadn't been with another man since the last time she'd made love with Brent in the week before their aborted wedding. She knew no man could ever measure up to this. To him. Her legs quaked as he slowly slid one finger into her honeyed depths.

She didn't want to think. She only wanted to feel. And feel she did as he withdrew his finger to move a little higher, to circle the swollen bud of sensation that begged for his touch before sliding back inside her again. He'd always known exactly how to bring her pleasure. Exactly how to send her hurtling into a realm where sensation ruled.

"I want you inside me," she moaned, pressing herself hard against the palm of his hand.

He had her so close already, but she wanted him inside her when she came. Somehow she managed to push his wet trunks down over his hips. He kicked them away from his legs and then lifted her against the wall. She hooked her legs around his hips. She could feel his pulsing heat against the core of her, feel the hardness of him as he positioned himself at her entrance.

He hesitated, and she groaned in frustration.

"Protection," he muttered.

"It's okay. I've got it. I'm safe," she ground out as she uttered a silent prayer begging forgiveness for her lie.

And then he was inside her. Gloriously filling her, driving harder and faster until her inner muscles clenched against him, until he probed that special place that sent her mindlessly screaming over the edge. She felt him pump against her, once, twice more, then his hoarse cry told her he'd let go and joined her on the ephemeral cloud of pleasure and sensation that rippled through her again and again.

The low afternoon sun was trying to break through the clouds by the time Amira woke. She watched as Brent slept on. She smiled quietly to herself. After their time in the shower, they'd managed to make their way upstairs, amazing really when she considered how boneless he'd left her after that first time. And it had been the first of several as they rediscovered one another, sometimes slow and painstakingly gentle, other times fast and desperate, as they'd been in the pool shower.

Her heart swelled as she watched him—committing

each line of his face, the fall of his hair across his forehead, the sensual fullness of his lower lip, to her memory. Her hand lay across her belly. Had they done it? Had they begun the miracle process to create a child? She certainly hoped so, because once she told him they could no longer marry he'd be angry. So angry he might never want to see her or talk to her again. But if they'd made a baby, she'd have a special part of him forever.

She rolled over on the bed of the master suite and looked at the clock. Nearly five. No wonder she'd woken. She was starving. She slid from the bed and padded naked through the room to get a robe from her own wardrobe.

"Where are you going?" Brent raised a sleepy head from his pillow.

"Just to put something on and get something for us to eat."

"Don't."

"Don't get anything to eat?"

"No, don't put anything on."

Brent sat up and swung his legs off the side of the bed. He crossed to where she was standing in only a moment. He bent to kiss her, his hand possessively snaking around her waist and pulling her against him.

"I'll help you."

Laughter burbled from Amira's throat. "Help me? Distract me is more like it."

She spun out of his arms and flew down the carpeted hall and then swiftly ran down the stairs, Brent hard on her heels. He caught up with her in the kitchen, trapping her faced against the kitchen bench. She could feel his arousal against her buttocks. Despite herself she couldn't help but squirm against him.

"Distraction, did you say?" Brent said, his breath hot against the side of her neck.

She was helpless in his embrace—helpless to refuse what he promised with the slide of his tongue along the cord of her neck. When he gently kneed her legs farther apart and pulled her hips back to him to position himself to enter her once more, she gripped the kitchen countertop and fought back the moan of pleasure that built from deep inside.

How could she not have been driven mad missing this intensity between them? This insatiable need to be together, connected as one. As Brent's hands slid up over her hips and around to her belly, skimming the surface of her skin until they cupped her full breasts, his fingertips and thumbs teasing and pulling at her nipples, she acknowledged that she'd never stopped loving him and never would.

A shaft of heat speared through her body, from breast to deep in her belly. She pushed back against him, matching his rhythm, urging him on faster and harder until he groaned, his body pulsing deep inside her, and her climax spiraled out to claim her every sense, her every emotion.

Weak with satisfaction, she leaned forward on her arms, bracing herself against the counter. She'd never be able to enter this kitchen again without remembering this moment. Brent coaxed her body upright, turning her around to face him.

Brent battled to get his heart rate under control, reminding himself that while sex was one thing, his self-appointed task was quite another. It would be all too easy to allow his mind to be as seduced by their near-insatiable desire for one another as his body had been. He had to keep the upper hand—to remember what she'd done to him and what he'd vowed to make her pay for. He had to remember how carelessly she'd put the Fulfillment Foundation in jeopardy.

He reached out a hand and smoothed Amira's tumbled golden locks from her face, cupped her chin and lifted it to present her for his kiss.

"You okay? That was…" His voice petered off, lost for words to describe the overwhelming need he'd had to possess her.

He'd thought the edge would have worn off a little now; instead, each time, it only whet his appetite for more.

"Yeah, it was…" She smiled. "I'm fine. What about you? Hungry?"

He kissed her again. "Always, but some food would be a good idea too."

He leaned back against the bench as she went to the fridge and pulled out a plate of gourmet cheeses and placed it on a tray on a side counter. She added some sliced fruit she'd obviously also prepared earlier, as well as a loaf of French bread and some crackers. A small jar of relish completed the tray.

"There's some wine in the fridge and glasses in the cupboard over there. You take care of those, and I'll take the tray upstairs. This can tide us over until dinner later on."

"Sure," Brent replied, grabbing the bottle of chilled Marlborough grown and bottled chardonnay from the fridge door and snagging two wineglasses from the cupboard.

Later on sounded just fine to him, because it meant something else came before, he smiled to himself as he followed Amira back up the stairs to his room.

By the time the launch arrived to take them back to the city on Sunday they'd eventually gotten around to finalizing their guest lists for the wedding and all the minutiae that Amira insisted were important. More than once Brent had had to quell the pang that he was setting her up for major disaster. It was what he had set out to do all along, he reminded himself. One way or another, it was going to happen, and with it he'd remove her power to devastate others' lives along the way.

He was surprised to see Amira had arranged separate cars to take them back to their respective homes.

"You don't want to come back to my place?" he asked.

Amira ducked her head, not quite meeting his eyes when she answered. "I'm sorry, not tonight. I've got a really early start in the morning."

"Yeah, me too," Brent said. But still he had the sensation that she was hiding something. It irritated him that he couldn't put his finger on exactly what that was.

Across the street from the wharf, Brent espied a particularly persistent photographer who'd dogged their every step in the past few weeks.

"Look, he's here already." He nodded in the general

direction where the photographer lurked. "Let's give him the scoop he's been waiting for, hmm?"

With that he pulled Amira to him and wrapped her in his arms. Her lips softened beneath his, opening for the sweep of his tongue, all reticence gone under his touch. God, he couldn't get enough of the taste of her, of the velvet of her mouth. When he broke off the kiss, his blood pressure had gone up several points and his breathing was ragged.

"If I didn't have an early flight to Sydney in the morning I'd be finishing off on the promise of that kiss," he growled against her lips.

"I'll just look forward to when you come back then, shall I?" Amira patted his cheek and gave him a swift peck before turning to get into the waiting limousine that would take her home.

Brent stood a while longer, watching as she was driven away, still intensely aware of the imprint of her against his body. His return home wasn't all she had to look forward to, he told himself grimly as he handed his bag to the driver waiting to take him home.

Eleven

Amira watched the color change on the indicator stick of the home pregnancy test she'd bought. Her heart raced as she laid it next to the other three she'd already lined up on her bathroom vanity. She sank to the floor, her legs tucked under her, as the reality of the series of positives rammed home.

Pregnant. With Brent's child.

She laid her hand against her stomach as if she could already feel the differences taking place inside her. Tears rolled down her cheeks. She hadn't believed it could be so easy—that the time they'd spent together on the island at Windsong had so swiftly brought the results she'd wanted. At some time in that sinfully hedonistic weekend they'd hit the jackpot. She hadn't wanted to believe it had happened so quickly. She wouldn't even let herself begin to hope when she missed her first period after that weekend. It was only now, after missing her second period, she'd begun to dream it could be true.

In the past month she and Brent had spent a great deal of time together, forging what she believed had been a new closeness. A closeness that to her was all the more bittersweet because she knew it couldn't last, despite her wishes to the contrary. They'd dined together most nights, slept together most nights—spending time together just for the sheer joy of it.

And now she had to rip all that apart and tell him she wouldn't be marrying him in two weeks' time. The tears increased in frequency as a sob ripped from her throat. She should be happy—ecstatic, even—she reminded herself. Sometime before the end of December she'd be a mother, well before her thirtieth birthday as demanded by Isobel's will. Her dreams for the Fulfillment Foundation would be realized.

Even so, she felt so dreadfully empty inside. Bereft. How on earth was she going to summon the courage to tell Brent the news that their wedding was off? She was cutting it fine. Two weeks to the wedding. What if she'd had to stand him up again on the day? Her stomach pitched uncomfortably, making her draw in a steadying breath.

Slowly the tears dried, and a sense of calm began to settle on her shoulders. First things first, she had to get official medical confirmation of her pregnancy. She pulled herself to her feet and swept the test results and their packaging into the bathroom waste bin. It would be tricky getting an appointment with one of Auckland's leading obstetricians without having the media get a hold of the information and effectually blowing her secret into the stratosphere of gossip.

She looked in the mirror and lifted her chin. She wasn't a Forsythe for nothing. She'd pull whatever strings she could to ensure her privacy, even if it meant having everyone attend to her here at the house.

Amira sat at the table of the famed Okahu Bay seafood restaurant on Auckland's waterfront and looked back at the city. It was a perfect mid-autumn day. A light breeze ruffled the sea and a dozen small yachts engaged in trying to make the most of the wind as they jostled about in the bay and beneath the sea wall. Across the road from the restaurant a school group of kayakers made a colorful splash against the blue of the water. In the distance, the towers of Auckland City punctuated the intense blue skyline.

She sighed. A perfect day to be doing the least perfect thing she'd ever had to undertake in her life. Today she was going to tell Brent the wedding was off—face-to-face. No text message this time. She'd deliberately chosen this public setting because she knew Brent wouldn't make a scene here. Not that he'd make a scene exactly anywhere else, but she knew she'd need the buffer of other people around her to at least keep the exchange on a civil level.

The hair on the back of her neck prickled. He was here. She turned and smiled as he walked toward her, immaculate in his black perfectly-cut suit, an open-necked turquoise, black-and-white-striped shirt beneath it. His eyes were hidden by the dark-lensed designer sunglasses he wore, but she could see he was pleased to see her. His lips curved into an answering smile as he bent to give her a kiss.

As brief as it was, she felt it all the way to her toes, and she hoarded the sensation to her. It was the last time they'd be so intimate. She thought of the life growing within her. At least she'd have that, she reminded herself.

"Have you chosen what you want to eat yet?" Brent asked as he lowered himself into his chair adjacent to hers and picked up the wine menu.

"Not yet. I thought I'd wait for you."

"I'm easy. I'll have the seafood medley. Why don't you try the scallops. I hear they're delicious."

When she nodded her assent he gestured to the waiter, placed their order and pointed to the award-winning Pinot Gris on the wine list that had recently become his favorite.

"Oh, no wine for me, thanks. I'll just stick with mineral water today," Amira interrupted as Brent started to order a bottle of the wine.

"You're sure? Well, in that case, just bring me a glass for now," Brent told the waiter. He turned his gaze back on Amira. "Are you feeling okay? You're a bit pale."

"I'm fine, really. Just a little tired is all." Amira rushed over the words.

She hadn't realized the strain of what she was going

to do was showing a physical effect already. They made desultory conversation until their main courses arrived. Amira could barely eat the delicately flavored seared scallops drizzled with a lime and coconut cream dressing. Instead, she slid them one by one off their skewers and pushed them about her plate. She jumped when Brent reached out and put his hand on hers.

"What's up? Something's bothering you."

Her stomach flip-flopped uncomfortably, and the words she needed to say clogged in her throat. Tears burned at the back of her eyes as she raised her gaze from her plate to meet his. There was no avoiding it. She had to tell him.

"I'm calling off the wedding. I can't go through with it."

There, she'd said it. She reached for her mineral water and took a sip, surprised to see her hand so steady as she put the glass back on the table.

"You what?" Brent's voice was deadly cold, but the heated slashes of color that appeared on his cheeks gave immediate insight to his anger.

His hazel eyes narrowed as he met her gaze, reminding her of the predatory stare in a panther's eyes before it struck its prey. Amira fought back the tremor that threatened to rock through her body and focused on her breathing, on calming the now erratic beat of her heart.

"I've asked Marie to prepare a statement to the media to say that we've both agreed to withdraw from our engagement."

Rage flared inside him, hot and fast, threatening to

consume the cool demeanor that was his trademark in business. Brent beat back the flames of fury before they could erupt. How the hell long had she been planning this? He chose his next words carefully fighting to keep his voice level.

"You talked to Marie about this before you told me?"

"I had to."

"You had to," he repeated. He lifted his glass and took a long sip of his wine. "And what made you decide you *had* to break our engagement? Hmm? Last I saw, my finances were still intact. Had a better offer, perhaps?"

He saw her flinch at his words and allowed a slither of satisfaction to slide beneath his anger. His vengeance was slipping through his fingers, and he was helpless to stop it. He didn't do helpless.

"Your financial position has nothing to do with it, Brent. Look, can we be civil about this, please?"

"Civil? You want me to be civil? How about a reason why, Amira? Wasn't last night good enough for you?" He leaned forward and pitched his voice low so only she could hear him. "Didn't you come apart in my arms as we made love, as I kissed your body? All over."

To his satisfaction, a flush rose in her cheeks and a tiny gasp broke from her lips. Lips that had in return touched him in places that warmed and roused to her touch with an alacrity that left him raging with a heated desire that showed no sign of abating. Not even now.

"I thought I could deal with it, go through with the wedding but I can't." She picked up the white linen napkin from her lap and dabbed at her lips, her knuckles gleaming white as she clutched the stiff white cloth. "It's over, Brent. Please don't make this harder than it has to be."

She slid her engagement ring off and put it on the table between them. He leaned back in his chair and eyed her carefully. She refused to meet his gaze.

"Harder than it has to be. That's a joke. And what about the money you owe me. I agreed to your terms. We signed a contract. If you don't fulfil the terms of that contract, cent for cent, I will sue you for breach of promise—and won't that make for some interesting publicity?"

He may not have the satisfaction of doing to her what she had done to him eight years ago, but he drew some comfort that his demand she fulfill the terms of their contract would destroy her financially.

"I'm a woman of my word."

He scoffed in disbelief. "Really? Then what do you call this?"

Amira rose from her chair, dropped the cloth napkin onto her seat and gathered up her handbag. If he'd thought she was pale before, she was even paler now. A pang of sympathy was swiftly quashed. Let her be rattled by his demand. She'd learn soon enough that she couldn't wriggle out of the contract. That every last word was binding.

"I fulfilled the first part of our deal. You have the consents you needed, and you will get your money. I personally guarantee it."

With that she spun on her heel and headed for the

stairs leading out of the restaurant. From his position on the balcony table he watched as she walked with clipped steps to where her BMW was parked and gracefully got in then drove smoothly away. Without so much as a sign of any distress. Had she planned this all along? If so, he'd seriously underestimated her.

Brent played her parting words through his head. *You will get your money. I personally guarantee it.* How on earth was she going to do that? He knew for a fact she had no personal wealth of her own. No hidden offshore accounts that could possibly meet the multimillion dollar requirements of their agreement. She was in no position to *personally* guarantee anything.

So what, then, was she up to?

Amira drove toward the city, her hands clenched tight on the steering wheel. She'd done it. She'd actually done it and walked away. She should be feeling a sense of lightness, of relief. Instead she wanted to howl in misery. For the second time in her life, she'd rejected the man she loved above all others. For the second time because of her grandmother's control.

"You won't have any control over me anymore, Grandmother. This is the last time you pull my strings," she vowed through a throat choked with emotion.

She swung into the underground parking lot in the building housing her lawyer's offices and parked in the designated visitor's parking space. For a few moments she just sat there in the artificially illuminated glare, forcing her breathing to settle and her body to stop trembling. The journey from the restaurant to here had passed in a blur; she had no memory of the road she'd traveled. The knowledge frightened her. She couldn't afford to be so oblivious again, she scolded herself. She had another person to consider now, and she couldn't afford to put that tiny life at risk by any means.

The ride in the lift to the eighth floor was swift. A quick glance at the mirrored walls of the car confirmed she still looked the same as she had when she'd left home this morning. Still as cool and poised as if she hadn't just ripped her heart and her dreams into shreds. At least she had her training and poise to thank Isobel for, she admitted with a self-deprecating shake of her head. If nothing else.

She was ushered into Gerald Stein's office by one of his administrative staff as soon as she arrived in the main office. Gerald rose from his seat and put his hands on her shoulders, dropping a kiss on her forehead in welcome.

"My dear. How are you?"

She couldn't exactly tell him she was a total wreck, now could she?

"I've ended my engagement to Brent Colby and," she said while reaching into her handbag for the letter from her obstetrician, "I think you'll find that this confirms that I will still be able to meet the terms of Grandmother's will."

She sat in a chair and watched as Gerald read the letter, his face changing from his usual calm demeanor to one of complete disbelief.

"You're pregnant?"

"Yes."

Gerald was speechless as he sat back down in his chair, shaking his head in denial.

"I can't believe you've done this."

"The terms of Grandmother's will were clear, were they not? Either marry before my thirtieth birthday or bear live issue before that date. Gerald, I'm not prepared to marry just any man to satisfy her dictates. No matter what hold she has over me I cannot do that. Nor can I just let my rightful inheritance slip into Roland's hands. You and I both know he'll burn through the immediately accessible funds before starting to sell off the other assets. A man like him would do irreparable damage, and then where would Grandmother's charities be?" Not to mention the Fulfillment Foundation, she added silently. "At least this way I'm not bound to someone I neither like nor respect, and I can still continue my charity work in Grandmother's stead. That *is* what she wanted, isn't it?"

"Well, yes, of course. But Amira, having a baby on your own is no small task. Are you sure you're doing the right thing? And what about the father? Who is he?"

"The baby's father is of no consequence." Sharp pain dragged through her chest. Of no consequence? He was everything but. Amira continued, "Besides, Grandmother left me no other option, did she?"

Amira reached into her handbag again and drew out her copy of the agreement she'd signed with Brent. She put it on the desk between them.

"Now, based on the fact that I am pregnant and can

fulfill her stipulations, I want you to raise a loan for that sum." She stabbed her forefinger at the amount written in words and in figures in the middle of the agreement. "And I want you to pay that to Brent Colby."

"What? You can't be serious. Amira, that's an enormous sum of money. It's not as if Colby needs it."

"Whether he needs it or not, it's what we agreed to when we became engaged. I'm still obligated to keep up my end of the deal." Amira tried to ignore the stab of pain in the region of her heart. Oh, how she wished it could have been different.

"Surely there's a loophole or an escape clause." Gerald slid his glasses down his nose and peered at her, realization dawning on his wrinkled face. "Oh no, Amira. Tell me you didn't sign this without a legal opinion."

"I read the document thoroughly. It encapsulated everything we'd agreed upon. There are no loopholes. Gerald, I was quite happy to marry Brent until you disclosed that additional clause. Had I known about that from the beginning…well, things obviously would have taken a different path, wouldn't they?"

"But Amira, this agreement says nothing about not having to meet your obligations if the wedding doesn't take place." Gerald read aloud the clause that looked like it was on the verge of triggering a coronary. *"And furthermore, the said Amira Camille Forsythe will make over to the said Brent Colby a sum of money being not less than ten percent of the amount Amira Camille Forsythe would inherit upon the occasion of her marriage.* Would inherit! This is disastrous!"

Gerald placed the paper on his desk and rubbed at his chin before continuing. "This has been so broadly phrased that it wouldn't have mattered who you married or even *if* you married. Amira, you are obligated to pay this money to Colby no matter what happens."

Gerald's words died on the air as the truth behind them slowly sank in. Brent had set her up all along. Whether she went through with their marriage or not, he'd stood to gain massively. Amira reached her decision quickly. No matter what Brent's motives, hers had been less than honest also. She'd promised to pay him, and now she could afford to. In every transaction there was always collateral damage to some degree. She could put this behind her now and move on.

"Gerald, you're my lawyer. Grandmother's estate pays you to take instructions from me unless I fail to meet the terms of my inheritance. Is that correct?" Amira fought to hold on to the final shred of control she had left.

"That's correct, of course. But I'm more than that, my dear, and you know it," Gerald said.

"Then, please, in this instance, can we keep emotion out of the equation. I'd like you to raise a loan for the money I promised to make available to Brent, and I'd like you to see to it that he receives that money as quickly as possible. Please defer repayment of the loan until two weeks after the due date of my baby."

"If that is your last word on the matter—"

"It is. I'm sorry to have to be so blunt, Gerald, but you know I have no other choice."

Choice, as she understood the term, had never been

hers. But, she thought as she pressed her hand against her belly, that would change with the advent of this new life, this new hope for her future.

Twelve

"There's how much been deposited?" Brent fought not to shout down the receiver at his bank manager.

The man repeated the sum. Brent thanked him then replaced the phone. How on earth had she raised that much money in less than a fortnight? Tomorrow would have been their wedding day, the day he'd been looking forward to as his *coup de grâce* in their relationship. The day where he'd finally extract his revenge. But she'd forestalled him in that quest, and now, it appeared, she'd preempted his attempt to drive her into financial ruin.

Something wasn't right. He paced to the window of his home office and gazed out across the estuary. She should be destitute and frantic, not calmly depositing several million dollars in his bank account.

There had to be more to her grandmother's will than she'd let on. Some other clause that had given her a different method of accessing the funds she so desperately needed. But what was that clause?

Brent spun back to his desk and punched in a series of numbers on his phone before switching it to speaker. When his investigator answered, he wasted no time in getting to the point.

"I need to see a copy of Isobel Forsythe's will. What will it take?"

"It's simple enough. A letter of application to the High Court together with payment of their fee and it's yours."

"Then what are you waiting for?"

"I'll apply to the registrar, Mr. Colby, but it may take some time."

"I don't pay you to keep me waiting."

"Yes, sir. When do you want it?"

"Yesterday," Brent barked at the phone before disconnecting the call.

He raked his hands through his hair, then clasped his fingers behind his head and stretched against the tautness in his neck and shoulders. What the hell had Amira been up to?

Later that afternoon an e-mail arrived with a scanned copy of the late Isobel Forsythe's will as an attachment. Brent glanced over the basics—the bequests to staff and to charities—finally he reached the part he'd been looking for.

He felt all the blood drain from his face as he read the subclause under the conditions of Amira's entitlement to inherit that stated in cold black and white that she was never to marry him under any circumstances. There'd never been any love lost between the old battle-ax and Brent, but this? This was proof the woman was nothing more than a manipulative monster. How dare she have toyed with Amira's life—her happiness—like that.

It made more sense about why Amira had canceled their plans and withdrawn from their arrangement. He didn't want to feel any pity or sympathy for her, but this gross influence over her life was unbelievable. He'd long believed that Isobel had kept Amira under her thumb for her own purposes, much like a personalized marionette, there to do her bidding. This was proof positive of his theory.

Another thought occurred to him. How long had Amira known about this? Surely she'd seen a full copy of the will. Surely she'd known even before she asked him to marry her that she couldn't do that and inherit at the same time. What the hell had she been up to?

There was more. Brent read on, and his earlier disgust was rapidly replaced with a new level of fury he'd never believed himself capable of.

Live issue. The two words swam before his eyes.

Damn her to hell and back. She'd cold-bloodedly allowed him to think he'd seduced her all so she could have a baby to access her inheritance. She'd played the ice maiden, being so inaccessible as to drive him to distraction and insisting on their arrangement being strictly business when all along she'd planned to have his child.

He clenched his hands in an attempt to control the

urge to pick up the top of the range laptop on his desk and hurl it through the nearest window. Oh, she was her grandmother's successor all right. He doubted even Isobel would have accepted a man in her bed for the sole purpose of procreation for financial gain.

A baby. *His* baby.

An overwhelming flood of emotion swamped him. A sense of connection to his as yet unborn son or daughter. No matter what Amira did, he'd make sure she didn't retain custody of the child once it was born. There was no way on this earth that Isobel's influence, through her scheming granddaughter, would taint his child.

He pushed his hands through his hair again and swore a blue streak. Amira would be sorry she'd ever deceived him. Sorry she ever thought to tangle with Brent Colby again. Oh, she'd pay for her deception. She'd pay dearly.

He picked up his phone again and punched in Amira's cell phone number only to hear the beeps that told him the number had been disconnected. He tried her home only to get the same.

He'd track her down eventually. She could run, but she couldn't hide from him forever.

The wind whipped around the headland, making the palms bordering Windsong sway and dance with a massive rustle of noise. Amira got up from the desk in the office she'd made her own since she'd left Auckland in an attempt to dodge the media circus that had erupted when the wedding had been canceled. The carefully worded request for privacy as they went their own ways was as casually discarded by the media as a day-old cup of coffee.

Two weeks after the announcement it had become impossible for her to stay in Remuera. Daily encampments of paparazzi made leaving the property a risk as her car was swamped and then chased by various means of transport. It had only been after she'd encountered a near miss with a photographer dangerously perched on the back of a motorcycle that she realized staying in her family home was putting both her and the baby at risk.

She'd made arrangements to be transported from the property in the dead of night in a removal van, which then took her to Mechanics Bay, from where a chartered helicopter had deposited her at the island.

For the past month that's exactly where she'd stayed—her only physical contact with other people being the small staff who maintained the property and the interior of the house. It was a lonely existence but a necessary one. No one had thought to see if she was here, instead fictional sightings of her in Sydney, Paris and London had effectively put everyone off the track.

She wondered what Brent thought. If he'd tried to contact her once he'd received the money. She missed him with an ache that went soul deep. Worse than the last time. She'd tried to keep busy, had submerged herself in the administrative duties she could manage to do with the Fulfillment Foundation and in the joys of discovering the week by week progress in her pregnancy.

Already she displayed the tiniest of baby bumps, and the other day, even though from her books she knew it was unlikely, she'd been certain the flutter she'd felt had been the baby's movement. Oh, how she wished she could have shared her excitement with Brent. But he could never know about the baby. She reminded herself again of the wording of the agreement—how he'd set her up to take her money, come hell or high water, no matter how much he said he didn't need it. If he knew about the baby no doubt he'd take steps to take it away from her too. She couldn't bear for that to happen. This was her child. Someone to call her own. Someone to love and who would love her unreservedly in return.

Tears flooded Amira's eyes, as they did so easily these days, spilling over her lashes and down her cheeks. She dabbed them away with one hand and focussed on the letter she had to e-mail back to her office in the city.

With the electronic and satellite setup Isobel had insisted on at Windsong, Amira had maintained contact with her staff at the Fulfillment Foundation. She swore them to privacy on the promise of a massive bonus provided no news of her whereabouts leaked out. So far so good.

Until yesterday morning.

She'd woken with a niggling ache low in her belly. After going to the toilet, she had been horrified to see a small amount of blood. Terror had torn through her. At fourteen weeks pregnant she'd thought she was past the worst of the danger time when it was most likely to lose a baby. She was well aware of the statistics, that as many as one in four pregnancies ended unexpectedly before the twenty week mark, but she'd been so well. Felt so safe.

Now, however, she was terrified. She'd gone straight back to her bed and called her obstetrician's office. The nurse she'd spoken to had been comforting, consoling her that the symptoms she'd experienced may well settle down, but she'd advised Amira to make her way to the specialist's rooms as soon as she could so they could do a scan and ensure that everything was as it should be.

Amira's next call had been to the helicopter company that had flown her out here. But due to the very high winds, it was impossible to get a chopper safely out to Windsong. Likewise, the swells that were running on the sea effectively trapped her where she was. Her island paradise, her sanctuary from the public eye, had turned into her worst nightmare.

She'd stayed in bed all day, and this morning, thank goodness, the weather had died down sufficiently for a chopper to be sent to bring her back to Auckland City.

She e-mailed the letter back to her assistant and shut down her computer. Then she grabbed her things. It was time to go out to the helipad at the back of the house and wait.

Her timing was impeccable. Just as she secured the back door, a sleek black helicopter came in over the ridge and hovered prior to setting down on the marked H on the expansive back lawn. Strange, she didn't recognize the logo on the side. It certainly wasn't the company she'd used to arrange her flight back to the city.

A tall dark form alighted from the helicopter. Sudden recognition dawned, and it was as if a shower of icy water had been dumped over her head. Brent. He'd found her.

He covered the distance between them in a few short strides, his jacket fluttering in the buffet of wind from the slowing rotor blades. There was no doubt at all that he was angry—very, very angry. With nowhere to run— or to hide—Amira stood her ground and fought back the rising nausea that suddenly surfaced.

"Amira. Running away again, I see?" He gestured to the small overnight bag the nurse had recommended she bring with her in case she needed to be admitted to their private hospital overnight.

"What business is it of yours where I am?" she replied with a snap in her voice she managed to dredge from deep inside. "I don't answer to you."

"Really?"

"Yes, really. Now, get off my property," she ordered in an attempt to channel her late grandmother's hauteur.

"Ah, but it's not your property yet. Is it?" he countered.

A wave of dizziness hit her, and she swayed slightly, battling to keep her balance. The sensation receded, leaving her feeling sick. Scared.

"Either way, you have no place here. Please, leave." To her disgust her voice wavered.

"We have things to discuss."

"We have nothing to discuss. I met my obligations to you under the terms of our agreement. You have your consents. You have your money. Now go."

The ache in her belly sharpened, and the bitter taste of fear flooded her mouth. How far away was her ride? She had to get to the specialist. She just knew it.

"But what about my baby?"

He knew? The realization slammed into her with the full impact of a freight train. The breath rushed from her lungs; spots danced before her eyes. Brent took a step toward her, his dark eyebrows drawn in a straight line across eyes that demanded answers.

"Were you planning to pay me for that too?" He said the words so casually, any bystander could be forgiven for thinking he was joking, until they saw the glare of intent in his gaze.

"That's ridiculous. I'm not pregnant. How could I be? Besides, I don't have time for a baby. I'm far too busy." Amira took a step back and rattled off her denial hoping he'd believe her.

All she wanted was to create space between them, but he was closing that space, stepping in until he was close enough that she could see the flecks of color in his eyes, smell the hint of cologne he wore, feel the heat emanating off his body in waves.

"Don't lie to me, Amira. I know the full conditions of Isobel's will. I know you used me and then discarded me like last year's fashion. Besides, you forget, I know you. *Intimately.* I can see the changes in you, even feel them."

He put his hand on the small swelling of her belly, the heat of his hand imprinting through the fabric of her winter dress, all the way to her skin. There it was again, that flutter, followed by another spear of pain.

"You don't know me at all. And, besides, you set me up all along. You didn't mean to go through with the wedding either, did you?"

His lips firmed into a straight line as he maintained a silence that told her more than any words.

"Just go. Leave me!" Amira cried on a sob.

He removed his hand and stepped back. "This doesn't end here. I will fight you with every last breath before I'll allow you to keep my child."

On that note, he turned and began to walk away. Amira raised a hand toward him in a silent plea as the dizziness returned again, as the pain increased.

"Brent?"

He turned at the sound of her voice. Something wasn't right. She was more than angry, more than defensive. She was frightened. And suddenly, so was he. She swayed, her eyelids fluttering. He closed the short distance between them in a flash, only to catch her in his arms as she lost consciousness. Gently he lowered her to the path, and cushioning her body against his own he checked her pulse, her breathing. As he did so he noticed the blood, and fear as he'd never known it before plunged through to his heart.

By now the chopper pilot was running toward him, with a first aid kit in hand. But this was more than any first aid kit could handle. Brent knew it.

"Call the rescue helicopter. Now!"

Brent smoothed her hair from her face and held her to him, desperate to impart his health and vitality back into her. He'd never before prayed in his life, but suddenly he was prepared to barter anything to keep safe the small life he knew was at risk before it was too late.

Thirteen

Amira looked around her hospital room and fought to swallow the sorrow that threatened to choke her. She could no longer hold on to any hope that her dreams for the future would come to fruition. She'd lost it all. Her inheritance, the Fulfillment Foundation, the man she loved and above all else, her baby.

And it was all her fault.

Oh sure, the specialist had said even if she'd made it the day before she'd collapsed there was nothing that could have been done. That some pregnancies are simply not to be. But deep down inside she knew she could never forgive herself.

She'd refused all visitors except Gerald. The colorful arrangements that had been delivered on a daily basis were an assault on eyes that had shed too many tears already, and she'd turned each display away, asking the nurses to move them to another room, another ward, anywhere people would appreciate them more than she.

She stood and walked to the window, oblivious to the leaden skies and the clouds that skidded along, pushed by powerful gusts of wind. She was still a bit shaky on her legs. The hemorrhage that had taken her baby had almost taken her life. Sometimes she almost wished it had, because what was left for her now?

The clouds burst open, the sudden downpour drenching all and sundry. Beneath the hospital, on the pathways, people scurried for cover. As she watched them, Amira had never felt more apart from the world than now.

"Are you ready to go, my dear?"

Gerald's voice stirred her into movement. He sounded as if he'd aged a thousand years in the past few days. Goodness knew she felt as if she had too.

"Yes, I'm ready."

"Are you sure you want to go to the mansion? There's been all sorts of speculation in the media about why you were admitted to hospital. Some have even hinted at miscarriage. They won't leave you alone."

Amira flinched then forced herself to relax her shoulders and speak in level tone. "Let them speculate. Before long I'll be old news."

She started toward the door but Gerald stopped her, gesturing to a lone card on her bedside table.

"Don't you want to take that with you?"

Amira looked across the room at the colorful handmade

card little Casey McLauchlan had sent when the news had broken of her hospitalization. Gerald took it off the cabinet and handed it to her, but Amira shook her head.

"No, please leave it."

"But isn't it from one of the children—?" Gerald gently laid it facedown on the bed. "Ah, I see."

But he didn't see. He'd never understand how devastating it had been to receive that message of cheer from a child she'd promised the earth and then let down. She'd failed in this as she'd failed in everything. Her grandmother had been right all along.

After Gerald had settled her back in at her apartment, he sat down in the chair next to the sofa where she'd flopped on entering.

"I hate to bring this up now, Amira, but there's something we really must discuss."

"I know. The loan. I can't think about that right now. Please, can you defer the finance company a few more days?"

"I'll see what I can do, but I have to warn you that they are pressing me for a response."

"Gerald, please?"

He patted her leg. "I know, my dear. I know. Now, if you're sure there's nothing more I can do for you right now?"

"No. There's nothing. Thank you for bringing me back, and thanks for arranging the meals in the fridge. I don't think I'll be up to going anywhere for a few days at least."

"Of course not," he answered, patting her hand absently. "I'll see myself out. Don't hesitate to call if you need anything."

Amira smiled in response. She wouldn't be calling him. What she needed he simply couldn't provide. No matter how things went in the months leading up to her birthday, she knew she'd never meet Isobel's terms. She couldn't bear to put herself through the fear and worry of another pregnancy just to fulfill her grand-mother's requirements; nor did she want to marry any man. The future stretched out in bleak silence ahead of her, the weight of worry about repaying the loan heavy on her mind.

As day turned to dusk, then night, she remained where she was. Eventually she roused herself from her stupor and went to the kitchen to make a cup of tea. As she passed her phone, she noticed the red light flashing on her message service. She pressed the button and gagged as Roland's voice filled the air.

"So sorry to hear about your miscarriage, darling. But never mind, if you play *nice,* I might still let you live with me. I've always fantasised about you. Would you like to hear it? Let me tell—"

Before he could complete his poisonous suggestion, Amira ripped the machine from its socket and threw it across the room with a cry of raw pain. Shaking, she slid down the wall, collapsing at the bottom. What on earth was she going to do?

The next day Amira roused herself into making an appearance at the foundation's offices. Anyone looking at her in her immaculately tailored dress, stockings and high-heeled boots would never imagine the turmoil that churned inside.

As she pushed open the front door to the office, she drew in a leveling breath, squared her shoulders and mentally rehearsed how she was going to tell her staff that it would probably be a good time for them to start looking for new jobs. Then, that done, she'd have to find the strength to personally contact each family on their register and apologize for failing them.

"Amira! I'm so glad you're here. I've been trying to call you all morning."

Caroline, her assistant, came racing through the main office, her face alight.

"You're never going to believe this. I didn't at first myself. But it's just wonderful, wonderful news!" Caroline bubbled with joy, her eyes gleaming and her face wreathed in a massive smile.

"Believe what," Amira asked. "Tell me. What's happened?"

Caroline's exuberance was infectious, and for a second, Amira could forget her grief as the beginnings of an answering smile began to pull at her lips.

"Come to my computer and see for yourself," Caroline said, taking Amira by the arm and tugging her past the other staff who all wore similar smiles and exuded the same air of suppressed excitement. "Here, sit down."

Caroline pushed her into her chair and pointed to her computer screen.

"There. See?"

Amira stared at the screen. Caroline was logged onto their Internet banking facility, their operating account's dismal record open for her to see. But what was that? Amira blinked to clear her eyes and looked again. That wasn't right. The sum in the account was massive. Seven figures massive. Her scalp prickled as she realized what this meant. The foundation could go on—for a while longer at least. But surely it was a mistake. The bank must have messed up somewhere along the line.

"Have you—?"

"Checked with the bank? Yes. They said the money was authorized by a benefactor who wished to remain anonymous."

An anonymous donor. Amira slumped in her seat. Could she dare to believe it was true? That finally her campaigning and soliciting for funds had borne fruit. Forget fruit; this was a whole orchard.

"That's amazing," she said weakly.

She got to her feet to face her staff, the people who she had thought only minutes ago she'd have to turn away. Beside her, Caroline began to clap and one by one each of the Fulfillment Foundation team rose to their feet and joined her in a standing ovation.

Tears gathered in Amira's eyes then overflowed down her cheeks—happy tears this time—and the ache in her heart began to ease a little. She might not have foreseen this solution to the foundation's financial woes, but she sure as heck wasn't going to look a gift horse in the mouth.

"Come on, everyone," she finally managed to say through her tears. "We have work to do!"

As everyone cheered then returned to their desks, Caroline threw her arms around Amira in a massive hug.

"You did it. I'm sorry I didn't believe you would," she whispered. "I'm so proud of you and of what we're doing here."

"Me too," Amira answered, lost in the comfort of her assistant's embrace. "Me too."

Amira settled at her desk and started to sort through the unopened mail that awaited her arrival. One in particular caught her eye. Marked "personal and confidential," it bore the logo of one of the inner-city law firms. Curious, she plucked it open and slid out the single sheet of paper inside. She scanned the words, first telling her about the anonymous donor and his generosity. Her eyes flicked back to the date of the letter. It was from before her time in the hospital. No wonder the sum in the bank had come as such a surprise to her staff. None of them would have opened her personal mail.

The small smile on her face froze as she continued to read the letter and read the next sentence. *This donation is being made under the condition that Amira Forsythe withdraw and step down from her association with the Fulfillment Foundation effective from the date of deposit of funds.* There were other sentences, but the words all ran together before her eyes.

Ice ran through her veins. Step down? Immediately? She didn't think anything could hurt her any more than she was hurt already, but this, the foundation, was all she had left. But the letter was clear. If she stayed, all financial assistance would be rescinded; if she left, the foundation would be assured of a regular influx of funds to ensure it continued its mission in the community.

Amira pushed her chair out from her desk and stood on shaking legs. All she had to do was countersign the bottom of the letter and fax it back to the firm in acceptance. Her hand dragged a pen across the page, and she went through the motions to ensure the fax went through.

She managed to get through the rest of the day encased in a state of numbness. Not even Casey's excited voice when informed of the details of her family's dream-come-true trip penetrated the frozen shell. By the end of the day, she was the last to leave the office. She put the letter she'd faxed to the anonymous donor's lawyers on Caroline's desk. Tomorrow would be soon enough for them all to know.

For the last time she wandered through the office, turned off the lights and locked the front door, pushing her key through the slot to fall silently to the carpet mat inside the door.

By the time she arrived back home, Amira couldn't care less that she bore little resemblance to the perfectly coiffed fashion plate who had left in the morning. Her hair was more out than in its twist, her lipstick had long ago worn off on the rims of countless cups of tea and her mascara lay in smudges under her eyes. Nothing mattered anymore.

She dragged her feet up the few steps to her private entrance and inserted her key in the front door. As she turned her key in the lock, it occurred to her that she was completely and truly alone. Alone and bankrupt. For the briefest time today she'd realized that her annuity wouldn't be needed to fund the foundation, but there was still the loan she had to repay.

Her annuity would barely touch the surface of the sum she had to repay, and all hope she'd nurtured of a future, died. Whatever money she had and whatever money she could potentially earn would be tied up for a very long time.

But at least the foundation would go on. She had to hold on to that dream. So what if it wouldn't be her dream anymore—she'd made it happen. She'd brought it to life.

Inside the house she forced herself into the shower in an attempt to warm her body. Afterward she changed into a fleece sweatshirt and track pants and sat down with yet another mug of tea, a notepad and pen. It was time to start seriously planning how she was going to manage—survive was more to the point. But nothing would come, and her paper remained blank. Eventually Amira picked up her mug and went through to the main house.

The furnishings shrouded in dust cloths had never been more eerie. She'd tried to make a habit of walking through the house at least once every couple of weeks to check that everything remained secure, but it had been a whole lot longer than that since she'd done so.

Ignoring the bottom floor, Amira trailed up the staircase, stopping to toast her grandmother briefly on the way up.

"You win again, Grandmother. I hope you're happy, wherever you are."

She took a sip of her tea and wondered anew at what had driven Isobel to be so harsh toward her only granddaughter. Whatever it had been, Amira had no way of ever knowing. She carried on up to where her father's portrait hung and sank to the floor, desperate for some sense of connection to the handsome smiling man whose eyes were so much like her own.

How different would things have been, she wondered, if he and her mother hadn't died that day? She shook her head. She could no more change the past than she could satisfy Isobel's posthumous demands.

She searched her memory for the sound of her father's voice, the feel of his arms around her, but somewhere in the last eighteen years she'd lost all that. All that and so very much more. Yet, on the periphery of her mind lingered the sensation of being loved, of being happy. She wanted that again; oh how she wanted to feel like that again.

"Amira?"

She knocked over her mug on the carpet runner as she struggled to rise on feet that stung with pins and needles from the way she'd been sitting.

"Brent? What on earth—?"

She drank in the sight of him. Dressed in faded jeans and a heavy black woollen sweater, he was a feast for her eyes. But she had to remember his betrayal, his anger. Amira forced herself to clamp down on the surge of emotion rocketing through her.

"You didn't answer your front door—it was unlocked so I let myself in. I was worried about you. You wouldn't see me at the hospital. I had to see for myself that you were okay."

She drew herself up to her full height and met his gaze, summoning every shred of Forsythe sangfroid at her fingertips.

"Well, you needn't have worried. As you can see, I'm fine." *Please leave now, before I break down again.*

"I…I wanted to say I was wrong and," he said and sighed deeply, "I'm sorry."

Sorry? The word tore the breath from her throat, making it impossible to speak. He shifted under her incredulous stare, as if for once in his life he wasn't the strong and confident man she knew him to be. As she watched him, he made as if to speak again, then shook his head slightly and turned to go back down the stairs.

"Wait!" she cried out, anger blooming in her chest where before only pain had resided.

Brent stopped on the stairs.

"You can't just say you're sorry and then leave. So you're sorry. So what? Why? You made it perfectly clear what you thought of me. You even planned to set me up for failure. Is that what you're sorry about? Because if that's all it is, you can take your apology and you can sho—!"

Brent ascended the stairs lightning fast and reached out to grab her shoulders, giving her a little shake before pulling her now shaking body against the hardness of his.

"I know. I was a bastard. A total and utter bastard. I can't ever ask or even expect you to forgive me for that.

It was inexcusable what I did—what I planned to do. But, Amira, I'm begging you, please give me—give us—another chance."

She pushed away from his hold. "Why should I? How can I trust you again? How do I know you don't have another strike against me up your sleeve?"

"I need you to trust me, like I should have trusted you. Please, can we talk about this downstairs?"

Amira gave a short nod and bent to pick up her mug before leading him back down the stairs and through to her apartment. She dropped into a chair and gave him a baleful stare. She still couldn't believe he was here. While her heart leapt in her chest, her mind still warned her to tread carefully.

"Go on then," she said flatly. "Talk."

Brent lowered himself onto the couch, his body dominating the piece of furniture.

"There's a lot I need to say to you, but before I start can you tell me why you broke off the wedding?"

"The wedding?" She looked startled. "You know why. Because of the proviso in Grandmother's will. I didn't know about it until it was too late—not that it mattered anyway."

"No. Not this wedding. The first one."

"What difference does it make? You weren't interested back then. Why now?"

"I came here straight from the church. Did you know that?"

Amira's expression told Brent she had no idea, confirming his belief that Isobel had orchestrated the whole thing as effectively as a military maneuver, including training her staff to head him off at the pass.

"Why?" She wasn't giving him an inch.

"To try and talk you back into going through with the wedding for one thing."

"If you were so keen to talk me into going through with the wedding, why didn't you try and contact me when we got back?"

"By then I was angry. At you, at Isobel. The whole damn world. When your housekeeper told me you and your grandmother had gone away, I wondered how long you'd been planning it. It all just seemed a little too slick for it to have been a spur of the moment thing. I was told you'd gone to the airport and that you wouldn't be back for a month or more. I ended up pouring all my frustration into work. By the time you got back, I was so busy trying to hold my business together that I wasn't prepared for anyone's excuses. It was wrong of me. But all I could focus on was protecting my name and my future." He rose and paced the carpet. "I'm not saying it was right. If anything it was probably a totally immature reaction. But that's done now. I can't turn back time, but I do concede I handled the whole situation very badly."

"Why didn't you tell me about the business?"

He stopped pacing and shoved his hands in his pockets. "At the time, I didn't want to worry you. Looking back now, I probably was feeling too insecure to want you to know—to give you an excuse to back out. Your grandmother had made it clear often enough that she didn't approve of me, that my financial position was no more than a drop in the bucket as far as she was concerned. I knew if she found out what was happening with my business before the wedding there was no way she'd let us go ahead. I didn't want to take that risk." He sat down in the chair opposite Amira, his forearms resting on his thighs as he leaned forward. "I didn't want to lose you, Amira, but I couldn't compete with her, could I?"

A flush stained Amira's throat, and her lower lip trembled. Damn, he hadn't meant to upset her again.

"She told me you'd deliberately withheld the information from me. From the moment I woke in the morning, she went on and on about it, waving the newspaper under my nose and telling me it wasn't too late. I was dressed in my gown, ready for the photographer. We were still arguing over it when she suddenly started to complain of chest pains. Our doctor came straight away and insisted she go to the hospital, but she refused to go unless I promised not to go ahead with the wedding.

"I had no choice, Brent. I was terrified I would kill her if I married you. I was incredibly hurt that you hadn't told me about what you were going through. I thought that if you kept that from me then what else were you hiding from me? That maybe Grandmother was right all along—that you only wanted to marry me because of my family's fortune and position in society. You were my first real boyfriend, my first love. We were about to be married. If I couldn't trust you, who could I trust? So I sent that text.

"After we went to the hospital, her tests came back

clear, and instead of coming home afterward, she'd arranged for our luggage to be brought to us and for a car to take us to the airport. She'd planned it all along. When I asked her about it, she told me she knew you'd let me down. Eventually I believed her."

Brent groaned. By trying to protect her, he'd ended up destroying them both.

"I had my reasons, my insecurities," he said quietly. "They were what drove me to succeed. I was too stupid to realize that I was driving you away at the same time." He thought back to his upbringing, to that sense of being beholden to his uncle for providing his education and then doing his utmost to pay him back. Of wanting never to have to rely on anyone for help in any shape or form. "How could I tell you my deepest fears? I didn't think you'd understand, coming as you did from a background of wealth."

"But that's what couples do. They support each other. Help one another. Stand together against their fears," Amira argued.

"I had to be able to give you what you already had, and more. How do you think I felt when I realized I was losing everything I'd worked so hard for. I couldn't lose you too."

"Money isn't everything. We would have managed."

"You say that when you've never wanted for anything. When you've never had to check a price tag or consider the cost of what you're wearing, what you drive, how you eat." Brent got up and paced again. "I felt I had to compete with all that, and when the papers blasted my news all over their pages that morning, I held on to the hope that you loved me enough to marry me anyway. I needed you more then than I'd ever needed you. And that's why I took the chance to have my revenge, to pay you back for choosing money over me."

Amira paled, her hands clenched into fists in her lap. Brent leaned forward and grasped her hands, slowly unpeeling her tightly knotted fingers and threading them through his own.

"Believe me. I am deeply sorry for what I put you through. Back then and now. I should have known Isobel wouldn't have given you a choice."

"I should have stood up to her," Amira whispered.

"How could you when she'd been manipulating you for so many years? She's gone now. She has no hold over you any longer."

Amira laughed—a raw sound that struck straight to his heart. "No hold over me? You know exactly what kind of hold she has over me. You've read her will. Even in death she's still trying to force me into motherhood or marriage, but not with the man I love. I honestly admit I used you to have a baby, but it was because I couldn't bear to think about marrying anyone else."

Brent latched on to the words he'd been hoping against hope to hear. *The man I love.*

"So if you couldn't marry anyone else, Amira, would you still marry me?"

"Don't!" She pulled her hands from his grasp and covered her face, her shoulders shaking as a sob racked her body.

"You said Isobel was trying to force you into marriage to someone you don't love. But if you could, would you marry me?" he pressed, determined to hear her answer.

"Yes."

He barely heard her through her tears. His heart twisted because he was once again causing her so much grief; but her answer sent a positive punch of hope through his body. She loved him. The knowledge suddenly made him feel ten feet tall and invincible. This was what he'd missed in his life. This was what had made that weekend at Windsong so special in those moments when he'd forgotten his vendetta against her.

And he knew without doubt he loved her too. Now all he had to do was convince her of it.

"Amira, look at me."

He reached out and took her hands, tearing them off her tear-streaked face.

"We can't let her win. Not now. Not when we still have the rest of our lives to be together. I love you too much to let you go again." He felt her stiffen at his words. Undeterred, he pressed on. "I was so wrapped up in paying you back for what had happened eight years ago that when I figured out you must be pregnant I had to see you. Had to see for myself that you'd hidden our baby from me. On top of everything else, it was the ultimate betrayal. I'll freely admit all I wanted to do at that stage was rip everything from your grasp.

"I already knew about the Fulfillment Foundation, and I'd set plans in motion to see you removed from the administration."

At Amira's shocked gasp he squeezed her hands firmly in his, drawing them to his lips and pressing a kiss to each.

"That was you? You took that from me too?" She wrenched free of his hold and rose on shaking legs.

He tried to stop her but she moved out of his reach, looking at him with eyes full of pain and accusation.

"I was a man bent on revenge. I had no thought for what it would do to you aside from take from you something personally important. To make sure you knew loss on every level the way I'd known it when you left me. In the past few years, whenever I've seen you featured in the papers or on TV, you've always been a figurehead, and I thought that was as deep as you went. Taking the foundation from you would have been nothing, especially when I saw the financial difficulty it was in. I arranged to make a sizable donation. But the donation was on the condition of you stepping down from your position there."

"How could you do that to me? It was all I had left." She turned her back on him. "Get out. Please just get out, and leave me alone."

"No! I've learned what a total idiot I was. I've seen that you're more than just a face on these charities you work for. They're a part of you as much as you're a part of them and their success. I couldn't take that from you now. I'm ashamed I ever dreamed I'd do that in the first place."

He stood up, staring at her back, his arms helpless at his side. He wanted nothing more right now than to drag her into his arms and try and comfort her for the hell he'd put her through—to make up for the pain he'd caused. But he had so much more to say to her first. To convince her they belonged together.

"Believe me, Amira. This past week I've learned a great deal about myself. Most of it I don't like. But one thing I have learned is how much you mean to me. How much I love you.

"When you collapsed on the island, I'd never been more scared or felt more helpless in my entire life. It was a wake-up call I hope never to get again. I thought I was going to lose you. One minute we were arguing and the next you were unconscious and bleeding. I would have given all my wealth and my right arm to know you were okay. I went with you to the hospital, but they separated us at emergency."

"I don't remember any of that. The first thing I remember was waking up in a recovery room and the doctor telling me—" Her voice broke off, and she shoved a fisted hand against her mouth.

A piece of Brent's heart tore away at the gesture, at the helplessness in her voice. He lifted his hands to take her into his arms to try to comfort her; but her body was stiff and unyielding in his embrace.

"Please, Amira. Don't reject me now. I tried to see you at the hospital. I waited, day after day, but they wouldn't let me near you. I had to see you. To tell you what a fool I'd been. To tell you how much I love you and how sorry I was for everything. Especially for the loss of our baby."

"But don't you see," Amira cried out, "it wouldn't matter. None of it matters anymore. I have nothing left. You've stripped me of every last thing that was mine."

"My solicitor told me this afternoon that you'd returned the foundation proposal letter, signed. I told him to tear it up. That the foundation was nothing without you. And I've instructed my accountant to return the money that you paid out to me. Your solicitor should have it in his trust account as we speak. I could never have kept it. Not even if our baby had lived. Let me make up my misjudgment to you. Let me love you as you deserve to be loved. Please, Amira, give me one more chance."

"I don't know if I can do that again, if I can trust you again."

"Do you love me?"

"What does that have to do with anything? I've always loved you, even when you've hurt me. What kind of pathetic person does that make me?"

"The kind of person who deserves the best of everything. The kind of woman I want to spend the rest of my life with. Marry me, Amira. Let the past go. Let Isobel and her ridiculous dictates go. Please, if you can find it in your heart to forgive me I promise you I will make it worth your while."

A crazed laugh shuddered through her as he repeated to her the words she'd uttered to him a few short months ago.

"I don't want you to make it worth my while."

Brent dropped his arms, let her go, his heart pounding. He'd lost her. Forever. The pain was indescribable. He stepped away from her, every cell in his body screaming at him not to.

"I'm sorry. You'll never know how sorry." He slowly walked toward the door. "I won't bother you again."

"Brent, stop." She ran across the room and threw her arms around him. "I said I don't want you to make it worth my while, but I never said I didn't want you to love me for all my life. We can't change what we've done to each other. But it's more than enough to me to be the woman you love. I love you. I'll always love you—every day and every night for the rest of my life."

"Will you marry me even though it'll mean saying goodbye to all of this?"

He swept an arm to encompass the home she'd lived in for eighteen years, and Amira suddenly understood that the bricks and mortar meant nothing to her now. Yes, it had been where she'd grown up. Yes, she was the last of the Forsythe line. And that was where it all ended. With her. Right now.

"Yes."

She looked around her. Aside from her father's portrait in the main house, there was nothing here she wanted to keep, nothing that was intrinsically hers. Nothing but the man in her arms.

"It doesn't matter anymore. Let Roland have it. Let him have it all. As long as I have you, I don't need anything else."

"I will look after you, you know—you and the family we're going to build together. And if you want, we can make Roland an offer he can't refuse for the place. Gerald Stein told me about your plans—how you wanted to turn it into a respite center and head office for the foundation. We can still do that. I'll make it happen if that's what you want."

Amira lifted her hand to stroke his face, the face that was so dear to her. She lifted her lips to his and kissed him, trying to imbue into her caress how much she meant what she'd just said. And he understood. She felt it in his body, in his kiss, in the way he held her.

"I want you," she said gently.

"Let's go home, then."

Brent took her by the hand and led her to his waiting car. As they walked out into the night, Amira realized the sensation of joy and lightness that suffused her was freedom. Freedom from Isobel's expectations, freedom from doing what had always been expected of her by others.

Freedom to love the only man she'd ever wanted.

* * * * *

Don't miss the second book in
ROGUE DIAMONDS, Secret Baby, Public Affair,
available March 2010 from
Mills & Boon® Desire™.

millsandboon.co.uk Community

Join Us!

The Community is the perfect place to meet and chat to kindred spirits who love books and reading as much as you do, but it's also the place to:

- **Get the inside scoop from authors about their latest books**
- **Learn how to write a romance book with advice from our editors**
- **Help us to continue publishing the best in women's fiction**
- **Share your thoughts on the books we publish**
- **Befriend other users**

Forums: Interact with each other as well as authors, editors and a whole host of other users worldwide.

Blogs: Every registered community member has their own blog to tell the world what they're up to and what's on their mind.

Book Challenge: We're aiming to read 5,000 books and have joined forces with The Reading Agency in our inaugural Book Challenge.

Profile Page: Showcase yourself and keep a record of your recent community activity.

Social Networking: We've added buttons at the end of every post to share via digg, Facebook, Google, Yahoo, technorati and de.licio.us.

www.millsandboon.co.uk

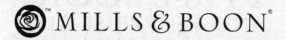

2 FREE BOOKS
AND A SURPRISE GIFT

We would like to take this opportunity to thank you for reading this Mills & Boon® book by offering you the chance to take TWO more specially selected books from the Desire™ 2-in-1, series absolutely FREE! We're also making this offer to introduce you to the benefits of the Mills & Boon® Book Club™—

- **FREE home delivery**
- **FREE gifts and competitions**
- **FREE monthly Newsletter**
- **Exclusive Mills & Boon Book Club offers**
- **Books available before they're in the shops**

Accepting these FREE books and gift places you under no obligation to buy, you may cancel at any time, even after receiving your free books. Simply complete your details below and return the entire page to the address below. You don't even need a stamp!

YES Please send me 2 free Desire stories in a 2-in-1 volume and a surprise gift. I understand that unless you hear from me, I will receive 2 superb new 2-in-1 books every month for just £5.25 each, postage and packing free. I am under no obligation to purchase any books and may cancel my subscription at any time. The free books and gift will be mine to keep in any case.

Ms/Mrs/Miss/Mr_____ Initials _____

Surname _____
Address _____

_____
_____ Postcode _____

Send this whole page to: Mills & Boon Book Club, Free Book Offer, FREEPOST NAT 10298, Richmond, TW9 1BR